Love Lust

And

A Whole Lotta

Distrust

A Novel

By

DeiIra Smith-Collard

ISBN 978-0-9818-1320-2

Cover Design by:
Oddball Dsgns

AriSiri Publishing
P.O. Box 681973
Houston, TX 77268-1973

Printed in the U.S.A

This book is dedicated to all those who believed in me, encouraged me and lifted me just when I thought I would fall. I love you all.

Acknowledgements

Firstly, my thanks go to my Father, God has blessed me with an incredible gift and I will forever give Him praise for all that he has done and bestowed upon me.

To my awesome husband John, who has encouraged me for years to see my dreams through, I love you and appreciate you.

To my mother, Cheryl Chism and family who support me always and push me to be the best that I can be, thank you. Thanks for encouraging me to use my gift.

To Jennifer Leviston, Josephine Brown, Khahelah Williams, and Iris Greene, thank you guys for being my shoulders to lean on. It's not every day you find a real friend who will love you at your best and your worst. I have found that in each of you. Thanks for your honesty and proofreading, it's greatly appreciated.

A special thanks to my extraodinary publicist, Torrian Ferguson, of the Ferguson Literary Group. With your help I've gone further than I ever imagined. Thank you for all of your efforts on my behalf.

To my dear friend Michael Lewis, writer and friend your help is priceless, Thank you.

A special thanks to Toinetta Norris and your countless suggestions, you will never know just how much your support really meant to me.

To Jovan Shaw and all of those who have given me constructive criticism, thank you because you have helped me to become a better writer. Everyone who has given me an encouraging word, thank you.

Lastly, thank you to those who are reading this. I appreciate this opportunity to entertain you and I hope that you enjoy.

DeiVra Smith-Collard

A bird doesn't sing because it has an answer, it sings because it has a song.

-- Maya Angelou

This is my song.

$\mathcal{P}\,\imath\,o\,\ell\,o\,g\,u\,e$

Nicole Neatherly-Edwards

I sat up in the bed instantly as if I had forgotten something. My heart is pounding in my chest, screaming to be released. I don't know what it is about today that's making me so uneasy, but I am. I blinked my eyes in an attempt to focus. I turned to Jason's side of the bed, but he wasn't here. Letting out an exasperated sigh, I squinted to see the clock. It's three in the morning and Jason's side of the bed is cold. Anger began to swell as I sat here all alone in our king sized sleigh bed. The satin covers were warming my body, wrapped around me in every way I wanted Jason's arms enveloping me. Kendra and Cory were keeping Jaden so that Jason and I could have quality time together. We had the entire week to spend with each other and he had started it by not coming home.

I moved myself out of the bed to look for my cell phone. My fingers trembled as I pressed the buttons. The phone rang once and went to voicemail and I immediately knew he had ignored the call. I walked to the kitchen and surveyed my home. It was beautiful to me. This two-story home was furnished with nothing but the best. From the imported area rugs that covered the mahogany hard wood floors, to the Italian silk upholstery that covered my sofas, my home was immaculate, even extraordinary. I paused to look at the large 16X20-wall portrait of my family. Everyone seemed excited and happy. On the surface everything was calm, but I knew underneath a storm was brewing. Jason and I had come a long way in five years. I found it amusing the way things have worked out.

The garage door opening interrupted my thoughts. Total darkness surrounded me as I waited for Jason to walk through the door.

"It's nice of you to join me at home. You do remember what that is, don't you?" I stood up and walked towards Jason. I could smell the stench of alcohol on his breath and the scent of perfume lingered on his shirt. It was a fragrance unknown to me.

"Cole, look, I'm not trying to hear that now. It's late and the only thing I want to do now is curl up in our bed and go to sleep. Kill the drama." He started to walk away from me. Even through my anger, I was desperate for his love. What I really wanted this man to do was take me in his arms and hold me like he really cared for me.

"Jason, stop walking away from me." My voice was barely audible. I found myself pleading with Jason like I have so many times before. My mind said he loved me; I at least know that he cares, but I also know that he never meant to settle down. He never meant to be married to me or any body else for that matter.

Jason and I still worked in the same center, in different departments. I saw how the women flirted with him and just wanted to be near him, and I tried not to let it bother me. I refuse to pretend that it's not hard to watch women lust over him. It was more than hard; it was extremely difficult. Remembering the first time I saw Jason brought a smile to my face. I thought he was the most gorgeous man I had ever laid eyes on. Instantly I knew I wanted to be with him and I was willing to go through anything to be his woman.

I sat down on the sofa and curled my feet up under me. The thought of my bed was inviting but I knew I couldn't go to sleep now. Our marriage was not one built on trust, or love for that matter. I loved Jason, but he didn't fall hopelessly in love with me. I thought about all the secrets and lies told to convince him to be with me. The saddest thing about that was even though I had him on paper and the rock on my finger to prove it; I understood I didn't completely have Jason at all. In some way, he was still that man I met all those years ago. He was still the man that thought he would never settle down. He never thought he would be exclusive to anyone. At least that's the way I felt he wanted to be. I pondered the thought of Jason not wanting to be with me and it hurt like hell. The idea of my life without Jason was foreign to me. My heart ached at the thought of losing him. All I ever wanted from him was to return the love. My emotions were running amuck and I knew they were coming. The tears are beginning to stream down my cheeks. He's the only man that can make me happy and the only one that can make me cry.

Carmell Devereaux

"I love you too." I said to my fiancé as I ended my call. It had been five long years ago when Dr. Alejandro Escalante entered into my life. My life has some major changes since that day. I smiled to myself. Alex was everything that a woman could want. He was gorgeous, successful, and very well off. As if that wasn't enough, he was filled with patience and kindness. Any woman would be happy to be in my shoes.

I walked towards my new Mercedes, another gift from my husband to be. He was like that; he wanted to give me the world and a whole lot more. So why did I have a nagging feeling? I couldn't put my finger on it, but there was something bothering me. I shook my head; no good ever came of lying to yourself. My wedding was a month away and I couldn't get an old flame out of my mind. I had convinced myself I was through with him. I thought I didn't want anything to do with him, but that was another lie. After telling myself repeatedly I hated him, I started to believe it, but the older I got the more I realized that my hatred was just to cloak the love I felt.

I pushed thoughts of him out my head because he was the last thing I needed to be thinking of. I had a man; a successful man that would spoil me and love me unconditionally.

I pulled my car into PF Chang's to get dinner for Alex and me. When I walked through the door, my heart dropped along with my face. I didn't believe I was seeing them. After the fiasco with them, my life was left in ruins.

It was hard not to hate people who went out of their way to be cruel to you. If I had learned anything from Alex, it was forgiveness. I'm unsure how I managed to stand still and not revert to my old ways as pain flooded my heart. Seeing them here brought back memories, memories I wasn't prepared to deal with. Attempting to hide, I slid behind a pole. He was the very man I had just pushed out of my mind, she was the woman he had dated, and then married, while I thought he was my man.

I stood here in a trance thinking of how I had been so foolish. I was willing to do anything and everything for that man and when I tried to prove it to him I found out the joke was on me. I remember feeling used and betrayed. Nothing has changed; I still harbor the same feelings.

I ordered my food and waited. It was weird. I couldn't take my eyes off them. I couldn't stop watching them. It was like watching a wreck on the highway, even though you wanted to look away it commanded your attention and you couldn't turn away for fear of missing something. I was a little envious even though I knew I shouldn't be. I had the better man. I had come out on top. I was the one who had risen even though that couple did everything to hold me down. I knew all those things but I couldn't understand why I felt this way.

I exhaled.

"No use worrying about that now", I thought to myself. It was old news, happened many years ago, but the pain, the pain was still fresh.

Natina Mayes

She thought I hadn't seen her. I laughed to myself, she wasn't my sworn enemy anymore but she wasn't on my list of favorite people. She had actually been a very good friend to me at one time, until it all went down south. My husband was here with me. This was just another one of the many steps that we had taken to get back together. After seeing her, my mind flooded with memories. I still worked at the same place that we met. Even though she worked for the same company, she had taken a position with our marketing department in a completely different building. I haven't seen her in almost five years.

I started to mention to Louis that she was here but decided against it. I wasn't prepared to start down that road again. After her, our relationship went to hell and back. I had even left him, but being away from him was torture. We're meant for each other and he knew it just as well as I did. So we were here working on being together again. This time we were guaranteed to make it work. I knew no other way. When I walked out the door I thought I would never come back to him but it was inevitable. I would always return to him and him to me.

I looked towards the front of the restaurant and saw she was watching us. I watched her even though I pretended not to see her. I remember the days when I thought of nothing but her, then I thought of nothing but ruining her. When it came to her I had done many evil things. After everything was said and done I went through hell and I couldn't help but think it was because I had wronged her. After all the things I had to endure I knew that I had paid for my misdeeds. I'm not going to sit and pretend she was innocent in it all, because she wasn't, but after five years it all seemed senseless, maybe even worthless.

I stood up, my bulging belly hitting the table as I attempted to stand. Having a baby inside of you was a true miracle but learning to maneuver with the extra weight was torture. I was on a path to the restroom and it was leading me straight to her. As I moved closer she noticed me and we made unavoidable eye contact, and that's when I saw the look on her face. I looked deep in her eyes and they spoke an undeniable truth. She was still hurting. What we had done still haunted her.

K endra Dubois

Damn. I all but cursed aloud when I heard my cell phone begin to ring. I don't know why I had left it in the bedroom. I shook my head as I dressed my godson, Jaden. He looked more and more like his father every day. I smiled at him. He was almost five and he brought so much joy into our lives.

I didn't know who that was that was calling me but I do know that I didn't want him, him being my husband, to have my phone. She would be calling me soon and I was hoping that she wasn't calling me early.

"Kendra, your phone is ringing." Cory said that as if I couldn't hear it. Then I heard him answer it. My heart began to beat fast, uncontrollably fast. I slowed my breathing. If it was her she knew to block her number before she called me and if he answered she better just pretend to be a bill collector. Still it made me nervous. I knew that she was off limits and even though we had somehow maintained a platonic relationship with one another, my husband would not approve. I walked into the room where he stood.

"We're about to go to Chuck E. Cheese's, baby. I walked over, kissed him on the forehead, and took my phone from him. "Who was it?" I asked.

"I don't know they hung up. Bring me some pizza back please." I kissed my husband again then we left.

I got into my car and drove off. I was almost certain that was her calling me. I was running late, we should have been at the pizza place but I was always late and she should be used to it. She was back in town. It seemed she was always in town and she always wanted to see me whenever she came back.

When we arrived I parked the car and immediately spotted her. It was amazing to me that even after all these years seeing her still stopped my heart. I tried extremely hard not to fall into our old ways but I couldn't let her go. I had tried but she called out to me. She was one of the rare people who got me, who understood me.

Years ago she had gone toe to toe with my husband and even though she didn't win she has kept on fighting. I tell her that we shouldn't see each other and she ignores my words. She finds them to be meaningless and they probably are. I know what I should do. I also know what I tried to do five years ago when my world came tumbling down, but I still hadn't found the courage to walk away from her.

I know I am greedy. I wanted it all, my husband and her. It wasn't fair for me to have two and force people to share my love. When I was with my husband he was the only thing that mattered, and when I was with her I rarely thought of him. Could you love two people? They say no but why did I feel so strongly about her? Having her had caused a whirlwind of events in my life that could have very easily cost me everything. I loved my husband and I know she knows that. I also know, she knows, when it comes down to it, I always choose him. I looked at her and wondered if this would be the time, could this be the place where I tell her I won't see her any longer and truly mean it.

Love Lust and A Whole Lotta Distrust

The Beginning

Nicole

Another Day Another Dollar

•————————————————————————————————•

"Thank you for calling Synergy Wireless, my name is Nicole how may I help you?" I opened my call as I always do. I wonder what kind of nut I would have on the line today.

"You can help me by fixing my damn bill!" Okay see obviously she didn't know who she was talking to cause I wasn't going to put up with this drunk who's bill was probably right.

"OK, I'll be happy to help you. What is your cellular number starting with area code first?"

"You don't have that already? I put it in. You people are so stupid." I could not believe that she said that and who in the hell was she calling stupid? I ain't got time for this.

"I definitely apologize for any inconvenience, your number is requested in our automated system for routing purposes, and I need your number so that I can view your account and bill. Trust me ma'am if I had it I would not be asking for it." So just give me the damn number I thought to myself. I wasn't about to play this game with her.

"281-507-0347." She spat the number at me as if she could not get it out fast enough. I pulled up the account and made her wait. I placed the phone on mute and began conversation with my neighbor. I wasn't going to reward her ignorance. She needed to marinate for being stupid.

"Hello, Hello." I heard the idiot woman say. I removed myself from mute and then responded.

"I apologize for the inconvenience" I started in the nice-nastiest voice that I could find, "I seem to be having a problem with my system. May I place you on hold?" I didn't wait for a response it was more of a statement than a question but for quality purpose I had to ask to place her on hold. I hit the button and let her listen to the hold music. I decided I was going to go get a coke out of the vending machine. I started to look for some change when Jason walked up to my desk. I loved looking at this man and at this moment he was a much-needed distraction.

"Hey there sexy, we still on for tonight?" I asked.

"That's what's up! What time you want me to pick you up?" He was walking with me to the break room.

"Eight is good for me." I responded. This man was the sexiest man in this call center. He probably was close to the sexiest man in Texas cause I had never seen a man as attractive as he was. I leaned down to retrieve my coke from the machine and just as I reached for it I felt a soft touch caress my behind. I started to sing a verse of Black Eyed Peas, *My Humps*, as I moved it back and forth seductively.

"You like that don't you?" I said as I turned and faced him. "It can be yours if you prove you got some act right!" I laughed.

Jason leaned close enough to kiss me. I thought that he was about to kiss me and I moved in to kiss him but he pulled back. Tease. "Everything I do is right." He said as he turned and walked away.

That man had left me wanting more of him. How he had managed to do that I don't know.

I stood in a trance like state. Then I remembered I was on a call. I hurried back to my desk and put my headset back on. I half expected her to have hung up the phone by now but that had not happened. She was still hanging there on my line, refusing to go away. I know she was going to be pissed off. I think she had been holding for more than five minutes. I hit the hold button to go back to the line.

"I apologize for the long hold time; I was having some system trouble and had to pull my entire system up again. I now have your information again. What is the name on the account?" I asked her. I knew that my nice nasty attitude was bound to get her.

"It's my damn name. Mary Steinbrook, you left me on hold for an eternity and you expect me to be alright with that? Just fix my damn bill!" It truly amazed me how ignorant people could act when it came to a cell phone. This woman was demanding that I fix her bill and I hadn't even had a chance to look at it. She never even considered the fact that her statement was correct. She saw her statement picked up the phone and immediately called me with her theatrics.

"Ms. Steinbrook there is nothing to fix on your bill. You exceeded the minutes so you have to pay for the overage. There is no credit due." See if she had been nice I might have hooked her up, but she had to call here and be Billy Bad Ass. This call was getting old. "Is there anything else I can help you with?" In other words get off my damn line. Oh how I wish I could say that without losing my job.

"Look you black bitch. If you don't issue me a credit then I am gonna jump through this phone and whoop your nigger ass." Who did she really think she was? I know she didn't think her idle threats were gonna get to me. Especially since she had threatened to do something impossible like jump through a phone; who in the hell said things like that anyway? I guess in some weird universe that was supposed to scare me into doing what she wanted me to do. I looked around to see if my supervisor was around. She was nowhere to be found. The fact that I didn't see her didn't mean a thing; many times the supervisors and managers did meetings where they randomly listened to calls. They had the ability to call in from home and listen to our calls, and one associate director went as far as to listen to the calls on the way home from work. I would just have to take my chances and hope I wasn't being monitored because I was finished with this nut job.

"Thanks for calling Synergy Wireless. Have a nice day." I hit release to disconnect the call. She could kiss this black bitch's nigger ass. It was time to go anyway. I put in my seven point five hours. "I don't know how I put up with this." I mumbled to myself on the way out the door. I saw my supervisor on the way out.

"How is your day going Nicole?" She asked. She looked at me in a way that made me feel so guilty. As if she knew what I had just done. Maybe she could tell by the look on my face that something was wrong. I hope she wasn't monitoring me. I didn't want her to see me sweat so I answered her just as I always do. I was upbeat, cordial, and full of bs.

"Oh my day is going splendid; even better now that I'm on my way out the door. You know me, another day another dollar."

Carmell

Same Shit Different Day

I was putting on my favorite t-shirt, it is Friday and I am ready to get this week over with. I am looking forward to my last day in transition. I'm ready to get away from the people that I have been training with. At first I thought that these people where keeping it real, but that was hardly the case. As I pulled my socks and shoes on I thought about last nights events. Tina, one of the girls that I work with, had wanted to treat me to a night on the town for my birthday. Of course, I didn't mind cause I never mind when someone is spending money on me. Besides, it was my birthday and I didn't have any other plans.

Tina picked me up and took me everywhere I wanted to go. We went to the strip club and then out to eat. She even got me my own private dance. I was having so much fun. Since I wasn't one who had many female friends I was happy for the sisterly company.

When we got back to my house Tina insisted that she come upstairs saying it was late and she did not feel like driving back to the southwest side of town. That was cool with me cause I wanted to do nothing but go to sleep anyway. I took my shower first and hopped right into bed. I made a mistake of sleeping in the nude like I do when I'm home alone. About two hours into my peaceful slumber, I felt a gentle touch across my thigh. My first response was a soft moan. I still had not awakened fully. I felt the warm softness of a tongue run across my most personal area. A series of moans escaped my lips before I realized that I didn't bring a man home with me and although my toys were great none of them felt this damn real.

I opened my eyes and focused. There was Tina going at my coochie like a Chinese buffet. Ohhh, this felt so good I almost didn't want it to stop. Wait a minute, what the hell was I saying? I'm definitely no dike. I regained my senses, jumped out of bed and proceeded to whoop her ass.

"What the hell do you think you are doing?" I asked, although I knew exactly what that bitch was trying to do. She never responded, just looked at me with this amused smile on her face. That look was saying yeah you know you liked it. Yeah I liked before I realized I was being molested by some damn girl. I tried to break every bone in her body before I kicked her ass out of my apartment.

I stormed out of my apartment. Reliving that night pissed me off all over again. On my way to work I had to find a happy place. I popped in my Sade CD and let her smooth sound take me away. By the time I reached work I had calmed down a bit.

"Are we busy?" I quizzed a coworker of mine.

"No not too bad but steady." Kendra replied. That was fine by me. It was the weekend and I planned to drive to Galveston and get some rest. After what happened last night, rest and relaxation was a much-needed event. I sat down and signed on to the phone. As Tina walked in, she looked dead at me, smiled and licked her lips. I hate that stupid dike.

I did my work and politely ignored her harassing emails. I looked up and I had an hour to go. Tina's emails had stopped. She was talking with Ed our transition supervisor. Her stupid ass is probably in trouble. Maybe she will get fired. I silently laughed to myself.

"Carmell, I need you to sign off on an approved exception for me. Human Resources would like to speak with you." Ed said to me as he stood near my desk and waited for me to follow his instructions. I did as instructed and followed him to HR.

"Do you know what this is about Ed?" He didn't really answer me.

He just mumbled something about not knowing people. It made me wonder if he was smoking something. I walked into Lakisha Martin's office and took a seat. Ed took the seat next to me.

"We have a formal complaint of sexual harassment filed on you by Natina Mayes." Lakisha stated to me. I looked at her with this puzzled look on my face. Somebody needed to tell me what the hell was going on.

"Sexual harassment? What are you talking about? I did not sexually harass anybody." So that is what Tina was over there talking to Ed about. She was over there lying her ass off.

"Natina filed a complaint stating that you exposed yourself to her in the women's restroom and that you tried to kiss her. Was she aware that you were a lesbian?"

"I am not a lesbian, nor did I expose myself or try to kiss her." This girl was trying to get me fired. I cannot believe this. I wouldn't give her some last night so she decided she was going to get me fired. I was trying to think back in my mind to see if I had done something that she may be able to use against me like this. A light bulb went off in my head.

"I never kissed her and the time that we were in the bathroom she asked to see my piercing as well as show me hers. I bet she didn't tell you that. I cannot believe this is happening. She is just mad because she came on to me and I turned her down. I am not gay!" I was getting frustrated. I began to tell them the entire story of last night's events. I could not believe that she had sunk this low to get back at me. She is messing with my income and that ain't even much funny. By the time I finished my story I was about near tears. Someone that I thought was my friend was causing tremendous pain in my life.

Ed started to speak. "Their shifts are about to change starting Sunday. I have never seen any inappropriate actions between the two of them. There is no need for anyone to lose a job. Carmell you just avoid her and she will be instructed to do the same." I looked at Ed, thankful that he had spoken on my behalf. As we left the office and got on the elevator, I thanked him.

"A word of advice sweetie, watch your back. There are all kinds of people in this world and some of them are ruthless." Ed said with concern in his eyes. I smiled thankfully and exited the elevator. I went to my desk and grabbed my purse.

"Bye Carmell. I will see you Monday. By the way, what does the SSDD on your shirt stand for?" Kendra asked.

"Same Shit Different Day." I said as I left the building. I could not wait to hit the beach and relax.

Natina

All Is Fair in Love and War

—————————————————•

I saw Carmell walk in and get her purse and she looked pissed. I wonder if she was fired. I hope so. That will teach her to play with people. For her birthday I took her out to eat and paid for the club and everything; she could have at least let me finish snacking on her. I know she didn't expect it to be free. I learned a long time ago that nothing is free. That night she went to bed naked. She paraded around in the nude as if it were nothing. Flaunting her body for me to see, I now understood what guys meant when they say the girl was asking for it. Even though she teased me with it, I had to admit her body was more than nice. Her skin was bright and vibrant with hues of gold, as if the sun had kissed her. Her hair was the longest, silkiest hair I had ever seen on a woman of color, with hints of auburn and brown. I wanted her. When she turned me down last night and then had the nerves to hit me I knew that bitch had to learn a lesson and I was going to be the one to teach her. She didn't know who she was playing with. I didn't like being told no and I was going to get to her any way that I knew how. That's why I turned the tables on her and took my story to our sup. Only I made it seem that she sexually harassed me at work. All I wanted to do was kick it with her and expose her to more than just heterosexual sex. I had never told her that I was bisexual but I thought that she would figure it out. Actually, I thought she was feeling me. I always made comments about how good she looked and how soft her ass looked. I guess she ignored the hints that I gave her. She didn't

·

seem to mind me spending my money on her. All this time I've spent taking her to lunch, paying for things when she didn't seem to have any money. All of that and she has the nerves to try and fight me, that's cool. You get what you get and I hope she got fired. I bet if I had been a man she would have gave it up without hesitation. I looked at the clock and saw it was almost time for me to go too. I started to shut down my system. Just as I was about to sign off Ed walked up to my desk.

"Can I talk to you for a second?" I wonder if he wanted to tell me that she had to pack her box.

"Yeah sure Ed, what's up?" I asked. I was waiting on him to deliver the news that she was gone and that I had nothing to fear. When I told him my story I made it seem like I was the victim. I mean I had the tears and all. My major should be theater in school instead of Sociology. I was about to burst because I just knew my scheme had worked.

"Well basically I wanted to inform you that Carmell denies all of your allegations. Since it is virtually your word against hers then what HR has come up with is that you all are to avoid one another. You are to have no contact with each other. None whatsoever" Ed stated. This was not at all the message that I hoped to get. She was to no longer be employed by Synergy Wireless.

"Ok. That is fine with me as long as she can keep her clothes on and her lips to herself." I said. Just to make my story still seem true. Ed just looked at me and walked away. I know he was not taking her side. So she had gotten to keep her job. That's fine I will have to just find another way to get to her. Unless she changed her mind about giving it to me, I was going to make her life hell. I was gonna get what I wanted one way or another.

I began to send text messages to her phone. I was going to harass the hell out of her if I couldn't get her fired. The first message I sent her was telling her how lucky she was that she kept her job. When she responded to me she called me a sick dike. Why was she so quick to use that word? I didn't respond to her after that. After thinking about it I thought it would be best just to change my approach, the direct approach just wasn't going to work for Carmell. I guess I had to be sneaky about it. The opportunity hadn't yet presented itself but when it did I was going to be all over it. I was going to have what I wanted. She could give willingly or I could make her life hell. Either was fine with me because all is fair in love and war.

Kendra

Packing My Bags

Today has been such a good day for me. I guess the best thing is that it is Friday. That means the weekend is coming. Not only was I chosen to go to Atlanta and train for a month, I am supposed to leave Monday morning. The only problem that I have is that I haven't told my husband about it. Okay let me rephrase that. I had not told him the complete story. I told him that I might have to go. I know he is gonna act like a baby. When I told him about it the first thing out of his mouth was what about school. I looked at him like he was stupid. It is the beginning of July. The fall semester wouldn't start for another month and a half. I had talked to him about going back to school because I didn't know if psychology was what I wanted to do and at the time I didn't even think he was listening, but now all of sudden he has become concerned about me and school. He would do anything to keep me here in Texas.

I grabbed my bags and headed out. Just as I did my cell phone began to ring. I looked at the caller id and saw it was a 404 area code. That could be only one person.

"Hey My Cherry." I used my nickname for Gia.

"Sweetness, whatcha doing?" I loved the way she would come up with nicknames for me.

"Guess what. I'm coming to Atlanta. I delivered the news to her. I knew she wasn't gonna believe me right off so I prepared myself.

"Whatever yo, tell me anything." There she was playing the role of little miss hard.

"I'm serious. My job is sending me out there for a month to do some training. You know we have an Atlanta call center right." I was extremely excited about finally meeting Gia face to face. We had met one day about eight months ago through a yahoo chat room. She sent me a page and we have talked every day since. In the beginning it was innocent. She was open and let me know right off that she was a lesbian and I in turn told her that I was as straight as an arrow. Even that did not stop her. I think it made her even more persistent. She would flirt with me and we both loved to read and write poetry. We began to exchange writing thus the games began. Every time I talked to her, I became more and more attracted to her. It was mental and when she sent me a picture it became physical. I had never been attracted to a woman but it was something about this woman. I mean she was beautiful. I called her cherry because of the color of her cheeks. Her skin was the color of French vanilla ice cream and her cheeks full of color. It looked like two cherries on the side of her face. I thought it added to her natural beauty. Being attracted to her was a new experience and I know that her great personality also had much to do with it. There were so many qualities in her that I wished my husband possessed.

"Hello?" Gia said.

"Yeah I'm here. So are you ready to see me?" I asked fully knowing the answer to that question.

"You already know babygurl. You don't even need to ask that. What hotel are you staying at? Hotel Gia?" She laughed.

"Well I have a room reserved but I am quite sure a few of my nights will be spent at Hotel Gia." I flirted back with her. "How was your day at work?" I asked. I liked to ask her about her day. I liked when she wanted to know about mine.

"It was fine. You know how that goes. I had to fight this one guy out of my office cause he was drooling over your picture." She told me she had a picture of me on her computer at work. It made me feel special. "What about yours?"

"Well my day was great. I found out I was coming to you. This girl today filed some type of harassment charges at work. Supposedly this one girl Carmell kissed and fondled this girl Natina that I work with. I know that they were friends but I didn't know that they were getting down like that." I laughed at my own joke.

"Can I fondle you Sweetness?" She loved to sneak little things like that into our conversation.

"Only if I can fondle you back My Cherry." I know when I said things like that it caught her off guard. I think she was still in shock. I mean her flirting had been successful. "I am pulling into my driveway. Can I call you back when I get inside and settle down?"

"Sure. Why don't you call me back around eight o'clock your time? I will be home by then." She answered. I blew her a kiss through the phone as we said our goodbyes. I hopped out of the car. I needed to tell my husband. I would do that when he got home. I knew the response I was going to get out of him. I contemplated cooking one of his favorite meals and telling him over dinner. Maybe I would take him out to Saltgrass Steakhouse or Joe's Crab Shack instead. He loved to eat there. I was a little confused on just how I was going to tell my husband I was being sent to work out of town. It wasn't telling that I was working out of town. That much was true. What I didn't want him to see was that I had an ulterior motive for wanting this assignment. He had a way of seeing through me and I wasn't that great of a liar anyway. I didn't want him to pick up on the real reason I was so exited about going to Georgia. I dismissed those thoughts quickly. I will deal with that when the time arises. First things first though, I ran to the closet and began packing my bags.

Nicole

Getting Yo Honey Where You Make Yo Money

•───•

It was almost seven-thirty. Jason should be here at eight. I was looking for my mascara when the phone began to ring.

"This is Nicole." I answered my cell without even looking at the caller id. I hated to do that but I was in a rush.

"Hey girl what are you doing?" I knew immediately who it was at the first sound of her voice. No one else I know sounds like a chipmunk.

"Hey Kendra, I'm getting ready for my date. Jason should be here any minute." I held the phone between my ear and my shoulder as I applied my makeup. If it's one thing I knew I knew makeup. My mother had taught me all about make-up. She always said that it was a sure fire way to get a man's attention. She told me to make my pretty face work for me and that's exactly what I did. I would look like a movie star when I was done. I mean I could give Halle Berry a run for her money.

"Jason from work? Girl didn't I tell you that boy was nothing but trouble. I heard he has just about knocked off everybody in that call center. Are you gonna become another one of his statistics?

"Hell yeah if it is as good as they say it is. Besides why do you always assume that I'm gonna give it up to somebody. Did you ever consider the possibility that this is nothing more than a date? "I laughed at my thoughts of showing Jason how a real woman got down and putting an end to all that sleeping around that he does. Even though that's what I was thinking, I didn't have to let her know.

"Girl cause you so nasty. You a nasty girl and we both know that as soon as he tries your legs gonna open up like the automatic doors of a quickie mart." Kendra laughed into the phone.

"That was just mean you know. I know that you are jealous of me." I joked back with Kendra. "You just mad cause you can't be nasty since you got married. Hey you coach in Transition Queue with Carmell and Natina right? What was that all about? I heard they got caught kissing in the restroom."

"I really don't know the full story I don't think they got caught kissing. Carmell stormed out of there so fast I didn't get a chance to ask her. Tina never said anything about it. I heard Tina filed sexual harassment charges and said that Carmell tried to kiss her or something." Kendra finished.

I was thinking to myself why would any woman want to kiss another woman when dick was so good? The doorbell rang and interrupted my thoughts.

"Hey Kendra that is Jason outside I'll call you back later."

"Hey before you go. The reason I was calling was because I'm going to Atlanta. I need you to do the follow ups on my calendar. Can you do that for me?" Kendra said.

"Sure, whatever girl I gotta go. I will talk to you later okay. Bye-bye." I hurried and disconnected my phone cause I knew that girl would start talking again if I let her. We had both started the same time. She worked in transition queue training the new hires. She was destined to be somebody's supervisor. Me, I preferred to do the least amount of work I could for the most amount of pay. That is why I was hiding out on the phones and I sure as hell didn't want to go to ATL. I would have to work too damn hard. Many of the trainers that went took reps or coaches as they were called to assist with training. More often than not, the coaches ended up doing all the trainers work, teaching classes, expense reports and depending on the trainer you were assisting you might have gotten stuck being their chauffeur. I know that just ain't me now, nor will it ever be me. If I'm gonna do extra work I'm gonna get paid to do it.

I checked myself in the mirror before I opened the door for Jason. Man, not bad at all. I was rockin' my new Gucci dress I got from the Galleria. It was my little secret that I had left the tags on and it would go back bright and early in the morning. I needed to look my best and what said it better than a little black dress with an Italian designers name on it. When you mixed me and designer clothes together it couldn't get any better. I was a size five with all the curves in the right place. My jet-black hair was layered hanging below my shoulders, with just a few tracks to give a little thickness and body, and my makeup was flawless. I opened the door to find Jason standing there looking scrumptious. His creamy skin and soft eyes made him more than cute he was handsome. Jason's hair was cut low with a very nice trim on his mustache. It was so sexy. He smiled at me to show a perfect row of white teeth. His smile was alluring and sexy and his deep dimples gave him an innocent like quality. I marveled at his height, standing at six foot four he towered over me. His body was toned and well defined. He was just the way I liked my men, somewhere in the middle. I could tell by his biceps that he worked out. They screamed for attention through the shirt he wore. It was a blue button down shirt and on the pocket there was the Sean John insignia. The man also had good taste.

"Damn girl. You are rockin' that dress." He said as he walked through the door.

"You don't look too bad yourself." I loved the way he always smelled and looked good. Not only was this man handsome he was also confident. He took a seat while I added the finishing touches to my makeup.

"Ready." I said as I grabbed my purse and we walked out of the door. My date with Jason was unreal. I mean he was so damn smooth and I felt so comfortable with him. Just as a man should be he was a perfect gentleman. He took me to a nice restaurant and we had a wonderful seafood dinner. The wine we had for dinner began to talk to me and I was ready to party. We decided to finish the night off by heating up the dance floor at a club.

This is where I would begin my seduction. I knew how to dance and use my body. When R. Kelly said move your body like a snake he was talking about me. I shook my milkshake and gained his undivided attention and the attention of numerous men passing by. I was so into dancing I had a crowd of onlookers standing around me throwing dollar bills on the floor. Through all of this I never broke eye contact with Jason. In my mind, I was making love to him on this dance floor. Through the smoked filled room, surrounded by hundreds of people, I only saw him. He was my only concern at this moment, I wanted him to read my body, my movements, and understand my desire.

"Girl you sure know how to work that thang!" I could tell by the bulge in his pants that he liked my movements. I slid close to him and started grinding on him. We would have been having sex if we didn't have our clothes on.

"Where did you learn how to dance like that?" He asked me, obviously impressed by my dancing.

"I used to be a stripper for a hot minute. I needed money to pay the rest of my tuition and I needed it fast." I said. He looked at me with a certain excitement in his eyes. I just knew that he was picturing me in nothing but a thong working the pole. I saw it in his eyes along with a great deal of lust. My little seduction plan was definitely working. The stripper story always turned men on. Every man wanted a lady in the street and a freak in the sheets and I was going to give him just that.

"Is that right? Well can I get my personal private lap dance?" Jason was looking at me with desire in his eyes. I could tell that he was thinking the same thing that I was thinking.

"That depends on how fast you can get me back to my place." I said teasingly.

"Now that's what's up." He grabbed my arm and the next thing I know we were in his car on our way back to my apartment. When we reached my front door he pulled me close to him. I was so close that I could feel his breath on my skin. The mixture of his cologne and the scent of alcohol further intoxicated me. I was drunk off this man and I wanted him more than imaginable. He took my face in his hands and began to kiss me. It was deep and passionate. It was a fairytale kiss; the kind of kiss that I had yearned for my entire life. I unlocked the door.

"Make yourself comfortable. I will be right back." I ran to the bedroom and began to undress. I found my French maid outfit and put it on. I grabbed the remote to the stereo and hit play. R. Kelly began to sing. When it came to setting the mood, no one could do it better than my friend Robert Kelly. He was freaky with a capital F and I took in every note of his music. I followed every freaky movement the song directed. I began to move my body erotically. I lowered my body to the floor as I began to move my hips like I was riding the floor. I was giving Jason a little taste of what this ride would be like. I was a girl that knew exactly what she was doing and after tonight this man would be sprung. I started to move my body like a snake twisting and turning like a belly dancer. I stopped a moment to change the song on the disc changer.

I slowly walked towards Jason, as R. Kelly led my freaky seduction.

I stood in the middle of my living room. I could see the excitement in Jason's eyes. I danced on him, working every part of my body to please him. He was practically drooling over me. I began to remove my clothes one by one.

"You want me baby?" I asked although I knew the answer to that question.

"Shit yeah, girl give me dat?" He responded. I thought it funny that he answered me with the lyrics to a song, it was something I would probably do, and I laughed to myself and continued to work it. I was gonna make sure that I put it on him so good that he wouldn't forget this.

He stood up. I could see the bulge from his pants. It was calling me. He walked to me and began to kiss my breast slowly.

"Girl you are so fine!" He moaned. I was about to show him that I was not a girl that I was all woman. I led him to my bedroom where I began to undress him. When I got to his boxers there it was that dick that everyone raved about. It was thick and long. I know it was at least a full nine or ten inches. I could not wait to get it inside of me. He began to kiss every part of my body, touching me in places I didn't even know existed. He gently slid his head between my legs and began to taste my sweetness.

"Mmmmmm baby" I called to him, letting him know that I was pleased with the pleasure that he was giving me. Jason used his tongue to send shivers through my body. Round and around in circles the tip of his tongue went, gently stroking my clit. He pulled himself close to me and slid inside of me. Just his entrance sent chills through me. Position after position he found that special spot. When he entered me from behind he thrust all of himself inside of me. He was so deep I could feel him in my stomach. Now that was my kind of man. As Kendra would say, I was becoming a statistic and loving every minute of it. He was loving me right and everything about it was wonderful. The way he held my hands as he pushed himself inside of me. I love the way he wrapped his hands around my neck. It turned me on to feel him slightly holding me tight enough to let me know that he was in control, but gentle enough to show me that he wouldn't be too rough. My body began to move with his rhythm as I reached my third climax. Who knew that I could find honey where I made my money?

Carmell

A Day at the Beach

After what happened at work yesterday the beach was welcomed. I drove to my parent's beach house in Galveston to get the peace I needed. As I pulled into the garage I noticed that Craig and his family where at their beach home this weekend. When I got out of the car I saw him running over. He was a cutey but I think a little too eager to get into my pants.

"Hey Pretty Red. What's up with you? You gone be here by yourself this weekend?" He quizzed. I looked at him. I loved those pretty hazel eyes of his. They were slanted and tight. His mothers Chinese genes had been good to him.

"Yeah I had a hard week at work. So I decided to come out here and get away for a while." I smiled at him as I pulled my bags out of the car. He hadn't even offered to help with them. I hated impolite men. I had an idea of how a man should treat a lady and so far Craig wasn't doing that. Well he just lost points.

"Well, if you want to hook up tonight then let me know. You know today is my birthday. That is the real reason you come down here huh?" He started to walk back towards his house. I know he couldn't have been serious. Now how in the hell was I suppose to know it was his birthday when I don't even talk to him. I can't even remember what his last name was so there's no way I could remember his birthday. I just stared at him and then walked away.

"Okay, I will let you know." I yelled back at him. I knew that I was probably not going to call him.

I walked into the house and began to unpack. It was a good thing that no one knew where I was. I didn't feel like being bothered. After I finished I started the Jacuzzi tub. Ready for a hot relaxing bath, I climbed in the tub and let the water and bubbles surround me.

"This is what I need." I thought to myself.

I was falling asleep in the tub when I heard the doorbell ring. Quickly glancing towards the clock I saw it was ten thirty. I had been in the bathtub for almost two hours. I grabbed my robe and ran to the door. The only person it could have been was Craig. I looked out the peephole. Damn, I should work for Dionne Warwick and her psychic friends.

"What are you doing showing up at my house this time of night?" I was a little annoyed that he would just invite himself to my house.

"Awe come on baby, show a nigga some love on his twenty-seventh birthday." He pleaded.

"Okay, the only reason you got this far is cause it is your birthday." I stated. I opened the door wide enough for him to come in.

"Damn yall beach house is nice. It looks like it is bigger than ours. I notice part of it sits in the water. That is nice." I don't know why he was trippin. This was not his first time seeing the deck. When we purchased the house my parents had a deck built that extended into the water. That place use to be my refuge. I loved to just sit out there and watch the stars. Whenever I felt sad or hurt I ran to my deck. Not only had that deck been my heaven but my hell. Things I didn't care to remember had happened to me on that deck. I snapped out of my trance realizing that I was wearing nothing under my robe.

"Hold on a sec okay. I will be right back." I said as I headed towards the bedroom. I didn't plan on having any company but I was kinda bored. I removed my robe and searched for my long nightshirt.

"Damn Carmell, you working with a lil something. Girl you fine."

Craig was standing at the door gawking at me. I could not believe that he strolled his ass off in here.

"What the hell are you doing in here? I thought I told you to wait yo ass on that couch." He was really pissing me off.

"Wait lil momma I just want to taste you. Just allow me to savor your sweetness please?" He began to lick his lips. Oh so he wanted to eat it huh. That just may be what I need to take the edge off. A man, emphasis on man, to send me to Pleasureville and then I can send his ass on his way.

"So you want to taste me. You gotta promise that is all you want to do." I looked at him with a seductive look while twirling on the end of my hair like an innocent schoolgirl. Yeah that was all he was gonna do and I hope he wasn't getting ideas.

"Yeah, that is all I want for my birthday." Craig started to come close to me. He started at my forehead and made his way down. Next, he began to nibble on my neck, sucking softly but just hard enough to send chills up my spine. After that he began to tease my nipples, softly running his tongue over them as they became harder and harder. The next kisses were planted on my stomach as he headed south of the border. He began to please me with his tongue. I got to give it to old boy he had skills in that department. He had me going and after my third orgasm I was ready to give in and let him have it all.

He started to pull off his clothes as he continued. I could only speculate that if he ate it this good that what was to follow was going to be mind blowing. He pulled off his boxers. I could not wait to see what he was working with. Whether he was going to get it or not was definitely dependent on the size of his tool. I lifted myself up before I made the decision to do this I needed to see what ole boy was packing. I needed to know that his size was at least worth my time. Once I saw it I immediately made my decision.

"What are you doing?" I was not about to waste my time with him and his mini me dick.

"What?" He asked as if he did not know what.

"I told you only eating. It was good thanks but now you gotta go." I said looking at the clock.

"Come on baby. You can't just work me up and let me down." He started to move towards me, his two-inch dick in hand. He started to try and climb on top of me.

"Get back!" I see he thought that I was playing.

"You know you want this." He reached for me. I jumped up and pulled out the nightstand drawer.

"What you looking for?" He was still stroking his pencil-sized pokey. That is what will be doing tonight cause he wasn't getting none from me.

"Nina." I said.

"Nina?" I turned around just in time to see the question mark on his face turn in to fear.

"Like I said, it is time for you to go. Since you don't want to do it the easy way we can do it the hard way." I could see the terror in his eyes. He thought I was little miss sweet. My father was an FBI agent and I been shooting since I was twelve. He was an easy target. I could shoot his dick off with my eyes closed.

"I, I, I." Craig stuttered.

"What's the matter cat got your tongue? I asked. No pun intended. "This could have been simple but you had to make it hard. I see it this way. If you don't get out of my damn house Nina gone put you out. So if you want to leave with your dick still attached there is the door. I will not hesitate to shoot you and then pistol whip yo ass for wasting my time." I was walking towards him.

Craig began to trip over things. He struggled to put his clothes on. As he walked towards the door I followed. He stepped outside the door.

"Bitch, I don't need you!" He yelled. I guess he felt safe since he was running across the walkway.

"Good, cause yo dick too small for me anyways!" I yelled back as I slammed my door. Just as I was locking the door, my cell phone began to rudely interrupt my newly found silence. It was evident I wasn't going to have that relaxing day at the beach.

Natina

Cause I got High

Since I was so pissed about Carmell I decided to find the neighborhood weed man and get blowed. My weekend was pretty much going nowhere. I had not accomplished in getting her fired and I failed at trying to get with her. So I needed a break from all this drama.

"Hey DeeDee. You seen Reggie around here today?" I walked towards DeeDee, if any one knew where the weed man was, she would.

"Why girl you trying to get high?" she asked knowing full well what the answer to that question was.

"Yeah. I've been having some problems and I need to smoke them all away tonight."

"Well, Reggie gone to make a run. He won't be back for a couple of hours. But you know what today's your lucky day. I got a sweet, you want it you can have it. Just don't forget when I need a favor!" DeeDee said. That girl was crazy.

"For sho!" I said taking it from her hand.

"As a matter of fact, I'm gonna need that favor today. I need to go pick up some stuff from the South Park and ain't no telling when Reggie gone come back. You think you can take me over there?" I shook my head yes. I didn't have anything else to do so why not. It might even take my mind off Carmell. She hopped in the car and we drove off blasting Trina in the cd. As soon as we hit Highway 610 some fool started acting stupid. This fool just cuts me off and shoots me the finger. Oh hell no, what the hell is his problem.

"Obviously he doesn't know what kind of day I had." I yelled as I sped up to catch up with the Suburban. I pulled up on the side of the over sized truck. My plan was to simply shoot this dumb ass the finger and speed off, but DeeDee had a different plan. She rolls down the window and started shouting obscenities at them.

This shouting match didn't last long. The guy in the front seat pulls out a gun and begins shooting towards my car. Oh Lord I sure didn't plan on dying today. I tried to drive off but the beast of a truck wouldn't let me by. Then as if this situation can't get any worse Dee Dee is strapped.

"Who these niggas thank they playing wit? When I shoot I don't miss." She pulls out her gun and proceeds to aim. Round after round she lit into the twenty-twos the truck wore. She managed to hit one tire before I hit the gas as hard as I could and did almost 100 down the freeway until I hit Highway 59. I was in a hurry now to get this girl to her destination and out of my car. As we were pulling up into the apartments her cell phone rings.

"Girl that was Reggie, he's over here now so you don't have to worry about dropping me off back home. Thanks for the favor and I'm sorry about the shooting girl, but I just can't let nobody punk me like that." She said.

I looked at Dee Dee. "Don't worry about it chic. I knew better than to act a fool on the freeway with yo looney ass in the car. See ya girl." I said whatever I needed to say to send this loony bitch on her way.

"Alright then. Get high enough for me." She laughed as she walked off. My initial thought was to curse her out, but she was carrying a gun and she just showed me she ain't afraid to use it. As soon as I get home I'm gonna take her advice and get as high as a kite.

I headed home and began to fire it up. This is what I needed after a long hard day. I laid back on my sofa and began to think about Carmell. She was fine as hell. I had never felt this way before about a woman. She was the one that I thought I wanted to be with. Man I must be trippin' but I think I love that girl. Now I had to be tripping or it was the weed talking.

That inner voice that only speaks when your state of mind is altered began to chatter. It kept telling me to call her even though I knew that would be out of the question. Instead, I called a guy I had been kicking it with to come over. I needed to release some frustration and sex was the best way I knew to do it.

While I waited for him, that voice started to persuade me to call her. That damn voice told me she wanted to talk to me just as much as I wanted to speak to her. I could not stop myself from picking up the phone. I began to dial the number but quickly disconnected the call. Finally, I got the courage to complete the number.

"Hello" a frustrated Carmell answered the phone.

"Hey sexy, I just wanted to hear your voice." I hoped she would not hang up the phone in my face. I needed just to hear her voice.

"Natina? What the hell do you want?" Carmell screamed into the phone. Okay I could see she was still upset.

"I want to taste you again. Can I hold you and feel your soft body?" The narcotics gave me a sense of courage. I waited for her to reply to my last comment.

"Look bitch don't be calling me with that sick shit. I already done told you that I don't get down like that. So why the hell you gone call me? To top it all off you tried to get me fired. I know damn well you don't think that you have a chance in hell with getting with me do you?" She stated. Why couldn't she just be nice?

"Alright, if that is how it is. You know what, by the time I finish with yo ass you gone wish you would have just gave me some. You didn't seem to be saying that you didn't like it with all that moaning that you were doing when I was going down on you. So don't sit here and tell me no shit about you don't get down like that. You don't know who you messing with." I slammed down the phone. I could not believe her. Just a week ago we were chilling together. I just knew that she was feeling me. Maybe it was she was just feeling having a friend and I misread the signs. No, that couldn't be it. With the way she flaunted her naked body around and flirted back with me, there was no way I had misread the signs. Damn, this weed was steering the wheels of my mind in the wrong direction. I was pissed at myself for listening to that damn voice.

Why in the hell had I called that girl anyway? Oh yeah, I thought as I walked to the door to let my friend in, cause I got high.

Kendra

Love At First Sight

The warm summer air caressed my face as I stepped off the plane. I was so nervous about meeting Gia. I couldn't really figure out why I was so nervous. I have been talking to this girl for months and months but now that I am here in Atlanta I can't seem to calm myself.

I grabbed my bag and walked toward the passenger pick up of the Hartsfield Atlanta International Airport. I could not stop myself from thinking what if she didn't pick me up. I had to go to work tomorrow so I would just take Sunday as our day. I looked around the airport. I did not see anyone that looked remotely like the picture that she had sent me. I quickly dismissed the thought that maybe she was lying to me.

I pulled out my compact to look myself over. I examined my face for any imperfection or flaw, but my makeup was flawless. The eyeliner I had chosen complimented my smoky gray eyes perfectly. I began to run a brush through my shoulder length hair, as I brushed the layers feel framed my caramel colored face perfectly. I was ready to meet her now. I began to search for a familiar face.

Then, I noticed her. She was standing alone near the door looking like an angel. She wore a long black strapless dress with a split as high as her mid-thigh. She looked like the perfect woman. I didn't know whether to envy or admire her. Her hair lay gently against her bare shoulders nicely, her long layers accenting her beautiful face. I had never seen a woman this pretty before. I walked up to her. She had the prettiest eyes. They were a deep amber color with just a touch of green.

"Hey Sweetness!" She leaned in and gently kissed my lips. I thought I was going to faint right here. My palms were sweaty and my heartbeat quickened. I quickly looked around to see if anyone had seen our first intimate moment. I was a bit concerned about who saw and what they saw. I had to remember that I wasn't the only person working this special project and there were others arriving the same time that I did. I tried not to think of that. It was useless, it was done and we had shared a kiss, our very first kiss.

She grabbed my bags and led me to her brand new cherry red Tahoe. I could not help thinking to myself that this was a big truck for such a little woman. I got in. I just could not stop staring at her.

"Cherry sweetie you look so pretty." I looked at her beautiful face.

"You do too babygurl." She looked at me and smiled. She was so country and when she said girl it sounded more like gurl with a "u". Normally, it would bother me when people mispronounced things but her beauty and intelligence more than made up for her country grammar. I knew that when it came down to it, she could speak with eloquence. I gazed into her eyes and was simply mesmerized by her beauty. I could see the lust in her eyes and I know that she could see the fear in mine.

"We don't have to do anything that you don't feel comfortable with okay. Do you remember when I told you that I could just sit and look at you and I would be content? Well I meant it." She said to me as we pulled into my hotel.

My company had gotten me a room that had a kitchenette so that I could cook my own meals and it would seem more like home for the month that I was here. Gia had made her self comfortable on the bed as I prepared steaks for the two of us. While I prepared the salad, Gia ran a hot bubble bath for two. I knew that I would feel funny about baring all in front of another woman but this relationship is different from any other relationship that I have experienced with a female. This relationship was different from anything that I had experienced male or female. This woman, she got me, she understood me and when we were together it was like we were the only two that existed. Standing here preparing this meal I forgot all about my outside world, my other world. I didn't think about the part of my life that Gia does not fit into. I didn't want to think about it. I wanted nothing more than to savor the moment and time that we were sharing together.

We ate dinner over candlelight and wine. I began to unwind as we talked. It was just like when we talked over the phone. I was so comfortable with Gia and totally enamored with her beauty. She was so exquisite and as intelligent as she was she could have any one she wanted, man or woman and she was choosing me.

"So are you okay?" She asked.

"Yeah I'm fine; you know we talked about this. I just feel a little anxious, nervous, and aroused all at the same time." I told her as I smiled.

"Like I said, you ain't gotta do nothing that you don't want to do. I can just hold you if you let me." Gia looked at me showing that perfect smile of hers. Her skin was so beautiful. Every time I looked at her I noticed more and more features about her. Her lips looked so soft and they were perfect to me. They were pouty, sexy even, maybe almost as sexy as Angelina Jolie's lips.

"How about this" I said hoping I was wording my sentence properly, "we will take it slow. Whatever happens happens. K" I hoped that she was not offended by what said. I didn't want her to think she was some test experiment or trial run. I just simply didn't know if I were ready to move forward and take this relationship to the next level. I knew once that line had been crossed there would be no turning back. Once the flood gates had been opened they could not be simply closed.

"You're reading my mind Sweetness." She grabbed my hand and led me to the bathroom where she slowly undressed me. We stepped into the pool of bubbles and relaxed, holding one another as we talked. We talked about everything and anything. She held me in the warm water the way I wished my husband would. I quickly dismissed the thoughts of him. I didn't want to think of him. I wanted to only concentrate on this moment that we were having. If I allowed the thoughts of him to slip into my mind I would began to feel guilty. I would save my guilt moments for my alone time.

"I want you to tell me about it." I said to her.

"Tell you about what?" She asked.

"Tell me about being with a woman. I want to know what it feels like. Why are you so drawn to women? You are so beautiful that I know you can have any man you want, yet you choose women. Tell me why." I was curious so I asked.

"Well I choose women because I don't like men. It's that simple. I don't want a man because I love women. Their softness and their scent do more for me than any man could. As for what it feels like, baby girl I can only say it is a feeling that you have to experience. It's provocative and tender. Women are gentle but they are strong and it's such a turn on. They nurture you and take care of you, and who knows the female anatomy better than a female?" She smiled and kissed my forehead when she was done speaking.

I looked her in the face. It was a beautiful face. I couldn't stress that enough this girl was gorgeous and it felt so good to know that she looked at me and thought that I too was beautiful. I was lost in her essence. I could only stare at her. From the moment that I saw her, it was love at first sight.

Nicole

Waiting on Your Call

⸺⸺⸺⸺⸺⸺⸺⸺⸺⸺⸺⸺⸺⸺⸺⸺⸺⸺

I came to work today feeling good. After the weekend I had with Jason I was ready to take on the world. I can safely say that it is true what they say. I mean that boy put it down. I thought of having him all to myself. We seemed like we belonged together; a perfect fit.

After Jason left Saturday night I had tried to call him three times. He must be busy or something. I didn't worry much about it because I knew that I would see him today at work. I knew his lunch was at three-thirty, mine is at three. I decided to wait an extra thirty minutes so that I can eat lunch with him. I needed to show him that I too could be spontaneous.

At three-thirty exactly I signed off the phone for my lunch and walked towards Jason's desk. When I walked up I saw something that I did not like at all. There was Tasha, the hoe of the call center all hugged up on him. I couldn't stand her and now I really couldn't stand her because she always seemed to be wherever Jason was. My mind told me he was my man and she should exercise extreme caution before she even thought about messing with my man. Mama told me a long time ago don't let nobody take what's yours and she wasn't going to take what I had already claimed. I stood still for a moment and watched them. Thinking of the things my mother had told me brought back a flood of memories. My mother's a fighter too, and I had seen her on more than one occasion willing to fight for her men.

"Hey Jason, are you about to go to lunch?" I interrupted. She looked at me with disgust. She didn't have to worry cause the feeling was definitely mutual. I was disgusted by her and I let my face expose my emotions. Jason spoke and broke my thoughts.

"What's up?" Jason said to me. He was looking at Tasha's ass as she walked away and she was twisting extra hard. If she twisted any harder, her ass would have fell off. Why did he even bother with her skanky ass?

"Excuse me, was I interrupting something between you and her ass, cause with the way you are looking at it I know that you can recognize it in a line up." He was about to piss me off.

"Naw girl. What's wrong with you? I thought your lunch was at three today." Jason said. I had managed to sway his attention from her behind. It was actually making me a little jealous. After the night we had together he should have been only thinking about us. Instead he was engaged in deep conversation with her and the center of his thoughts was some other woman's behind. I was trying hard to control my pisstivity level. I took a brief moment and decided to tell him he had been blessed with my company for lunch.

"Well I took it late so that I could eat lunch with you." I smiled at Jason. My plan was to get him all alone in the parking garage. We walked out the door and headed to his car, which was conveniently parked on the fourth floor in the corner. I got into his car. As soon as he sat back I went for it. I began to kiss his pillow soft lips. His lips felt so good against mine. When he kissed me he moved his tongue in a way that made my legs quiver. I could honestly say I had never been kissed like that. It was one of those soap opera kisses, the kind that anyone would envy. He could move his tongue in such a way that it gave me tiny little goose bumps all over my body.

"So what do you want for lunch?" He asked. I just looked at him and began to unzip his pants. Once I had gotten his pants unzipped I pulled it out and I had to simply admire it. It turned me on just thinking about it. I felt like if you got a good one let it be known and I was definitely about to show this man that I appreciated him and his tool.

"You." I whispered as I placed my lips around his more than ample love. I knew that I caught him off guard and that is exactly what I wanted to do. I mean I was out to let him know that I was the one that was going to be down under any circumstances. I stroked him with my mouth, letting the ball of my tongue ring tickle him. He grabbed my hair and pulled it back. That is just like a man to want to watch. I was more than happy to let him watch me work. I took him all into my mouth until it could go no further. His moans let me know that it was good to him.

"Dang girl, do yo thang!" I heard him moan. He let out an extremely loud moan and then I felt a warm substance in my mouth. It was gooey and sticky and I didn't so much like this feeling in my mouth. That is nasty. He could have at least told me he was about to do that. What gave him the idea that he could leave his cum in my mouth? I could feel the little needle on my mad meter beginning to move slightly towards annoyed. I opened the door and spit that nasty stuff out of my mouth. I grabbed a napkin and began to wipe my mouth and reached for my purse to get the tiny bottle of mouthwash that I carry with me. I looked at him. I wanted to slap him across his head, cumming in my mouth like that. That was my first thought but then I began to look at him and his great body and that perfect smile he had. I wanted to hit him but he was so fine. I tried not to let how angry I was show.

"Did you enjoy that? I asked. It was more than evident that he enjoyed it but just to stroke my ego a little I needed to hear him say it.

"Yeah you shocked the hell out of me." He replied.

"So that means you will be taking me out tomorrow night right?" I said with a smile. I know after the amazing head I just blessed him with I was worthy of another date and instead of waiting until another time to ask I decided to go for it now. Hell, he should even feel obligated to take me out after what I just did.

"I'll call you and let you know." Jason said getting out of the car. The thought that he hadn't said yes but he would let me know upset me. I thought about going off but decided to handle it in a different manner. I decided to be delicate and act as if it just didn't bother me.

I leaned in and tried to kiss him. He turned his head and reached for his keys. I looked at him trying to read his thoughts. I know he wasn't tripping about kissing me after I had just finished giving him head. I know he wasn't tripping after he just let his seed go all in my mouth. No that couldn't be it. He had to have not seen that I was trying to kiss him. That better had been what it was.

"Don't let me down; I will be waiting on your call." I said as I headed back to the building.

Carmell

The Man of my Dreams

After the week that I've had something good is bound to happen. I called in today because I just didn't feel like putting up with the daily drama that my job put me through. I was speeding down Interstate 45 when I noticed my gaslight shouting at me. I was riding on fumes. I exited and pulled into Exxon. I parked my midnight blue Camaro, reached for my card and got out.

Oh my goodness. Be still my beating heart. There he stood, the sexiest chocolate that I ever did see. He stood about six foot three weighing in at about two-o-five. His skin was rich and smooth like dark chocolate. His eyes were dark brown and beautiful.

"*FLAWLZ* is right." I heard him say. I could not believe I was talking to him.

"Excuse me." I said.

"I said that I agree. You are flawless." He pointed to my personalized plates. I smiled. When he smiled back I knew it was love. He had the hugest dimples. He looked like a little teddy bear, a teddy bear that I would love to hold.

"Do you want me to pump your gas?" He reached and took the gas pump from me. He was fine and a gentleman. Oh he gets extra points. Even though the gas pumps would pump themselves I allowed him to pump my gas for me. It was gentleman like for him to offer and I appreciated a gentleman in this world full of scrubs.

"My name is Carmell." I said extending my manicured hand for him to take.

"And I'm Louis" He flashed that million-dollar smile. He was finished pumping the gas. We stood there and talked about everything and nothing all at the same time. I felt so comfortable with him. I realized that I had been standing in this spot for thirty minutes. I gave him my number and in return he gave me his.

It was so hard to meet a man that had something to talk about. I was so excited about him and there was no way I was letting this one get away. I was a little more forward than I would usually be. I love for a man to chase me but I thought I would give him a little push.

"Make sure you use that number, Louis." I teased.

"Lil' Momma you don't even have to ask." He said as he leaned in and placed a soft kiss on my cheek. I waved at him as he walked away. I grabbed my cell phone and called my mom.

"Hey mom, guess what? I just met him. You would love him. He is handsome and so so fine. And he is educated with a BS in Business management from LSU. He's your future son in law." I screamed into the phone. My mother was always the first person I called when something exciting or devastating, for that matter, happened in my life. She was my mother but she was also like my best friend. I could count on my mom to be real with me and more honest than any body else out there. I knew she loved me and wanted no harm to come to me so she told me the truth. Since I was so taken with this man the only thing that I could do was share my excitement.

"Met who?" my mother questioned.

"The man of my dreams. I just met the man of my dreams Mom!"

Natina

Ménage Tois

Well calling Carmell this weekend had been a total waste of my time. I guess she was still mad. I looked for her at work and didn't see her. She must have called in since my plan to get her fired didn't work I knew she still had a job. I needed to find something to get into tonight. I wonder if any of the girls over here were going out.

"Nicole, what's up on tonight? What yall got planned?" I really didn't know Nicole that well but I knew she knew where the party was.

"Yeah Tina, we can find a spot to hit after work if you want. I don't have anything to do tonight." She answered.

"So what clubs are hot on Mondays?" I was curious to know what club this girl was taking me to.

"We'll see" was all that she said. I guess we were going to have to play the guessing game.

"Okay then I will meet you at your house at 9:30 or 10:00 how does that sound?" I said.

"That's cool." Nicole said. She gave me her address before I left. When I reached my car I decided that I wanted a new outfit.

I met Nicole at her house. I had to admit she was almost looking as good as me. She had on a strapless black dress that had two splits on each side. Her splits were so high that I could see her g-sting when she walked. I had to give her props but my dress that I found at the Galleria left her breathless. It was platinum and I must say that it looked good against my size twelve honey colored body. The front was v-neck that extended so that my pierced navel was visible. My back was completely out and I wasn't worried about anybody seeing my g-string because I couldn't wear any underwear with this. I only had one split on my dress but it was so far up my leg I could feel the wind caressing my thighs among other things.

"Tina, where did you find that dress?" Nicole said to me as we drove to the club.

"Now if I told you I would have to kill you!" I laughed. I wasn't going to tell her where I had gotten my dress from so she could try to go buy one just like it. I knew that trick.

I stepped out of the car in my three-inch heels knowing that I was stopping traffic. Nicole followed my lead. I didn't mind going anywhere with her; she was a showstopper too. I can't hang with ugly chicks. You are like the company you keep and I sure wasn't ugly. So when I made friends I had to make sure they were as hot as me. Well no one could be as hot as me, but they had to be attractive. Call me shallow I don't care. My friends are like an accessory and I would never wear an ugly accessory. We stepped into the club like we owned it. I had a lot on my mind so the first thing I did was hit the bar for an Amaretto Sour. Soon I would chase that with a Blue Hawaiian and a Long Island Iced Tea. I knew what got me buzzed.

I hit the dance floor to shake it fast. I was feeling so good that I didn't have a care in the world. I looked over to check on Nicole. She was dancing with a fine chocolate brother. I walked up and began to dance behind this sexy man. I could smell his cologne.

"Versace Dreamer" I whispered. I knew that smell anywhere. Sexy man turned and faced me.

"Louis! Boy I haven't seen you in forever. I thought you went back to Louisiana." I said I hugged my old boyfriend. I remembered back to those wild days we used to have. This boy was down for whatever. He is the one that turned me out by getting me to do a threesome with this girl. I remembered how timid I was at first and I remember just how understanding he seemed to be. He was also persistent. He wore me down until I did it and I was so turned on by it I went to him and asked him to do it again. I guess you can say he introduced me to my love for women.

"Yeah baby girl I'm back now. I went to finish my last year at LSU. What's up with you? And who's your friend over here?" Louis was already giving me that look.

"Oh I have been fine, and that is Nicole, a coworker of mine." I said returning his smile.

We danced until the club was almost closed. We had agreed to go back to my house and since I drove Nicole was going to stay the night and I would drop her off in the morning.

When I got to my house I broke out my last sweet, might as well go all out. I fired it up and let Louis hit it first.

"Puff, puff, pass. You messing up the rotation!" I yelled at him playfully. He passed it to Nicole and then jumped on top of me and blew smoke into my face.

"Your friend is kinda fine. So is she down?" he whispered in my ear. I already knew what was up. It's like he could read my mind and I could read his. I didn't care if she was down or not. I wanted to be with Louis, he new how to work my middle better than any other man, having Nicole here would simply make it more interesting.

"I don't know. Why don't you ask her?" I was trying to get something started. It had been a while since I had hooked up with Louis and it had been even longer since I had a threesome.

"Hey lil' momma, let me ask you a question. Would you ever have a threesome? Are you down with women, men or both?" Louis asked her so smoothly. He had a way of making it seem like he was asking her if she liked to watch sports or something. He made it sound like it was an everyday normal thing and the poor girlies fell for it every time. I knew she would fall for it thanks to this weed she would probably fall for anything.

"I wouldn't say never. I don't get down with women but as long as the woman didn't like try to finger me and kiss me and stuff I would probably be down, I would like to meet a man that could handle two women." Nicole said. Louis just turned and looked at me with that handsome dimpled smile. Now that's what's up. Nicole was so high she would probably agree to anything.

I walked over and sat next to Nicole on the couch. I left just enough space for Louis. I knew my boundaries with Nicole and I would behave a little. Louis came and sat between us just as I had anticipated. He slowly began to undress me. He kissed places on my body only he knew would turn me on. I found his special places as I kissed his nicely toned body. I looked at Nicole and motioned for her to join in. She moved slowly towards us, a little hesitant at first. She began to remove her dress. The look on her face was so seductive. No matter how slow she moved I know it turned her on. She was into it. I could tell by her eyes. It's always in the eyes and she wanted to do this. I surveyed her body. She did have a nice body. She was very lean but with curves in all the right places. And she had plenty of ass, which happened to be one of my favorite body parts. Louis always knew how to pick a beautiful woman. He began to caress our breast at the same time. I climbed on top of him positioning myself above his face. I knew that is how he liked to taste it best. He licked and sucked. He used his fingers to touch and explore and it was wonderful. I was riding his tongue and so turned on.

Nicole began to taste him. Just watching her technique it seemed she knew what she was doing. Even though I'm sure she wasn't as good as me, but then again it's hard to compete with perfection. I laughed to myself. I was loving every moment of this. It was wonderful being with Louis again. I was even able to sneak a few feels of Nicole's breast. I slightly touched her nipples as Louis worked his magic stick. The look on her face told me she was enjoying every bit of him and I could not blame her at all. His sex was simply amazing. I squeezed and pulled on her nipples and watched him bring her to a climax. After back-to-back orgasms and multiple packs of condoms we were spent. I see that Nicole is bout' it. I think I found my new best friend.

We fell asleep right there on my living room floor. I was on one side of Louis and she was on the other. After a night like that I was in a sexually induced coma. I slept better than I had in a long time cause when it came to sex Louis could work magic.

I was the first to wake so I got up to begin cooking some breakfast. I know that he loves breakfast after a night like that and after him putting it down like that I would do just about anything. It was quite a night and after last night I was more than sure that they both would be hungry. I began to cook some bacon, eggs and pancakes. I guess Nicole heard me cause she came into the kitchen with me.

"Good Morning" she said. I looked at her and smiled.

I handed her a plate of food. "Hey there sleepy head, not bad for your first ménage trois"

Kendra

Peace of Mind

These people in Atlanta are driving me crazy. They don't seem to know anything, but try to tell them something and they know everything. No wonder they sent us down here to help them. I could not wait to get back to my hotel room and rest. I went to join Katey in the break room. She was one of my co-workers that were sent to train also.

"How you holding up there?" I asked. Katey was pregnant and if you ask me much too far away from home to be with child.

"I am okay. I've been having these strange cramps all day." She answered.

We began to hold a conversation on how completely dumb these people seemed to be in this call center. Maybe we should not have gone that far, but I know that I definitely get a little aggravated when I am asked the same question ten different ways twelve different times.

"Katey, what's the matter? What is wrong you look like you are about to faint." I yelled. She didn't look to well.

"It's those cramps that I have been having all day. They are worst this time." She replied. I didn't know what to do. I looked at her. Below her seat was a tiny pool of blood that had began to form.

"Oh shit, can somebody call 911 she's bleeding!" I yelled to the crowd that had begun to form. Everybody was just staring at her like she was a peep show.

Finally the paramedics showed up. Could this day get any worse." I thought to myself. I silently prayed for Katey and her unborn child, hoping that she had not miscarried and that she would be okay as well as the baby.

I began to gather my things. My shift was almost over and I had to hurry. I had been promised a wonderful dinner especially prepared for me. I couldn't wait to talk to and be around Gia. I knew that she would know just what to say when it came to calming me down. This was way too much for me to deal with and my nerves had become bad. I just couldn't understand why she would travel being pregnant and away from her doctors. Maybe for a little while but we were supposed to be here longer than a few weeks. It was useless to think about that, I just hoped that she would be alright.

I hadn't talked to Cory since yesterday and we hadn't talked very long. I decided to call him and let him know that I was thinking about him. Maybe he would have more to say about it than just oh yeah. I hit speed dial two and called him on his phone, he should have been on his way home from work now. After four or five rings I got his voicemail and just left a message. Then I had an even better idea, I needed a dose of cherry.

"Call Cherry" I spoke the voice dial command into my cell phone. I had to tell her that I would be coming over. I hurried to the hotel to shower. I needed to get to my cherry because I needed to get to my piece of mind.

Nicole

On My Mind

The night that I went out with Tina just blew my mind. I have never done anything like that before in my life. Her ex-boyfriend was something serious though. He could almost compete with Jason. Speaking of Jason, I had not heard anything from him. I called all day yesterday. I even rode by his apartment a couple of times but it didn't look like he was home.

I walked into work that day with a mission and that was to find Jason. Although that night with Tina and Louis was fun, I was yearning for some one on one love from Jason. I mean it was strange to me how willing Tina was to share her man, but she did. I was so messed up I'm surprised that I even remembered what happened that night. I remembered quite a bit from that night. I remember having sex with that fine man of hers and I also remember her trying to cop a feel while I was riding him. I didn't say anything cause she didn't try to go any further than that and I'm glad that she didn't cause we wouldn't be friends anymore if she had.

The day was speeding by and still no sign of Jason. I wonder where he was. While I sat at my desk and ate lunch I heard that girl Tasha talking to another girl about Jason. It took everything I had to stop myself from slapping the taste out of her mouth. That same disgust came over me as I thought about her and Jason. Like I said before, in my mind he was my man and she didn't mean a thing. That skanky hoe was over there talking noise. I think she thought he was her man.

"Girl yeah, Jason came over and put it down." When I heard that it made me want to slap the teeth out of her mouth. That is why he had not called me like he said he would. I bet she would never go so far as to please him at work and he chose to go screw around with her when he had all this over here. He had to be out of his damn mind. She had to be lying and even against my best judgment I just had to go ask her. I tried to sit still, but the more that I heard her talk about all the things that he did to her the more upset I got.

"Oh so you kickin' it with Jason now?" I walked over to Tasha.

"And what if I am, who are to question what I do with him?" She looked at me and smiled sarcastically. She smiled as if she had won first prize at the carnival. Oh so this was suppose to be my payback from me having to dismiss her I guess.

"I just asked a damn question. I don't need all of your attitude!" I said to her. She was really pissing me off.

"Well stay out of my got damn business and you don't have to worry about my attitude." She turned to walk away from me. As she walked, I again thought how nasty her walk was, and she might want to pull that wedgey out of her ass. I really can't stand her now and to know that she was the competition really bothered me. I thought back to that day that they were talking and I interrupted. That is why he never called me to go to the movies he was too busy doing her. Well she will never be able to compete with me. Never.

I needed to talk to someone about this. I knew that Kendra wouldn't be available so I decided to call my mother. She could tell me how to handle this.

"Hey Ma, how are you?" I asked when she answered the phone.

"I'm good baby, what's going on you sound stressed." She asked. I could hear something going on in the background but I hadn't quite figured out what.

"Some skank is messing with my man Mama and he is obviously

messing with her too." I could still hear sounds in the background. I could tell I didn't have my mother's full attention. "Ma are you there?" I asked. The sounds had started to sound like moans. I know this woman ain't having sex while I'm on the phone with her. That was some sick shit.

"Baby look, Mama gotta go take care of her man. I'll call you back later." Before I could say anything else she had disconnected the phone. That was my mother for you. I've never had her undivided attention; she's always been ready and available for her men but never for me. I vowed to myself that I wouldn't be that way. Not wanting to think about it I decided to force those thoughts from my mind and the best way to do that would be by hearing Jason's voice.

I picked up my phone and began to dial Jason's cell, maybe he would finally answer.

"What's up?" He seduced me with his sexy voice.

"What's up to you stranger? Where you been?" I quizzed him, trying not to show how upset I actually was. When it came to Jason I was always reserved. I felt like our relationship was new and fragile and I didn't want to go off on him to early.

"Who is this?" Jason said.

"What do you mean who is this? It's Cole." I said sounding a little upset. He could have at least allowed me to talk long enough so he could figure out who I was. He just came straight out and said, "who is this", like I didn't mean enough to at least learn my voice or program my number into his phone.

"Oh hey girl what's up?" He said.

"Nothing, where have you been I been calling you like crazy and you ain't returned my calls." I was trying to control my temper but it was beginning to be harder and harder.

"I'm in Atlanta. One of the girls that were here went into labor and they sent me. Why, you been looking for me?" I could hear the smile in his voice.

"Yeah I have. I've been missing that good love that you been giving me." I started to mention to him that I knew about him and Tasha, but I decided against it. He wasn't my man yet, even though I had mentally claimed him I knew better than to tell him that now.

I was okay now that I was talking to him. I was gonna make this man mine at all cost. He was going to be in Atlanta a month at the very least. I don't know if I could make it that long without him. I thought about him all the time. Every night he invaded my dreams and I yearned for him more and more with each passing day. I sounded like I was sprung, and I had to admit that I was. I was sick without him. I tried not to think of him but he was always on my mind.

Carmell

Couldn't Believe My Eyes

It had been a couple of days and still no call from Louis. I decided that I would treat myself to a dinner and a movie. I was really upset that Louis hadn't called me. All that mess he was talking and he couldn't pick up the phone and call.

All day at work that is all that I could think about. I tried to put it out of my mind.

As I was leaving I saw Natina. Just the sight of her disgusted me.

"Hey sexy" I heard her whisper. "Have you changed your mind yet?" She licked her lips as she walked past me. I just wanted to reach out and knock every one of her teeth out of her mouth. She knew how to work my nerves, but I ignored her stupidity. If I let it get to me it would just make me more upset. I jumped into my car and headed home. I had to get ready for my special night just for me.

Against all of my rules I pulled out my cell and searched for his name. I had to call him. I don't know what the problem was but I needed to remind him of just what could be his. I let the phone ring four times before the voicemail picked up. I decided to leave a message.

"Hey there stranger. You gonna capture my heart and then disappear like that. Well when you get this message give me a call back." I intentionally did not leave my name. If he had that many females he has given his number out to then he wasn't for me anyway.

When I got to the theater and took a look at that line I had to question whether or not I wanted to stay. I stood here, waiting. I had to admit I would rather be here with Louis but he never returned my call. So I am here. Alone. I stopped by the concession stand to get some popcorn and an Icee and then took my seat. I could hear the loud whispers of the couple behind me. I was two minutes from knocking the mess out of both of them. Why did people have to be so dang rude? You come to a place like a movie theater and you want to keep up all the noise in the world. I thought about moving but I paid for my ticket just like them and I deserved to sit wherever I wanted to.

They quieted a little and then I began to hear soft moans. I sat there. I know they couldn't have been having any form of sex behind my head. I mean were people really that rude and were they really that nasty?

"It's none of your business Carmell," I said to myself. The couple began to get louder and louder. There wasn't anyone in the back row but them. Maybe they had made a mistake and thought they were the only ones in the theater. I guess it was up to me to remind them. I turned around and faced the couple. I didn't plan on exchanging words with them; I just wanted to simply ask them to keep it quiet, please.

"Would you shut the ..." I could not finish my sentence. What I saw left me speechless. There was Natina going down on Louis in the middle of the movie theater. How and why was he here with her? I could have fainted right here. The blood rushed to my face and if this were a cartoon steam would be coming from my ears.

"Oh hey Carmell, you wanna join the party?" She smiled at me. I just looked at her trying to decide whether or not I was gonna finally slap her. I was begging for her to give me a reason.

Natina looked at me and then at Louis. I guess she sensed that we knew each other. Natina looked at Louis and then kissed me. She literally shoved her tongue into my mouth. What was with this girl? Every chance she got she was shoving her tongue somewhere on or in my body. She was worse than a man, cause she was a woman and she was just going to take it. I couldn't stress it enough that I wasn't gay and she just didn't get it.

"Bitch, you must like having your ass kicked." I screamed at her. I was ready to kick her ass. I pushed her away from me, shoved is more like it. I hated being tested by her and she seemed to always do it.

"No I just like being spanked by you!" She still had that stupid smile on her face. That was it I had enough. I jumped over the chair and proceeded to kick her ass. I scratched and kicked and did any and everything. Before I could get a good lick in people were beginning to crowd around and Louis jumped between us.

"Move out of my way!" I yelled at him. My dream come true had turned out to be a nightmare. Security had come to escort all of us out of the theater. I tried to get my money back, I didn't even get to watch the movie, but I guess when you are fighting in a public place you should just be happy not to go to jail. They told me I had to leave and no, I couldn't have my money back. I had to go first and then they would leave. As this rent-a-cop walked me to my car I thought about what had just happened.

It reminded me of the day I had come home from school to what I thought would be an empty house. I causally walked into my home as I always do. I thought I was mature, at twelve I was allowed to come home from school and be alone for a few hours until my parents got home. I wanted to go to my favorite place in the whole house and do my homework. I ran to the deck but when I got there I could have passed out. My father was standing outside holding a woman tightly as he pressed his body against hers. I was too young and naïve to know what was going on then, but I had long since realized my father was having sex in our home with another woman.

Once my father realized I had witnessed him in his transgression he ran in to talk to me. There is no way I could forget that conversation.

"Hey pumpkin, are you home from school kind of early?" He waited for my response but I didn't have any words for him. I couldn't speak so he continued. "Look baby, what you saw out there you could never tell your mother. It's between us only. I know it may hurt right now but sometimes we have to take on pain for those we love. You understand what Daddy's saying?" He sat there staring at me. I never gave a verbal response I just shook my head. I was trying to figure out how I, at twelve years old, could make it better. After that day, I tried extremely hard to make my daddy happy. Everything I did I did for his approval. I didn't want him to get another wife and I didn't want him to get another daughter. I felt my father had betrayed our family, and today I felt Louis had betrayed me. He wasn't the man of my dreams. How could the man of your dreams break your heart so soon? How could the man of your dreams allow himself to become involved with your worst nightmare?

I sat in my car and let the tears run down my cheeks, I was still in shock, even though I saw it for myself, I still couldn't believe my eyes.

Natina

Let the Games Begin

I smiled silently to myself the entire way home. I couldn't believe that Carmell and Louis knew one another. I could have never planned it better. If she wasn't going to give it to me then she wasn't going to be giving it to anyone, especially not my Louis. If she did I would have to be in on it. I laughed to myself.

"So Louis where do you know her from?" I turned and looked at him. He had been silent ever since we left the movies or got kicked out I should say. He looked at me with this blank expression. It felt like ten lifetimes before he actually replied.

"What are you talking about?" He asked.

"Come one now. Who are you talking to? I know you better than you know yourself. I saw the way you looked at her. You knew who she was." I just smiled and waited on his explanation.

"Yeah I know her. I met her at an Exxon the other day. She kinda looked pissed huh? What did you do to her?" He laughed. She did look pretty upset. She had turned bright red and her eyebrows had connected somehow as she jumped over her seat towards me. If she had been anyone else I would have to kick her ass, but it was something special about Carmell. Those little stunts that she pulled and her aggressiveness only made me want her even more. That was the thing with me. I want to obtain the unobtainable, if that makes any sense. I began to tell Louis about our encounter.

"We work together and for her birthday I told her I would take her out. I did take her out; I mean dinner, club, strip club and everything. When we got back to her house she took a shower and started walking around naked in front of me. She told me I could spend the night, hell I took it as an invitation. So I crept into her room that night and went down on her. You should have seen her Louis, she was moaning and shaking and everything. I was doing the damn thing and then she just snapped and fought me the same way she did tonight. So when we went back to work I tried to have her fired by making up some story, but it didn't work." I laughed to myself as I told Louis our story.

"I can not believe that you actually did that? I always knew my girl was bout' it though. You just gonna take what you want I see. Girl you know that's rape right" As he laughed he reached over and rubbed my thigh. I knew what was going down tonight. It was something about Louis and they way he touched me. Each touch had a different meaning and depending on the intensity of his grasp I could tell just how badly he wanted me. This touch told me he was about to put it on me until I couldn't walk and that was fine by me. I was always ready for him to work his magic on me. Although I was excited about the all-nighter we were about to pull, I could not help but think about Carmell. I had something she wanted.

"Hmmm", I thought to myself. "Let the games begin."

Kendra

Hold Up Fool

Gia had to work late tonight, so I was left in my room by myself with nothing to do. I sat here trying to figure out what my next move would be. I started out my room to get something to eat.

"Kendra?" I heard a voice behind me. I turned around to see who it was.

"Oh hey Jason. What are you doing here?" I asked, surprised to see him. I know that Nicole had a little thing for Jason, but so did every other female that I worked with. He was really easy to talk to so maybe if he wasn't busy we could kick it. I was feeling a little lonely.

"I'm replacing Katey." He said. I just smiled at him. He did have the cutest dimples. "So where are you going?" He questioned.

"I'm running downstairs to get something to eat. If I sit in that room by myself a moment longer I will go crazy. Wanna come." I asked hoping he would agree.

"Yeah I would like to cum! You gonna help me out with that." He laughed.

"Look at you being nasty. No I'm not gonna help you with that, from what I hear you don't need any help in that department." I joked along with him. He was no Cherry but he would have to do.

"So you believe everything that you hear?" We laughed as we walked towards that hotel restaurant.

"When it comes to you, yes I believe everything that I have heard about you. You know it's true." I teased him.

He was actually a lot of fun to be around. I see why the girls went crazy over him. He was handsome, intelligent funny and straight. You could hardly find all those qualities in a man. We decided to go back up to my room and watch some movies. I was happy for the company.

Jason was going through the movie listings that we could order from pay-per-view.

"So what do you want to watch?" He asked me as he scrolled through the listings.

"Oh it doesn't matter." I walked to the bathroom and got into the shower. Gia was going to drop by when she got off work.

After I finished my shower I went back into the room.

"So what did you decide on?" I asked Jason. He turned to me with this smile on his face. I looked towards the television. There were two women giving pleasure to a man with a very big blessing.

"A porno movie?" I laughed.

"Yeah, there was nothing else on and I thought this would be the most entertaining out of all the choices." He smiled. I sat on the bed beside him and we laughed at the porn stars. I wished my husband would sit and watch a porno with me. It wasn't for any type of sexual gratification, just because I found them funny. The facial expressions these people made and all the weird grunts and growls, it sounded more painful than pleasurable. Besides sometimes they made good instructional videos. Some men should actually watch them and take note of some of these guys technique.

"So do you like oral stimulation?" Jason caught me completely off guard with this question.

"Doesn't everyone?" I laughed trying not to show how uncomfortable I was. Why would he be asking me that, it seemed like a very odd question for someone that you are not intimate with.

"Well show me how much." Jason moved towards me taking my

legs and spreading them apart. I felt the tip of his tongue rub my inner thigh. What did he think he was doing? What was I letting him do? He began to taste me. I knew I had to stop him but part of me wanted him so desperately to let him finish. This hadn't been done in a long time and Kendra was craving some gratification, I needed to be satisfied but there is no way I was going to allow Jason to be the one that satisfied me.

"Jason, stop." I said pulling away from him. He was persistent. The more I squirmed the stronger he held me.

"Why do you want me to stop?" He said with his head tucked between my legs. I was trying to push him away but he was strong. I don't know if he was used to girls saying no but meaning yes, but I really meant no. I pulled my legs together. I was trying to clink-clink. I had made a very bad decision putting on this t-shirt. It was long but still I knew better. I had to get this boy off of me before I ended up doing something I had no business doing with this guy.

"Well I can think of several reasons, but the biggest being I'm married." He kept on as if he did not hear what I said. I knew I was going to have to get forceful. I pushed as hard as I could to get him off me and then scooted back to give myself room to get up. Once I stumbled to my feet I was about ready to fight him. I was upset with him.

"Damn, hold up fool! Did you hear what I said? You gonna have to stop. I am married and you are talking to my best friend. This is not happening." I jumped forward from the spot I seemed to be rooted in and showed Jason the door.

Nicole

The Golden Rule

•————————————————————————————————————•

"So you have anything planned for tonight?" Natina and I were going to get something for lunch. She was really a fun person to be around and we had become buddies. Since Kendra was out of town I didn't have anyone to talk to and now that Jason was gone too I guess you could say I was a little bit lonely. "Well if you want to go out you know that I'm game." Tina was laughing. I really think that girl can party every day of the week. Any time that I asked her where the party was she was ready to go. "I'm sure that we will think of something." I said as we pulled into the restaurant. As we sat here eating, my mind could not help but drift to Jason. It was funny how he seemed to creep into my mind. It didn't matter what I was doing or when I was doing it, he was always there, in the back of my mind. I thought about him on a daily basis sometimes two and three times a day. When it came to him I was so gone. I pulled out my cell so that I could call him. He answered on the second ring. "Hey there what's up?" I said to Jason. "Who is this?" Jason asked. "Me, Cole. You better start acting like you know who I am. I'm tired of you asking me who this is every time you answer the phone. What you need to do is program my name and number in your phone so it will tell you that I'm calling and you ain't gotta ask me that no more." I said. I had to admit I was a little hurt that he did not yet know my voice. We talked some but it seemed like his mind was somewhere else. "Hey Nicole hold on." He said. I heard some rustling sound and then I heard him call Kendra's name. I could barely make out what he was saying. I had to tell Tina to stop ranting and raving so I could be nosey.   "Kendra wait up!" I heard him say. Why was he trying to catch up with Kendra? Maybe it is work related. I mean that is the only thing that it can be. What else would they have to talk about? Perhaps it was about me. I smiled that maybe he had told her how he really felt about me. I heard Kendra speaking.

"Yes, Jason." She sounded like she was pissed. She responded to him with what I called the tone. I teased her all the time. She would get so matter of fact, so stern when she took the tone that it literally scared me at times. She could hurt your feeling using nothing but the sharpness of her words when the tone was involved.

"Kendra, let me take you to dinner. I want to apologize for the way that I acted last night. I was totally out of line, but ever since we started training I have been so attracted to you and you wouldn't even give me the time of day. I could get any of these chickenheads to pay attention to me and want me but you never even looked like you entertained that thought. I just thought that last night you were feeling me. I'm sorry." Jason had said a mouthful. I became furious. What the hell was going on with him and Kendra? She acts like she is just so faithful to Cory. Humph. I waited for her reply.

"That's fine Jason. I am not mad I just felt a little bit uncomfortable, you know with you talking to Nicole and all. I'm married and it just can't go down like that. I understand now that I threw out a lot of mixed signals like the shower and the t-shirt, but I wasn't trying to hit you over the head with any clues. But that's cool, let's just drop it, where you wanna go for dinner?" I heard Kendra say.

"Damn, Hello?" Jason said. I can't believe this nut forgot me on the phone. He had me sitting on hold for almost five minutes while they had their little heart to heart.

"Well I am glad that you remembered that I was here. What was that all about? Whatcha taking her to dinner for, when you have never so much as offered to take me to Mickey D's?" I quizzed him. I didn't care if it wasn't any of my business. What the hell were they doing going to dinner together. I can't even get his ass to take me to McDonald's. After our first date all we ever did was sex. Just like any woman who wanted a relationship with a man I wanted more than that. I was so pissed off. I couldn't believe what I had just heard and he wasn't responding to my questions, like they didn't matter.

"Hey let me call you back." I heard him say right before the phone went dead. No he didn't just hang that phone up on me. This man was straight losing his mind.

I turned and looked at Natina. "I can't believe this shit. I am on the phone with Jason and there he is chasing Kendra begging to take her to dinner." I was so upset now. "I thought that Kendra was married!" Tina stated.

"She is married. I want to know what happened with them. I'm gonna call her right now. She is supposed to be my best friend." Tina started laughing when I said that.

"So is your best friend getting it on with your man? Some best friend." She continued laughing, finding the whole situation funny. I didn't think it was funny at all. Actually, the more that I thought about it the more upset I became. Would Kendra actually do anything like that to me? I was her Ace, friends since high school, we started this job together, and I just couldn't make myself believe that she would do something behind my back. Even though I couldn't believe it, I couldn't ignore the signs either. I hit five, which was the speed dial for Kendra's cell.

"Hello." I heard Kendra say.

"Hey girl what's up? You got something you need to talk to me about?" I needed to get straight to the point.

I was giving her the tone now. "What are you talking about? I'm eating, can I call you back?" Oh so she was going to act like nothing was happening? Well I would fix her.

"Who are you eating with?" She was probably going to lie to me anyways.   "Jason, wanna talk to him?" Kendra asked.

"No, I want you to tell me what the hell is going on with you and him. What are you doing at dinner with him? So you just gonna stab me in my back like that?" I was fuming.

"Nicole, what are you talking about? Nothing is going on with Jason and me. Have you forgotten that I'm married and furthermore you are my best friend? I wouldn't sleep with your man girl. You know me better than that now don't you?" Kendra replied.

"Whatever Kendra, whatever. I heard him talking to you earlier. What is he so sorry for if you guys don't have anything to hide?" I sat silently waiting for more lies.

"Look Nicole, there is nothing going on with us. We had a bit of a misunderstanding that's all. I will call you back when I get to my room and we can discuss it. Okay. Calm down girl, do you seriously think that I would do anything to hurt you?" Kendra sounded like she was begging.

"Whatever." I hung up the phone. I didn't even give her time to reply. What good was it going to do; she was going to keep acting like nothing at all had happened. I was too busy trying to think of ways to shatter her world like she has shattered mine.

"So what did she say?" Tina asked.

"A whole lot of nothing!" I replied. I was too busy plotting my revenge. She knew how I felt about Jason and there was no way I was going to let her come between us. I was going to repay her for all the pain that I was feeling now. Do unto others as others do unto you. That was my golden rule.

Carmell

When Two Souls Touch

Here I am standing in front of the mirror getting ready for my date. I couldn't believe it myself, but when Louis called me and started apologizing for what happened I couldn't resist. He told me he had just gotten back in town from school and ran into Natina at a club. He told me all about how they used to be together. I decided to give him another chance. I was lost in thought when I heard someone knocking at the door.

I peeped out the peephole and saw Louis. He looked scrumptious. I opened the door and let him in. He smelled magnificent.

"What are you wearing boy. You smell so good." I could not resist asking him this question. He made me want to cancel dinner and have him instead.

"It's my secret. You have to stick around to find that out. How about we make it a blockbuster night? You game. I really don't want to be around a bunch of other people. I want to focus on nothing but you and your flawless face." I couldn't help but smile.

"Sure, do you want to go get a movie? It is Blockbuster down the street." Louis just shook his head no to my question and walked back outside. He came in with three movies and some Chinese take out. He had already had that planned. Okay Louis gets two points for spontaneity. He was going to need all the points he could get so he could make up for the big mistake he made.

"So you had this planned right? Are you trying to seduce me?" I asked, hoping that the answer was yes. No matter how angry I was I still couldn't deny that this man was fine. I looked him up and down, then down and up and prayed that he didn't see the lust in my eyes. I didn't want to seem to anxious or even worse like a slut.

We sat on the couch and talked. Until now I had not understood what people meant when they said it felt like they knew each other. He was soothing me with his conversation, massaging me with tenderness, and best of all he was touching my soul. I felt an instant connection as we sat here; it was as if we had known each other for years.

I got up and put on my Olivia cd. I had to hear *When Two Souls Touch* because now I fully understood that song. Louis walked up behind me and grabbed me by my waist. He gently kissed my neck and then my shoulders. He pulled my hair gently as he motioned his lips towards mine. He had the softest lips and I just didn't want to let go. He began to undress me. When he had managed to get all of my clothes off he stopped.

"Carmell, stand here for me. I want to just admire your beauty I want to admire your beautiful hair and body." He slowly walked towards me. Once he reached me he brought those pillow soft lips to mine again. Only this time it was more passionate and even more intense than the first time. He picked me up and carried me to the bedroom. He laid me down against my satin red sheets, then Louis stepped back and appreciated my body. Oh I wanted him now. I could feel the tingling sensation between my legs. My nipples began to swell with anticipation and my very own tiny lake began to form as the wetness seeped from my middle. I needed to have him. I couldn't remember the last time someone had touched me like this. His touches were soft but strong. His hands were like a paintbrush and I was his canvas. Louis began to undress slowly, never taking his eyes off of me. His eyes penetrated me down to my very soul and I became mesmerized by the seductive gaze. I was his prisoner. His stare was my handcuffs and with it he could command my every move. He continued to remove his clothes and finally, he was completely naked. He was beautiful. His skin was so smooth and his body toned. His muscles seemed to be chiseled or etched into his skin. They were perfect and best of all this man was packing. He started at my feet. He took my toes and gently began to kiss them. Then he kissed the soles of my feet and ankles too. He worked his way up to my thighs, kissing every spot that was visible to the human eye. He then began to taste me. Louis used his tongue like no other man has done before. It made tiny circles around my clitoris and then I could feel it move up and down. Whatever he was doing it was making my toes curl. I could feel tiny chill bumps form on my arms and legs and then my body began to shake. He kept pleasing me until I felt like I was about to burst.

"You taste so good." I heard him moan. He moved his body towards me until we were face to face. He kissed me and entered me at the same time. I was lost in him. Our bodies began to move together as if we were one. He moved my legs and placed them on his shoulders. I could feel every inch of him like this. Then he did something different. He turned my body to the side and pulled me close to him and thrust deep inside of me. Louis had my body bent like a pretzel but it felt like ecstasy. After he had given me an orgasm like that he flipped me again and positioned my body on top of his. He wanted me to ride him. He sat straight up then moved my legs around his waist. Once he had gotten me into position he began to rock back and forth, causing an incredible feeling. He didn't need me to do anything he was doing all the work and he was working me. From this positioned he rolled me back onto my back and again spread my legs so that he was deep inside of me. This time I came so hard I could feel the wetness all over my body and where it had spilled into the bed. I had no words, just wow. This is the kind of lovemaking that could make you fall in love after just one time. This feeling was nothing short of ecstasy. I lay there in his arms fully satisfied. I had to be careful or I would fall in love, people always fell in love when two souls touched.

Natina

Waiting on My Gift

I sat at home waiting for Louis to come home. We had decided that it was best for us to move in together. I loved having him around and he loved me. It worked out perfect. We were made for one another and I was happy to have a man that was fine with my sexuality. No one would come before my Louis and he would put no one before me. That is the way that it has always been that is the way that it will always be. The thought of their men and other women would intimidate most women, but it doesn't scare me. I know that he's mine, just like the song said, "They may have had him once but I got him all the time." I was lost deep in thought when I heard the key turn in the door.

"Hey baby." I said as he walked through the door. He looked so handsome. He leaned in to kiss me. No one I knew could kiss me the way that this man could.

"Your girl Carmell is a freak." Louis said heading towards the bathroom. "Wanna take a shower with me?" I followed him into the bathroom.

"So you say Carmell is a freak? Do you think my little plan will work?" I asked referring to the conversation that we had yesterday.

"I think after dicking her down real good for about a month; I will have her so sprung that if I told her that pigs could fly she would believe it." I laughed at him. Louis was so silly. He held me as the water kissed both our bodies. I knew that this was the man that I was going to marry. He kissed me, holding me tightly as he began to slowly make love to me in the shower. He pulled me close to him, as he did I wrapped my legs around his waste. With my back pressed against the wall he entered me. Moving back and forth, in and out of me as the water erotically bounced off of our skin. Each time was better than the last when it came to Louis. No man or woman for that matter could satisfy me the way that Louis could. We made love for hours. Afterwards I lie there in his arms and let my imagination amuse me as I listened to the rhythm of his breathing. My thoughts of having him and Carmell together were getting me aroused all over again. I had told Louis that I wanted her and he had been more than willing to convince her to have a threesome with us. He said that we would have to take it slow since she hated me so very much, but he felt that if he could get her to fall in love with him then she would probably do anything. Deep down I knew he was right. Louis was always coming through for me, always trying to make me happy and give me what I wanted. I decided to give him a little extra loving as I went under the covers to find that special magic stick. He wasn't hard but I would soon change that. I took his tool into my mouth and began to stoke it. I know that I could give really good head. I stroked it and let my tongue ring softly touch the tip. I know that always turned him on. He softly moaned. He was still asleep. Then I began to use my hands and mouth. I stroked him and he began to moan louder and louder. He touched my hair and then I knew I had his full attention. He motioned my head up and down and I let him have full control. I deep throated it which was no easy task since this man was larger than average. I could tell he was about to cum so I allowed him to cum all over my breast. He loved seeing his seed glowing on my chest.

I walked to the bathroom to wash up then climb back into the bed. I fell asleep thinking of the day that I would have her. I was anxious but I had decided its best that I waited patiently on my gift. I smiled as I drifted off to sleep.

Kendra

The Very First Time

Gia walked in the door using the key I had given her. I knew that it was time. I was ready to go all the way with her. I had all the lights turned off with nothing but the candle lit path to light her way. Between each candle there were rose petals to create a path that led to the bathroom where I had a bubble bath waiting for her. I had brought special sheets for this bed for this special night. The drab cotton comforter and sheets were not enough. I found antique gold satin sheets and a matching comforter that I just had to have. I had them pulled back and the bed was fully covered with red rose petals. It had taken me all afternoon to get all of this done. I lie there in the middle of the bed in the sexiest red lingerie that I could find in this city. I knew that red was her favorite color and that was mainly the reason that I had chosen it.

"Kendra?" I heard Gia call my name. She followed the path to the closed bathroom door. There I left a note that read: *After your bath come to bedLet's make a reality of the words we said.*I heard her chuckle just a little. I smiled as I heard her enter the bathroom. I lay there waiting nervously. Her thirty-minute bath seemed more like an eternity. I heard the bathroom door open. I had left another note on the bedroom door along with a neatly wrapped box. That note read:*Open the door only if you dareOnly if you are prepared to shareYour love with me, I won't fightI want to make love with you tonight*I heard the door open and there she stood. She was so beautiful. Her hair lay against her shoulders as she stood there smiling at me. She looked stunning in the satin black teddy I had gotten her. It fit her size eight figure perfectly. She looked around the room.   "All this for me?" She asked as she walked to the bed.   "Yeah cause you are so special." She leaned in and kissed me. This time we kissed it was much more intense, it was so sensual and I soon lost myself in her softness. She began to caress my body, touching me in ways that my husband never had. She used her hands to softly touch me below. She made tiny circles with her tongue around my nipples. They began to get harder and harder. The harder they were, the stronger her kisses. She gently bit them, making me quiver with anticipation. Our bodies pressed against one another as she slowly placed her fingers inside of me. She started with one, then slowly increased them as I became more and more aroused. This was delicious. She was so patient and loving and completely fulfilling me with just the touch of her hands. She found her way to my center and began to love me with her tongue and with both her hands and tongue she took me to places unknown and unseen.

She placed my legs on her shoulders as she found my lips. I could taste my sweetness, exciting me more. She used her body to press her fingers deeper inside of me, while taking my breast into her mouth. She stroked me gently teasing my clit with her thumb.

"Gia, damn that feels good." I spoke through heavy breaths.

"Is it good to you? Is it better than good?" She whispered in my ear. She had turned my body to the side, pressing inside of me, tickling my g-spot. She placed her free hand on my hips and pulled me closer each time she thrust inside of me.

"Baby it's amazing!" I responded. I felt myself about to climax. I was skeptical at first, that she would not be able to please me but she had no problems in that department.

Turning me completely on my stomach and then pulling me closer to her, I was now straddled across her lap with my back to her. I moved up and down, back and forth as I rode her fingers. Gia moved them in small circles tap dancing on my spot. I could feel her breath along my neck, perspiration making our bodies moist.

"Tell me you like it, I wanna hear it." Gia commanded.

"I like it, I like it!" I obeyed. She then gently pulled my hair, tilting my head back as she nibbled on my ear.

"You love it, don't you. Cum for me baby, show me you love it." More commands streamed from Gia. It turned me on the way she took charge. I loved even more the way she made my body feel. My body obeyed her command and I released a steady stream of my juices as I exhaled.

Our mental connection had heightened this physical experience. I could feel her love as she touched me. I could hear her thoughts as she made love to me for the very first time.

Nicole

Protecting My Interest

I was still upset about whatever was going on with Jason and Kendra. She had called me later on that night but I wasn't trying to hear any of it. She gave me some story about kicking him out and nothing happening between them. She was supposed to be my best friend and she had stabbed me in my back. I sat at my desk at work trying to figure out what I was going to do to get her back. I didn't know what it would be but it had to be good because I wanted to hurt her the way that she had hurt me. Even though they denied it, my heart says something happened between them. I called Jason back and he said he overstepped the boundaries by coming on to her. That was the same story that she told me and I wasn't buying either way. He was just trying to protect her. I picked up my cell phone and went through my phonebook. I came to Kendra's home number. I knew just what I was going to do. I called Kendra's house hoping that her husband was home.

"Hello Cory, I'm sorry to bother you." I said. I was trying to control my tone I didn't want him to suspect anything. "This is Nicole."
"Hello Nicole, how are you? Is everything alright?" Cory said. His concern was touching. I had always thought that Cory was an attractive man but I knew if I tried my first plan he would never go for it because Cory was the forever-faithful husband. Instead, I thought best if I just go with this plan.

"I'm fine. My call is about Kendra. Oh, Cory she misses you so much. Yesterday she called me crying cause she misses you. It would be great if you visit her one weekend. That would be a nice surprise for her."

"Yeah when I talked to her she told me she missed me but I didn't think it was that much. I tell you what; I will plan a weekend to surprise her. I will fly down." Cory stated more to himself than to me.   "Okay, well I can get her room number and everything. It is probably best that you not tell her. Make it a surprise. I will call and pretend to be Kendra and ask them to leave an extra key at the desk for you. That way you can just walk in to the room and it will really be a surprise. Oh yeah, make sure to take her some roses. You know how she loves roses." I added. I wanted him to catch her with Jason. That would put a stop to all of it; whatever it was that they were trying to do they were not going to get away with it. I was going to make sure of that. I hung up the phone with Cory. He was going to try to plan to go to Atlanta this weekend and if not this one the next weekend. I sat there content as ever. I was going to repay her for the pain she was causing. I had to admit I felt a little bad, but I was only protecting my interest.

Carmell

Falling

It's happening. Just like I said that it would. I am falling for that chocolate man. Being around him does something to me. I can't explain it. When I see him, my heart starts to beat fast. The closer he gets the faster it beats. His smiles and kisses are all I need to make me happy. We have been dating for two weeks and Louis hasn't missed a beat. He has fully redeemed himself. I questioned him about Natina but he said that they were a thing of the past. I was willing to accept that. For some reason I trusted Louis. It had been long time since I was able to trust a man. Actually, I hadn't full heartedly trusted any man besides my father and even he had let me down. So when it came to men I always guarded my heart. This man was different, he had opened up to me about Natina and I doubted that he was seeing her. I mean how he could be spending time with her when every moment of his free time he spent with me.

We were planning to go out tonight. I wonder if Tina knew that I had stolen her man. I would love to see the look on her face once she knew she was outdated and had been traded in for a new improved model. That day in the theater she looked at me as if she had him and I never would. Well wouldn't you know the tables have turned? I've seen her many times at work and she just smiled at me, like she held a secret from me that amused her. Well I have a secret too and I knew my secret was much better than the one she held. I shoved thoughts of her out of my mind. I didn't want to waste valuable brain cells on something as undeserving as Tina.

I glanced at the flowers that Louis had sent to me. He was so sweet and he made me feel like I was the only woman in the world or at least the only one that meant anything to him.

Natina walked by as I was looking at the roses.

"Who sent you those?" I heard her ask.

"Why in the hell are you talking to me? It's none of your business but if you must know Louis did." I bluntly stated. I wanted to piss her off by letting her know that the man that you thought you had is after me. Besides, he knows the better woman when he sees her. I would choose me over Natina any day.

"Oh that's nice." She smiled. She was much too calm for me. It would have infuriated me if he were sending her flowers. She didn't say another word just smiled and walked away. I thought that was odd because I would have hit the roof if I knew that my man or my supposed man was trying to charm another woman. Furthermore, if the woman were my enemy that would just make me livid. I quickly dismissed my thoughts. I don't have time to concern myself with her. Louis was keeping me much too happy. I checked the time and noticed it was almost five. Louis was meeting me to take me to a late lunch. I walked outside to look for him. He was standing by the car on his cell phone. I looked at this gorgeous man. As I marveled at his beauty I realized I'm falling for him.

Natina

Good Things Come to Those Who Wait

Okay Sweetie, I love you too." I said to Louis as we ended the call. He was about to take Carmell to lunch. He is bound to get her to go through with the plan. He thought that we should wait just a little bit longer before he asked her to be with me. He was going to make sure that she was in love or infatuated whichever came first before asking and at the rate that he was going it would be no time before that happened.

I remembered the spacey look she had on her face when I walked past her desk. She looked like a lovesick teenager. She believed that Louis had sent those roses when it was actually me who sent them. It was all a part of the plan. We wanted her to trust him and be willing to please him. I was good at judging someone's personality and Carmell was the classic clinger. Once she felt she could trust Louis she would want to spend every moment with him and do anything to please him. She seemed to have abandonment issues and I exploited this flaw to my full advantage. Every step I took was carefully calculated to make her trust and love him, that's the only way that this plan was going to work. Somehow, she actually thought that Louis had left me for her. I would sit and listen to their conversations on the phone. She was pathetic. Since we lived together, we didn't want her to seem suspicious by not giving her his home number. To avoid suspicion Louis comes up with the idea of setting up a priority ring when she called. That way I would know it was Carmell, even if I wasn't by the caller id. I never answered when I heard the special ring and we had even taken my voice from the call notes. We wanted to give her no reason to be apprehensive.   When they talked on the phone, I would listen to her whine about her life. How she has been through so much blah, blah, blah and whole bunch of other bull. It didn't matter to me one way or another. Louis and I would sit in the bed, make fun of her, and then make love as the phone rang back to back. One time she actually asked why he didn't answer the phone, he gave her some excuse about seeing a man about a dog, and she believed it. She was so damn gullible.

It reminded me of a time when I too was just as gullible, but growing up in a foster home you learn fast. It didn't take me long to get with the program. I wasn't always the person that I am now but the streets make you hard. From foster home to foster home, I had no one to love me. Most of my foster parents were in it for a quick buck and I could accept those, but the one that changed me was the one that pretended that she cared. I was a damn fool when it came to her and she exploited me. I consider myself a victim of the system because I soon learned to hurt others before they hurt me. Carmell's smile reminded me of my first foster mother. She was so gorgeous to me. Being fourteen and in the system, I longed to have a parental figure, some one that would care for me unconditionally so I did whatever it took to win her love. The problem was that I didn't understand that she would never love me. Her fake smile and her conniving demeanor was all for her gratification. It was all for her. I'll never forget those things she did to me, but I tried my best to block them.

I shook my head as if I could shake those horrible memories out of my head. I had to push them to the back of my mind. When I thought of them, they could bring tears to my eyes and since I left her home, I never cried and I didn't plan to start any time soon.   Sitting here at my desk, I became anxious. I decided to show up at the restaurant that he had taken her to have lunch. It was a little Chinese restaurant close to the job. I walked in and took a seat. I was facing Louis who saw me and behind Carmell, who was so lovestruck by Louis that all she could only see him.

I winked at Louis and got up to go to the restroom. He followed me and met me in the ladies room. There was no one in the restroom and he soon accompanied me into the large stall marked handicapped and began to kiss me. It turned me on to know that she sat out there at the table waiting on him. He quickly pulled up my skirt and entered me. Even a quickie was great with him. His thrust was greedy, attempting to take as much as he could with each motion. He grabbed my breast as he stroked me and I loved every second of it. It was fast but satisfying and I loved just how adventurous he could be. He left out of the restroom first. As he left one of the servers was entering. I heard her gasp and then say something in Chinese. I just laughed to myself and fixed my clothes.

When I left out of the restroom, Carmell's eyes were still glued to Louis. She never even noticed me. I blew a kiss to Louis and left out of the restaurant without even paying.

I was thinking of my little plan and how Carmell would feel when she found out she was nothing but my prey. Just imagining the look on her face when she finds out he doesn't want her and he was only doing it for me brought a smile to my face. She will be devastated and I will still have her as I wanted. I was anxious for my reward, but I knew I had to be patient. Good things always come to those who wait.

Kendra

Caught in the Act

After that first night with Gia my mind was blown. I couldn't get enough of that woman. I wanted her every night. She would laugh at my untamable sexual appetite. I sat there in my room and waited for her. It was Friday night and she would be getting off early. We had planned for a night out on the town and then we would come back to my room. I'm surprised no one has seen us in the hallways. If they had, no one had ever said anything. It was almost to the point where I didn't care. I heard a soft knock on the door. I opened it and there was my beautiful Cherry.

"Hey there." I said as I greeted her with a kiss at the door. As my lips touched hers I spotted Jason walking by. We had become good friends since he got here. I knew that I could trust him. He was now the perfect gentleman aside from the little flirting that he would occasionally do with me. I was flattered with his attraction to me but that is as far as I would allow it to go. I waived at Jason.

"Can I join the party?" I laughed at Jason. That was just like a man.

"Maybe later little buddy! We can watch more of your freak movies." I laughed as I closed the door behind me. I had been telling Jason about my little tendencies. At first, he was a little jealous that I would be with her and not him. I tried explaining it to him that to me it was somehow different. I was glad that I had someone to talk to about it. It was an ongoing struggle that left me in turmoil. I knew what the Bible taught me yet I knew what my heart felt. Talk about being confused; I was lost. Jason had proved to be a good friend and perhaps if I weren't married already I probably would have given him a chance, however that was the farthest thing from my mind. I had no interest in this man and besides that, I knew how my friend felt about him and I would never do that to her.

"Hey there Sweetness, how about we skip going out. I would rather stay here and hold you in my arms." She pulled me close to her and hugged me. Her embrace was different from a man's embrace. It was sweet, tender, and tight even but there was still some difference in the way she would hold me, and the way my husband held me. It was just different. Neither one was better than the other, they were simply worlds apart.

"Sure. I would rather that too." We began to kiss and I could not wait to glimpse her beautiful body. We were overflowing with desire. We didn't even bother with going to the bedroom. There was no time. We pleased each other in the very place that we stood, barely stopping to breathe. I lay on top of her kissing her and massaging her with my tongue. I found my way to her special place.

"Wait, you don't have to do that." I heard her breathe.

"I know, but I want to. I want to give you just as much pleasure as you give me and possibly more if I can." I continued stroking her with my tongue, her moans only exciting me more. She gently pulled at my hair. She was so warm and soft. This woman had completely mesmerized me. I never wanted to stop. It was just something about her beauty, her taste, and her scent that held me captive. I was intoxicated by just the softness of her body. I was lost in her, touching her, kissing her and pleasing her.

"What the fuck are you doing?" I must be dreaming because that sounded a lot like Cory, my husband. I had just talked to him earlier, he said nothing about coming to Atlanta, and furthermore how would he get a key to my room. Maybe this was just my conscious getting the best of me.

I felt someone pull my hair and it wasn't the gentle tugging that had just taken place. No this was painful. I looked up and there stood my abductor, tall, handsome, and mad as hell. He pulled me off her and tossed me to the side. He threw the long-stemmed red roses he was carrying at me and charged at Gia. I couldn't believe that he was fighting her as if she were a man. He had never raised a hand to me and it surprised me that he would attempt to hit another woman as if she were a man. Clearly, she was no match for him. He towered over her and she was a woman. I watched him consumed with hatred and even though he scared the hell out of me, if there was any fear in Gia I could not see it.

"What the hell do you think you are doing?" He screamed at her.

"Well if you were taking care of your business then you wouldn't have to worry about what I am doing to her. Whatever it is you better believe that she likes it" Gia wasn't going to back down man or woman.

Cory walked over and slapped Gia. Her little frame fell against the wall. I ran over and grabbed Cory. If anybody deserved to be slapped around, it was me. I am the one that's cheating on him. She didn't pressure me into anything. Sorrow consumed me for bringing her into something like this. I just never thought that he would react like this.

"Cory stop it! Stop hitting her!" Cory grabbed me and tossed me again to the side. While his back was turned, Gia jumped up and hit him from behind. I managed to get up and jump between the two of them. I had to pry him away from her. I wasn't strong enough to pull his arms back so I jumped between them. If he were going to hit anyone, it should be me. If he wanted to fight a woman that badly let it be me. I was the one that had angered him and his ego had gotten the best of him. I could tell that anger is what powered his actions. This was so out of character for him.

"So you're taking up for your little bitch! You disgust me." He said. His eyes were filled with hurt, pain that I knew I was responsible for. I had never thought of the consequences of what I was doing because I never thought that I was going to be caught. I stood there watching as my life fell apart. I loved my husband and part of me loved Gia too. I stood there in disbelief. Cory turned and looked at me as he walked out of the door. I knew he meant the words that he had said. I could see the disgust in his eyes as he looked at me. I stood there naked and embarrassed as he looked at me. I wasn't embarrassed about the feelings that I had for Gia. I was embarrassed because I had been caught in the act.

Nicole

The Last Laugh

Cory had told me that he was going to Atlanta this weekend. It was Sunday and I wanted to know what happened. Kendra should be thanking me. I sent Cory to stop anything that was going on. Once I had Jason for my man, Kendra and I could become friends again. I decided that I was going to call Jason.

"Hello." I heard Jason say. I could barely hear him there was a lot of background noise.

"What's all that noise I hear in the background?" I asked. Jason told someone that he would be back and then the noise stopped.

"Hey girl, what's up?" He said.

"Was there someone crying in the background? Well anyways, did you and Kendra get my little surprise?" If there were nothing going on with them then Cory showing up would not have made any difference to him.

"What surprise?" Jason asked. I could tell by the tone in his voice that he had no idea what I was referring to.   "Didn't Cory show up in ATL? That was my little present to you guys. So if something was going on we would stop it dead in its tracks." I rattled off the story to Jason. Telling him how I called and got the room number and told them that I, Kendra, would be expecting my husband and to please leave an extra key.

As I told my story, Jason remained in complete silence. After a while he finally spoke. "What did you do that for? Someone's life is not a game and you have no right to toy with people. You don't know the trouble that you have caused!" Jason sounded angry. He had never spoken to me in that manner. He had never even so much as raised his voice at me. Jason was so easy going. When he talked to me, he was straightforward but never loud and I didn't quite know how to take the tone he had with me.

"Well I didn't see you worrying about it when you were toying with me. You and my best friend were sleeping together. Both of you were playing with me." I said to Jason, his concern for her was pissing me off. He was the one that had been doing wrong and he was going to try to lecture me?

"Nicole, I knew that you could not be trusted. You never deserved to have a friend like Kendra anyway. She never did anything with me. I tried and she kicked me out because of you. Now you have gone and done something that could damage her life beyond repair. You know, people told me you were a bitch, but until now I never believed it." Jason words cut like a knife. The phone went completely dead. He had hung the phone up in my face. I didn't understand. If there were nothing going on, how would sending him to Atlanta possibly ruin her life?

I picked up my phone again, this time to call my mother. I had learned my games from the master and for this I needed her input.

"Hey Ma are you busy?" I asked not wanting to intrude on another one of her sex sessions.

"Hey baby, what's going on? I have some time to talk." She answered me. I knew if she had time to talk then her man was not in the house. My mother was a piece of work but when it came to getting what she wanted and manipulating the circumstances she was the best of the best.

"I got a problem mom, my friend is messing with my man and I devised a little plan to break it up now he's taken her side." I began to tell my mom the entire sordid story.

"First of all baby I know I taught you better than to let anyone come and take what's yours. She may be your so-called friend but when it comes down to it, your man is more important. So stop sounding like a damn victim and get your man back. Use what I gave you honey, and believe me just like your mother, you have it going on. No man can resist the power of the Neatherly p-u-s-s-y!" My mother finished her version of a sermon. She always talked to me like a friend, never a daughter and now I see she was quoting Jay-Z. I took my mother's advice, thanked her and then disconnected the call.

This situation was confusing but I knew one thing, somebody wasn't telling the truth. It could be Jason and it could be Kendra. I didn't know. I knew one thing though; I was going to have the last laugh.

Carmell

Baring All

Louis was the man of my dreams. I remember telling my mother that when I first met him. Those were only words then but now I really meant it. I was falling in love with him. Okay, let me stop fooling myself I was in love with him. I didn't want to say it because it had happened so fast but now it was here and crystal clear. I loved him. I planned to tell him tonight. I had never let on to any of my feelings because I didn't want to play the fool. I know that three weeks wasn't a long time but some people married after a month. Who can put time restrictions on love?   I leaned against my headboard to get comfortable. I was about to call Louis and I wanted to be comfortable so there could be no distractions while I talk to him.   "Hello sweetie." I said when Louis answered the phone. He was so sexy.

"Hey there lady!" Louis said. We sat there and talked for a while. So many things were going through my mind. All of a sudden I was nervous about telling him how I felt. I mean it was a little fast to be saying that I was in love with him, but that is how I truly felt. It was going to be all or nothing. I hope that he felt the same way.   "Louis." I paused for a moment. "Let me not bush beat. We have been kicking it for a few weeks now. Do you believe in instant love or love at first sight? That is how I feel about you. I mean I am not trying to label you or marry you tomorrow, I am just letting you know that I care and that I am falling in love with you." I finished my speech. That was tough but now it was said. I sat there for what seemed like an eternity and waited for a reply. I was scared of the rejection that might follow. It sounded

like I heard someone laugh in the background.   "What was that?"   I
asked.   "Oh that was the television. Moving back to the subject, you know
Carmell I have been feeling the same way. You are perfect. I have been
looking for a down woman. Now you know being with me is a lot of work
though." He laughed and then continued. "You know I need a woman that is
down for me and there for me and willing to do things that please me even if
we don't see eye to eye about it. You think you can be that woman?"   I sat
there and smiled to myself before I answered his question. "Of course I can be
that woman. I am that woman. There is none that can compare, compete or
come near the type of woman that I am. As long as you can keep me happy
then I will keep you happy." I said to him. I smiled to myself. I had a silent
victory. Instead of saying those words to Natina he was saying them to me. I
was the one he had chosen. Even after all the history they had, he could see
that I was a better woman. I couldn't help but smile and celebrate my victory.

I was overwhelmed with joy that I had found some happiness in my
life. The last man I trusted was my father. I remember the day he left the
family, I begged him not to. I had done everything he wanted, all of my efforts
went into making him happy so he would stay with our family, but in the end,
he had left even though he promised me he wouldn't. I was going to allow
myself to trust again with Louis. I hadn't had any meaningful relationships
because I couldn't trust any man, but Louis was the one I believed to be my
soul mate and for him I would go the extra mile.

We talked a little while longer. I was just grateful that he was not
going to send me packing. I thought that we were feeling one another and I
guess I was right. It was a relief to know that he felt the same way. I was glad
that I was baring all with Louis.

Natina

Making Progress

"She said that she was in love with you?" I laughed as Louis told me what Carmell had said to him. I knew that she had it bad but I didn't think that bad. I had been lying in bed next to Louis when she called. I heard her say that and I could help laughing. I mean, after three weeks she is ready to say that she loves him. Was she desperate or just stupid? Well I guess Louis just had it like that. "Yeah baby, I think if I asked her now she might go for it. I think she will agree. She will feel the need to prove to me that she is down; especially after what I told her about needing a down woman." Louis said while massaging my back for me. He could be so sweet and he gave amazing massages. His hands worked magic on my body. He was touching pressure points that relieved all of my stress. The room was completely silent and my mind began to drift.

Carmell had been extremely mean to me and I don't allow people to hurt me, not since the day I left that foster home. I was only fourteen years old then but what happened to me forced me to grow up soon. Our next-door neighbor came into my room one day when I was alone. He violently took my virginity and my innocence, but what happened after that is what hurt me more than anything.

I heard her pull the car into the driveway and I jumped up to tell her what he had done to me. That he had touched me against my will and I wanted to tell the police. I hadn't taken a shower because all the Lifetime movies and after school specials said that you should be examined before you shower. I didn't want to wash away all the evidence. I opened the front door and I could hear her talking to the neighbor. I could hear him thanking her, and I could hear her asking for her five hundred dollars. That bitch had been paid to allow him to rape me. The pain still resided in my heart and I don't know if I would ever get over it. Vengeance hadn't even eased the pain, because I loved her and she had betrayed me. I stole the very money that she had been paid for my rape, and hired a pimp to rape her. I even gave him a key to the house. I didn't stick around for the show. I left her home with tears streaming down my face and vowed no one would ever mistreat me ever again. I would do the hurting, before anyone could inflict pain on my heart.

Carmell, like my foster mother had crossed me and she too would pay. I would have what she told me I never would. I told her she didn't know who she was messing with. I don't think she believed me when I said it, but she better believe it now. I tried to do it the easy way. She could have just willingly given herself to me. She gave it up to Louis on the first night and all he did was get some Chinese take out and a video.   I thought about how and when I would have her. I already knew that once I got what I wanted, Louis and I would be through with her. At first I thought she was someone that I wanted to be with but now everything has changed. Now it was strictly about proving her wrong. Having what she said that I would never have. Once this was over I would shatter her world into tiny pieces. Let her know that Louis doesn't want her and never wanted her. I can see it now; she was either going to start crying or start fighting. Either way, I knew how to handle her. I laughed to myself. I had allowed her to get away with trying to fight me, but after I got what I wanted it would be no more of that. I would take care of her for the last time. She would know that she couldn't hit me whenever she felt like it. I turned and looked at Louis.   "Louis, thank you for trying to make me so happy. I appreciate it. You have always been so good to me." I said to Louis. I had to let him know that I appreciate everything he is doing for me. I didn't want him to think that I was ungrateful. I was just as willing to give him everything he wanted. I was willing to go the extra mile for him just like he was willing to do the same for me. If the situation were reversed I would wine and dine any girl to bring her home to him if I thought it would make him happy.   "Baby, you know that you are more than welcome. I would give you the moon and stars if I could. I'm just happy that we are together again. I'm going to make sure that I don't lose you. Ever." I smiled at his words. I loved Louis for who he was and everything he did for me. He was making so much progress with Carmell.

Kendra

All Cried Out

•————————————————————————————————————•

My weekend had been a disaster. I can't believe what happened. Then to top it all off Jason told me that the reason that Cory came to Atlanta was because Nicole told him to surprise me. Jason ran into my room saying that he had just talked to Nicole and she had sent Cory to catch us. The only problem was that there was no me and Jason beyond our friendship. I told Nicole that and she had not believed me. That hurt as well. I know that I cannot blame being caught on Nicole. I owe that to nobody but myself. No one made me commit adultery, but Nicole could have talked to me. She did that to be vindictive thinking Jason and I had something going on and that was hardly the case.   I was lying in my bed. Gia had held me in her arms as I cried. Cory immediately left that night, refusing to talk to me. I had tried several times to call him but he wouldn't answer the phone. I sat there dwelling on that look of pain I spotted in my husband's eyes. It was much too late to be asking the questions that were going through my head. I should have asked myself was it worth it. I didn't though. Instead I jumped in headfirst thinking of only myself. Cory had never mistreated me. He never hit me and as far as I know never cheated on me. He did not deserve what I was giving him.   I turned to face Gia who was sleeping silently next to me. I was surprised that she had not left me alone also. She was so beautiful. I looked at the black circle that now adorned her face. Cory had hit her so hard. That black eye was the most visible of the bruises that he had given her. I was still in shock over the way he charged at her. I guess jealousy and anger could do that to a man. It could make the sweetest man the meanest man in the world.

Gia stayed by my side the entire time. She was there when I tried to contact my husband. She was there when I cried from the pain and she was there to kiss my tears away. She did not try to have sex with me. She only wanted to console me and help me through what I was going through. Although she never really said it, I knew that she cared just as much as I did. If she didn't she wouldn't still be around. This was my last week in Atlanta. I had to finish my assignment. I was scared to go home because I didn't know what to expect when I got there. I had some decisions to make, life-altering decisions that could not be ignored.   "Gia, baby you sleep?" I asked. I wanted to talk to her.   "Never too sleep for you. What's on your mind? You want to try and call Cory again?" She questioned.   "No sweetie, it's not that. I don't think he would answer the phone anyway. This is about us. I want to talk about us." I turned so that I could face her. Every time I looked at her I noticed just how beautiful she was.   "I'm all ears." She said sitting up in the bed.   "I don't know how to say this." I started. "I guess the best way it to just say it. I care so much about you. I really do. If I could have it my way I would have the both of you. If I had that I would feel complete, but I know that is not possible. I want to try to work it out with my husband, if I can." This was really hard. "I know that I cannot ask you to wait if things did not work out. I would never ask that anyway, but I do want to give you something to let you know that I care for you." I got up to get my purse.

"Kendra, I always knew there would be a time when you would have to choose between Gia and Cory. To really be honest I knew that it would always be him before me. I came into this with my eyes wide open, knowing that you were married. I made the decision and I will deal with the consequences." She looked at me with tiny pools forming in the corners of her eyes. I pulled out two jewelry boxes. I had picked these up on my way from work. She began to open the box.   "This is beautiful." She said. She held in her hand a bracelet that I had purchased for her. It was a solid gold bangle with two hearts intertwined. I had the inside engraved.   "Forever   in my heart, Sweetness" She read the engraving.   "Please   wear   this bangle. It is a symbol of the feelings that I have for you. You will forever be in my heart and our hearts will be forever connected. I will wear one also and I will never take it off. I know that you have been through a lot for me. More than you should have had to go through and I feel responsible for that, but know that it was not all in vain and this was never just about sex or me being bi-curious. This is about the feelings that two people share. We were too late this life time but we are bound to be together in the next one." I smiled. She was crying now. I decided that I had done enough talking. I took her hand in mine and then moved slowly towards her. I kissed her. There was sadness in this kiss because we both knew this was a goodbye kiss. We made love nice and slow, savoring the goodness of one another because both of us knew that it would be the last. We both cried out of pleasure and pain. I cried until there were no more tears; they spilled until I was all cried out.

Nicole

Big-Headitist

Kendra and Jason were back in town. She hadn't said more than two words to me. What made it even worse is that Kendra was my acting supervisor. Management had pulled her off the phones thirty minutes after she got in. Our real supervisor was on maternity leave. I hoped she maintained her distance. I had tried to talk to Jason. He never apologized for calling me a bitch. At least we were on speaking terms though. Maybe I still had a chance cause I still wanted him. I never found out what had happened when Cory went to Atlanta but Jason and Kendra seemed to be buddies. I saw them hugging in the parking garage this afternoon coming back from lunch. Kendra was crying and Jason looked so concerned. Why couldn't I get him to care about me like that? He was all up on her, holding her and telling her it would be okay and I couldn't even get him to program my number in his phone. What was up with that?

I must admit seeing them two together made me envious. It didn't seem that there was anything sexual going on between them. There was something else, something deeper. When Jason looked at her there was a certain glow in his eyes. It was as if he held her on a pedestal or something. I had seen him look at other females or even the way that he looks at me and it was different. I would give anything to have him look at me that way. Maybe I would start to email him and convince him to go to lunch with me tomorrow. I would definitely make it worth his while. I was thinking to myself when Kendra walked up to my desk.

"Nicole I need to talk to you." Kendra stated. Her demeanor was cold. I could see her eyes were not friendly and her mouth didn't smile or frown as she spoke to me.

"Why Mrs. Dubois you haven't said more than two words to me since you got back and now you wanna talk?" I was being sarcastic but deep down I knew that I was missing my friend. We talked on the phone all the time and now she didn't have more than two words to say to me. With no Jason and no Kendra I was felt abandoned.

"Nicole I am not looking for conversation with you. I wanted to let you know that I was monitoring you when you disconnected that customer today." Kendra stared down at me. Though her tone was polite and professional, I could see a hint of anger flicker in her eyes. "So what are you saying?" I wanted her to get to the point. "I'm saying don't let it happen again. I'm not writing you up but consider this your warning." She said. I don't know what her problem was but I know she didn't just think she could talk to me any kind of way. She was only acting supervisor. "Is that a threat?" I asked. She was starting to upset me. "It is what it is. Take it how you want to take it." She stood there with her arms crossed. It was definitely a threat.

"What's your problem Kendra? You act as if I did something to you, even my mother agrees with me that you over stepped your boundary with my man." I challenged her. She wasn't going to have the last word that easily.

"Maybe the problem is your mother Nicole. You always tell me how you would never be like her and how you hate the way her boyfriends take precedence over you. I suggest you take a long hard look in the mirror, I'm sure you'll see your mother staring back at you, and he ain't your man. Now, I'm done with this conversation. Take it as a threat if you want, but you just be sure not to disconnect anyone else, or you will be written up." If this were a cartoon Kendra would have had smoke coming from her ears.

She turned and walked back to her desk. She walked away from me so fast you would have sworn I had something on me. I looked at her as she sat down and placed her headset back on. She never listened to calls. At least she never listened to my calls when she was our supervisor's point of contact. She would usually let me know when I was being monitored. That's how I had maintained such good quality scores. She looked at me and then smiled, but this smile wasn't friendly; it was, I don't know, sinister maybe. It was contorted and it looked a little mischievous. I was left there, speechless. Kendra had never taken that kind of tone with me. She never takes that tone with anyone. I couldn't believe how she threw my mother in my face, how dare she talk about my mother and furthermore what gave her the right to compare me to my mother. I don't know what happened in Atlanta that's got her acting like that but she needs to get it together. I hope that she did not let this little acting supervisor position go to her head. I looked at her out of the corner of my eye. She was definitely coming down with a case of big-headitis.

Carmell

Anything Goes

Today had been anything but an easy day at work. There was so much tension on my team. Kendra was acting supervisor and from what I could see, Nicole didn't like it. I thought they were good friends but it hasn't seemed that way since Kendra came back from Atlanta. Kendra seemed down about something and I could tell she was drowning herself in her work. It looked like she was trying to keep herself busy. It was almost five and I didn't want to worry myself with their problems. I have a date with Louis, and when I talked to him earlier he said there was something important that he wanted to talk to me about.   I jumped in my car so I could get home to prepare for our date. I always wanted to be perfect for him. I went into my closet to get one of my baddest outfits. I showered and got ready. I couldn't imagine what Louis wanted to talk to me about but I would soon find out.   It was seven now. I leaned over to peek out the window and saw Louis walking up the stairs. I grabbed my purse and met him outside.   "Hey baby." I greeted him with a kiss. As we road to the restaurant I tried to find out what he wanted to talk to me about. He wouldn't tell me though. He said he would rather discuss it over dinner. Okay he was starting to scare me. I hope he didn't plan on telling me that he had some type of STD, or was gay, or some type of closet cross dresser. We went through most of dinner in silence before he finally spoke.   "Carmell, I have something that I want to ask you to do for me." He still had not said what it was.   "And what's that baby?" I was ready for him to stop. I stared at him blankly as I set my fork down.

"Well, you know I am into group sex. Not so much group sex as threesomes or ménage tois. I just love to see women giving pleasure to each other and I want to share apart of it with you. Is that something that you would be willing to do for me?" Louis asked as he finished the last of his chicken Alfredo.

"What?" I stammered. I couldn't believe that he was asking me that, as if I weren't enough for him.   "I know it seems like a big deal now but it's really not. I just want to see another woman please you. Well there is one woman in particular actually. I would love to see you and Tina." Had Louis just said that? Did he get high before he came or what?   "You know how I feel about Natina. I don't like the hoe and I don't dike. That is asking a lot of me. That's asking too much of me." I said to him.   "I know but just one time. I told you when we first established this relationship that it would be a lot of work and you said that you could handle it. Are you going back on your word? Just one time, that is all I ask of you."   I sat there taking all of this in. I didn't know how to respond to that. I just wanted to make Louis happy. I just wanted to be his woman and be happy like we have been. Maybe if I do this then we can go back to just him and me. Louis had always kept his promises to me. So what would make this any different?

"I love you." He whispered. Those sugary sweet words slipped from his lips and I melted.

"I love you back." I said to him. I could do this one thing for him. This one time and one time only, he dare not ask again. It might cost him his life.   "Okay, but I ain't licking, kissing, or fingering her. Just the thought of being with a woman turns me off but if it is what turns you on then I am willing to provide that for you one time. But I'm warning you this is the first, last and the only time you will ever have anything like this." I said to him. I was a little disturbed by my readiness to please Louis. Just as I am with Dad, I was willing to do things to make him happy, even if those things hurt me. I didn't feel that Louis would hurt me though, because my heart told me to trust him. It was unknown to me why I was so taken with him. If any other man ever asked me that I was liable to pull a gun on them. I couldn't understand why but with Louis anything goes.

Natina

Tonight is the Night

I don't know how he had managed to do it but he had. Carmell had agreed. Louis must be working some type of magic or working his magic stick rather. "I want it to happen tonight." I turned and looked at Louis. I had been patient throughout the week, it was now Friday and I was ready to collect. "Okay." Louis answered. He reached for the phone and called Carmell. I knew that it wouldn't take much for him. He had a way of coaxing a woman right out of her panties. Louis left to go to the store and I began to get things ready. Even though my motives were for revenge, I wanted this to be special for Louis and me. I pulled out my special candles and lit the entire apartment with them. After I had done that, I created a walkway of rose petals. I had gone as far as to buy rose petals for this one occasion. Next, I created a platter of chocolate covered strawberries and champagne and sat them on the nightstand in the bedroom. Just as I was putting the finishing touches on the room, the phone rang. I glanced at the caller ID and didn't recognize the number. Even though it was against my better judgment I answered the phone.

"Hello." I was annoyed someone was interrupting a night that I was busy planning for.

"TeeTee is that you." The voice that spoke to me was familiar. No one had called me TeeTee in years.

"Who the hell is this? Wait, I know who this is so I have an even better question. Why the hell are you calling me?" I knew that voice all to well.

"Now is that anyway to talk to your mother, the only mother you've really ever known." She asked.

"Patricia, stop calling yourself my mother. I don't know how you got this number but lose it bitch. A mother doesn't pimp her daughter out. No amount of money is worth what you allowed him to take from me." I was fuming. She had the audacity after all these years to pick up the phone and call herself my mother.

"TeeTee you need to let that go. I have forgiven you for what you did to me afterwards and I think it's time you do the same. Then we can both move forward and get back to being the way we used to be, like mother and daughter. I'm reaching out to you, baby." She sounded like she was pleading. What the hell did she mean I needed to get over it?

"Get over it huh. I'm not over it. I won't ever be over it and you can forget that sick shit about us being mother and daughter. Your ass messed that up when you took money to let dirty ass Rodney rob me of my virginity. You are sick you know that. I have nothing more to say to you." I slammed the phone down so hard it cracked.

The phone began to ring back to back. After all of these years she resurfaces and of all nights my special night. I was pissed at her for stirring up all of these memories.

"There is no way I'm going to let her ruin my night." I said aloud as I blocked her number. I looked at myself in the mirror above my dresser. I was fighting back tears. There was no way I was gonna waste any tears on that phone call. I thrust thoughts of her out my head. I was going to have a good time tonight.

I went to the bathroom to take a bath and redirect my thoughts. I was finally proving Carmell wrong. She said I would never have it, never touch or taste her. Well she was wrong. I had a secret weapon that she couldn't resist, Louis. I smiled at the thought. Lately she has been looking at me as if she has taken something that once belonged to me. I could only imagine the look on her face when she found out that nothing is what it seems.   To be honest, I really missed the friendship that we once had. I thought about the cruel plot I had concocted, but soon dismissed the guilt. It was her fault.   If she hadn't been playing with my mind I would not have been playing with her life. I warned her. I told her I was going to get what I wanted. I always did and there is nothing that she could do or say that would stop me.

Louis yelled into the bathroom to let me know that she was on her way. I didn't want her coming over here but once this was over I would be through with her. I reached for the towel and dried off my body.   I began to get ready. I pulled on my clothes and did my makeup. Soon I was ready to do this. I walked onto the living room where Louis waited for me.

We sat there gently teasing one another while awaiting Carmell's arrival. I wrapped my legs around his waist and said "I'm ready baby. Tonight is the night!"

Kendra

My World Came Tumbling Down

This week had been horrible. Leaving Gia on those terms was hard, but I knew that it was best. I had to try to salvage my life and my marriage. I knew that it would be hard. Cory still wasn't speaking to me.   I sat at my desk consumed with work, but I didn't mind. The work was a welcomed interruption to the mess that I had made of my life. I was acting supervisor, which meant supervisor work.

Even with all the work that I had to do, I could not help but think of my own problems. When I had gotten back in Houston, Cory was supposed to pick me up. I was nervous, I mean down right scared. When I exited the plane and found my luggage I went to the passenger pick up and looked for my husband. Bush Intercontinental Airport was busy as usual. I looked around trying to spot my husband's familiar face. If he was there, I never saw him.   I waited outside on the curb for two hours before I realized that he wasn't going to show. I could not believe that he would just leave me here, but then again, could I blame him? I then understood I needed to call a taxi to take me home. I had thought about calling my mother but I didn't want to explain to her why my husband refused to talk to me. My mother was such a big part of my life, but if she ever found out I was with a woman, and had jeopardized my marriage as well, she would be disappointed with me. I hated to disappoint my mother. For her, I wanted to be perfect. She raised me in the church and the foundation of our home is the Bible; my adultery and bisexuality had no place in my mother's Christian home and as a Christian, it had no place in my life. I knew these things, was convicted by my own actions, but for some reason couldn't walk away from Gia. Right or wrong, my desire to love her and be loved by her beckoned me to her.   I let the tears slide down my cheeks on the ride home. My house wasn't that far from the airport. I grabbed my bags and paid the driver. Cory's Escalade was parked in the driveway and out of pure curiosity I walked to the truck and touched the hood just to see if it was warm. It was cold which meant that he had not even attempted to come pick me up.   I put my key into the door and turned the lock. I tried to push the door open but the chain was stopping the door. He had locked me out.   "Cory come undo the chain please." I yelled into the quietness of the house. There wasn't any sound coming from the house. Just complete silence that said more than I cared to hear.   "Get   your dike to undo the chain for you!" I heard Cory yell back. I can't believe he was going to make me stand out here and play this game with him.   "Cory please, I have to go to the bathroom. We can talk about this." I was pleading with him to let me in the house.   "No we can't talk about shit. You can talk to your little girlfriend maybe she will listen but we ain't got nothing to talk about. Now go back to where you came from and get the hell away from my house." What did he mean his house? I had made damn sure my name was attached to those mortgage papers when I signed on the dotted line.

"Cory it is not just your house it is our house. We do need to talk so stop playing and open up the damn door!" I was becoming irate. Cory still had not moved. The garage door was open so I tried the entrance from it. That door was also chained. I guess he had thought of everything. I dropped my bags in the garage and grabbed my keys. This was a damn shame. I was going to have to break into my own house.   I unlocked the gate and walked into my backyard. I walked around to the guest room, picked up a stick, and broke the window. Then I slid my arm through the hole I had made and unlocked the window, lifted it and then climbed through it. I was as hot as a firecracker on the 4th of July, but as I made my way into the bedroom, I calmed down to face my husband. I understood his anger, but what I couldn't understand was his need to act like he was twelve. I mean locking me out, leaving me at the airport. That was down right childish. I counted backwards from ten and then entered my bedroom. "Cory, baby it doesn't have to be like this." I stood over our bed where he lay. He was so handsome, how could I have let this happen. Millions of thoughts ran through my head. I could have been more careful, I could have just said no. It was too late to think about those things, I had to think about moving forward with my life and my marriage. I didn't want it to be over so I needed this silent treatment to stop.

"Is that what you were saying when you were eating some woman? How many other times have you cheated on me?" Cory said looking just as hurt as he sounded.

"Baby that was the first and last time. I want our marriage to work. I want to be with you. Gia and I have already talked and said our goodbyes. It's over. Please baby just say that we can get pass this." I was pleading with Cory. I was on my knees nearly pleading for him to recognize how sorry I was.

"I'm not your baby. As a matter of fact, get the fuck out of my face. This conversation is finished. You can have the guestroom and by the way, you're paying to have that window fixed that you broke." He stood up and pushed me out of the room and then closed and locked the door.

I stood outside that door for at least thirty minutes begging him to talk to me. I was beating on the door, pleading for him to allow me re-entry into our bedroom. I had been dismissed and pushed out of the door. I pleaded until I had no voice. All of my cries were unanswered. He further ignored me by turning the television on and the volume up as loud as it would go. Just reliving that moment inflicted further pain on my broken heart.

Jason walked up, interrupting my thoughts. I would have to have my flashbacks later, people needed me in the present. "Hey there, you look like you are in another world." "Yeah I feel like it." I grabbed my purse and headed to lunch. I had to figure out how to win my husband back. I refused to stand by and watch as my world came tumbling down.

Nicole

Total Shock

_____

I had tried all day to strike up a conversation with Kendra. She refused to talk to me, but I knew that something happened in Atlanta. After I left work I decided to try and call her because I wanted my friend back and even more importantly I wanted to know what went down in A-town. I never would have thought that sending him there would have caused me to lose the only friend that I really had. I didn't mean to cause all this, I just wanted her to leave Jason alone. Kicking it with Tina has been fun, but her world was crazy and I was longing for the steady comfort that Kendra's friendship could provide.

I don't know how I let my lust for a man come between us. I wanted to be there for her and I wanted to know the 411. Maybe I could call Cory and find out what happened since Kendra wouldn't talk to me. He had always liked me, maybe he could convince her that our friendship was worth too much to lose it over foolishness. I reached for my cell phone to call her home number. She shouldn't be home yet but I will act like I don't know that.

"Hey Cory is Kendra home?" I asked when he answered the phone.

"No and if you see her tell her don't bother coming either." Cory said to me. What the hell was he talking about? I know for sure now something went down.

"Cory what the hell are you talking about boy? Didn't I tell you that crack kills?" I said to him. He would usually laugh at my stupidity. Cory never even acknowledged that I had attempted to make a joke.

"Cole why in the hell did you send me down there? Did you know about what was going on?" Cory questioned.

"I don't know what you are talking about. I suggested you go so that you and your wife could spend time together." I said. Cory was making me nervous. "Cory, what happened? Why are you so upset?" I couldn't help but think that he had really caught Jason and Kendra together. Whatever happened I had to accept that I was partially to blame.

"Nicole, you're her best friend, did she ever tell you about any desires for other women? Did she ever say that she had some dike tendencies?" Cory sounded as if he spoke through clenched teeth. I had never heard him use the word dike before. Cory never called anyone anything other than his or her birth given names.

"Are you asking me if Kendra ever told me she was gay?" What kind of question was that? "No she never said anything like that. Why should she? She is too conservative for anything like that. I mean every time we watched *Queens of Comedy* she replays Sommore's part over and over. It's her favorite line "We gone be fightin' cause I ain't dikin'"" I mimicked Kendra trying to talk like her favorite female comedian Sommore. She owned the DVD and when ever that part came on she was shouting about how she feel her on that and she loved pokey, her word for penis, too much. So with all that how could he ever suspect that she was gay?

"Well I guess she had both of us fooled cause I caught her with a woman when I went to Atlanta. I haven't talked to anybody about it. That shit's embarrassing. I mean what am I suppose to say *Hi my name is Cory and my wife's a down low dike.*" I sat there and listened to him as he vented.

Now I didn't know my girl was getting down like that and further more I couldn't believe it. Kendra was my girl, my ace, my number one and she had never so much as expressed any level of curiosity regarding women. I know that she could be outgoing but I didn't know that she was going out like that.

Cory told me all about how he walked in on Kendra going down on another woman. She was carpet munching and to me that is nasty. For her to get caught by her husband with her head between some woman's legs. Ohh, she was so nasty, but it was so funny. Now that's the kinda stuff you see on television.

"Cory what do you plan on doing? This explains a lot. Kendra has been crying a lot, I would see her in the garage crying and I never could figure out why." I sat there in silence and waited for Cory to reply. It seemed like five minutes had passed before either one of us spoke again.

"So can you come over?" I heard Cory ask.

"What?" I said. I could not believe that he asked me to come over and Kendra was not there. "Well Kendra is not really talking to me now. She is blaming me for what happened in Atlanta. I was just calling, I thought she would be home and we could talk about it." I hoped this answer was sufficient enough. I was hoping that this was a strong enough no and that me coming over there would be crossing a line. It was a line at this point that did not at all need to be crossed.

"Well I'm not asking you to come over for Kendra, I want you to come over for me. I want to talk to you face to face. Besides, Kendra is stopping by her mother's house. I don't expect her home for some time." Cory sounded different to me. I guess the word that I was looking for was sexy. His voice had suddenly taken on a deep melodious sound and his sexy baritone notes had began to sing a song of desire to me. I must be losing my mind but I was going to talk to him. He sounded like he needed a friend. If I went over and left before Kendra came home she would never know. We were both adults and we could be in the same room without anything happening. We were just going to talk I told myself.

"Okay, I'm on my way." I couldn't believe that I had just agreed to go over Kendra's house, without Kendra. During my fifteen minute drive there I remained in Total Shock.

Carmell

Enemy or Lover

Louis was eager for this little threesome that he has set up. I hated Natina with a passion, but Louis I loved with a passion. It was funny how the human mind worked sometime. I had convinced myself that this was okay because I was pleasing my man. If I only concentrated on him then it would be like she wasn't even there. I would direct all my energy and attention to Louis and Natina would be like a piece of unused furniture, in the room, but for decoration purposes only.

I finished curling my hair and applying the rest of my make-up. Louis told me that he wanted me to be beautiful. I pulled out one of my favorite outfits. This outfit accented my every curve and I knew he was going to like it. I hopped into my car and I headed towards Natina's house. I sipped on a raspberry Smirnoff on my way over there. I knew I was breaking the law but I needed this. There is no way in the world that I would ever be able to go through with this in my right frame of mind. Sobriety would offer clarity and I wanted clouded judgment at this time.

I pulled into the parking lot and waited because I didn't have the courage to move yet. I began to fix my hair, which was already perfect; I cleaned something imaginary from under my nails and then sprayed my body once more with a bit of Amber Romance from Victoria Secret. Finally, I have the nerve to go to the door. Natina answered the door.

"Hey sexy, you finally gone give me the ass, huh? I told you I would have it, one way or another." Tina laughed as she closed the door and walked towards the bedroom. I don't know how I am gonna do this. Every time I looked at that girl I wanted to knock the shit out of her. I had to catch myself when I walked in the door. Where was my man, he was the only person I wanted to see. He walked from the bathroom. He moved around this house like he lived here. It was a bit odd. I probably would have felt better at my apartment but he insisted we come here and we never went to his house because of his room mate.

Louis came and sat down next to me. "You ready baby?" He leaned in to kiss me on my cheek as he grabbed my hand and led me to the bedroom. When we reached the bedroom both Louis and Natina came towards me. She was like some type of animal and she had made me her prey. Louis leaned in and kissed me.

"Mmmmm. You taste good Carmell, so so sweet. I want you and Tina to kiss. I want to see you explore her body and allow her to explore yours." I looked at Louis.

"I told you no kissing got dammit." I yelled.

"Not even one tiny one for me?" Natina reached towards me before I could answer his question. She parted my lips with her tongue and I was surprised by the softness of her kiss. It was interesting. It was different from kissing a man. Her lips were not as strong and when I found myself accepting what was happening I pulled away from her.

Natina looked at me with that sarcastic smile that she always wears.

"Don't be scared boo." Natina began to remove my clothing with Louis eagerly watching. He walked up behind me and began to kiss my neck. He rubbed my shoulders and began to run his tongue along my spine. Louis picked me up and laid me across the bed and positioned his naked body on the edge. I took him into my mouth.

I felt Tina move. I cringed as she began to touch my body. Her tongue began to play between my legs. I had to admit it did feel good. She knew what to do with it. It was intense. I didn't want to enjoy her technique so I concentrated on pleasing Louis and tried to ignore the gentle strokes of her tongue.

Natina continued to taste me and Louis moved behind her and entered her from behind. We had not talked about them having sex and I was jealous. He was making love to her and he had entered her before me. I didn't understand. He shouldn't want to enter any woman but me.

"Louis baby, I need some special attention over here." I said. At that moment Louis moved Tina over, kissed her and shoved himself inside of me. His thrust was hard. These were not the same loving movements that he had given Natina. He was banging my back out, literally. Our lovemaking had never been so rough. I mean this felt almost violent.

Louis's body began to shake. When he had reached his climax he pulled himself out of me, letting that warm substance flow all over my face. Damn what was really going on? My man wasn't acting like my man and somehow my enemy had become my lover.

Natina

Cancel That Ho

Finally, I got what I wanted. I guess she never believed me when I said it but I got it. I turned over and looked at her pretty face, she looked like she was about to cry.

"Did you have a good time?" I asked. She looked at me with total disgust in her eyes. She was really pissing me off now.

"Hell no, I didn't enjoy myself. I didn't do this shit for you. This was for Louis and Louis only.   Now get the hell out of my face." She was screaming at me. I know she wasn't screaming at me in my own damn house. I was about to put this ho in her place.

"Who in the hell are you hollering at. You better check yourself. You in my house and you will not loud talk or disrespect me in my house. I will put yo yella ass out butt naked." I looked at her. I could slap her for the way she was treating me. I go all out of my way to get her and this is how she treats me. I share my man with her. Let her use him for a minute and she wants to cuss me out in my damn house. Aww hell naw! This wasn't even happening.

"Fine, I don't want to be here anyway. Louis you got your threesome, let's get the hell out of here." Carmell said. She jumped out of the bed and started to try to put her clothes on. I had to burst her little bubble. She was too damn sure of herself.

"You dumb ass, Louis ain't going no where. He is staying here with me. He is staying with his woman." I laughed as I stood to take my rightful place next to Louis.

"Louis what the hell is she talking about?" Carmell shouted.

"I live here baby girl." That was all Louis had to say before leaving the bedroom to take a shower.

I looked at Carmell. I actually felt pity for her. She could not peep the signs? I mean when the three of us were together it was me that he made love to, it was me that he embraced; It was always about me. Carmell looked at me. I could not help but crack a smile.

"I guess you thought he was yours huh? Too bad!" I laughed as I threw the rest of her clothes towards her. She stood there for what seemed like forever and then threw them back at me. If there was one thing that was not going to happen she was not gonna fight me in my own house.

"What the hell is your problem? Get your clothes and get the hell out of our house. You crazy bitch!" I turned to leave the room. Carmell came charging towards me. I turned around and slapped her ass as hard as I could. I was tired of being nice to her. Every time her loony ass got upset she wanted to take her frustration out on me. I was friendly about it, but that was over. I slapped her three or four time, enough to knock her ass out. I wasn't gonna play this game with her. I took all her clothes and threw them out the window, then I looked at her lying on the floor. How could I have ever fallen for someone like her? She's pathetic. Willing to do any and everything to have a man that's not hers. Things could have been so different between us, but she had to take it here. This was her fault. I kicked her with my foot to get her attention. She wasn't about to take her little siesta on my floor.

"Get out of my house. I suggest you do it expeditiously cause I ain't gonna ask again." I was through with the games and I meant what I said or I would slap the mess out of her again.

"What did you do with my clothes?" I ignored her. "Did you hear me, where the hell are my clothes?" Carmell needed professional help. She lunged towards me, scratching me with one of her many rings. I grabbed her hair and dragged her to the front door, all the while she was punching me in my legs. I opened the door and threw her out like a piece of trash. That is all she was to me anyways. I told her if she kept messing with me I would throw her ass out buckey naked. I heard Louis turn the shower off.

"Where did Carmell go?" He asked.

I walked towards the shower and replied, "I canceled that Ho!"

Kendra

An Eye For An Eye

I didn't know what I was going to do about my life and the mess that I had made of it. This was sad though. I had left my mother's house more than forty-five minutes ago and still had not reached home. My mother had a way of sensing when things were wrong with me. Even though I didn't care to discuss it with her, she knew it was Cory and she urged me to go home and work it out. I drove around in circles until I worked up enough courage to go home. Cory and I had so much to talk about, however he had nothing to say to me.

His anger was understandable and I never meant to hurt him. It seemed that I could do nothing right. I tried several things to bring my husband back to me. Needless to say, none of them worked. He was like a ticking bomb ready to explode at any given moment. I know that I hurt him deeply. That was not something that I ever meant to do and I desperately needed his love in my life. I circled the block a couple of more times before I worked up the courage to drive to my home. I just hoped that this time I did not have to break in to my own house. I pulled into my driveway. Corey had company. I got out the car and noticed a set of faded pink dice in the rearview mirror. I looked at the license plates. The words around the plated read "Always late but worth the wait." What the hell was Nicole doing at my home? I wasn't here and we weren't talking anyway. My temperature began to sky rocket as I ran towards my door. I was gone whip somebody's ass. I moved my hand towards my lock when I noticed the voices on the inside. I could hear Nicole between soft moans telling him to stop. I couldn't believe this whore of a friend I had. I welcomed her into my home, gave to her when I didn't have, and she has the audacity to come into my home and screw my husband. Hell no, that was crossing the line. I know what I did was wrong, but this shit was foul. Then I heard Cory's voice. He was saying he needed this. He needed to be with a woman that knew and valued the importance of a man.

I stood there and listened. Tears began to stream down my cheeks. This shit hurt. I stood there feeling the ultimate pain of infidelity. So this is what I had done to Cory that day. I had hurt him so much that he felt the best way to get back at me was to sleep with someone that had been close to me. I guess the sad part about it is that the little tramp would actually do it. Lately she has been talking to me acting as if she wanted to be my friend again. I didn't really understand but I guess it was not my place to understand. I wasn't gonna walk into this house. No if that was something that Cory felt he needed let him have it. In the end he would return to momma and I would be here waiting with open arms. I needed him in my life. I wanted him, I craved this man and there was no way I was living without him.

Then there was Nicole; she was an entirely different matter. This just proved that she was no real friend. She never had been my friend if she would lay with my husband. The thought of them together, him inside of her, made me sick to my stomach. The moans from inside became louder and the pathetic theatrical pleas to stop had long ceased. No she was fully enjoying the skill I had gradually taught to that man. I backed away from the door. I moved my car around the corner, grabbed my Cannon and sprinted back to my house. I checked the number of exposures I had left. Twenty-two, it was a brand new roll.

I didn't quite know what I was gonna do with these pictures. I don't even know why I am taking them, but my inner person kept telling me to get pictures, don't let them know that you know, stay one step ahead of the game. So I found an open space in my flowerbed and crouched really low so that no one could see me. This wasn't the best of views but enough was visible. Thank goodness the blinds were open. I began to snap away. Each picture was snapped with more and more force. I became almost oblivious to the passing neighbors and awkward stares. I had been engulfed by anger as I watched my husband make love to another woman; a woman who I once called my best friend. Hatred enveloped me. I was filled with homicidal rage and through all of this I could not help but think of the old saying "what goes around comes around". This was the oldest game of revenge he was playing.

"An eye for an eye." I thought to myself as I snapped away until all the exposures were gone.

Nicole

Two Ho's and a Slammed Do'

Two weeks had passed since that day with Cory. I have to admit I felt somewhat guilty but damn it was good. I mean I never knew Cory would have been working with that. I lay against my sofa, lost in the thought of his sweet loving. It was almost enough to take my sway my thoughts away from Jason. Almost.

Jason hadn't been returning any of my calls. He was always there to comfort Kendra but when it came to me he only spoke to me if it were an absolute necessity. I didn't go to work today and I really want to see him. I have been sitting here all day thinking of a way I could see him or at least get him to talk to me.

Then all of a sudden it came to me. I would just show up at his house. How could he turn away all of this if I just put it in his face. I jumped up to get dressed, well as dressed as I was going to be.

The entire drive to his apartment I was nervous. When I finally arrived I called his number just to play with his head. I didn't want him to even suspect that I was close, I wanted to surprise him. I sat in the parking lot and dialed his number, but no one picked up. I knew that he had to be there cause I was parked right next to his car and it looked as if the light in his bedroom was on. I don't know what the reason was, but he was not answering his phone and it was driving me crazy. I hate being ignored. I hated even more feeling this dude the way I did and getting the cold shoulder.

I gathered all of my strength and courage then jumped out the car. I pulled my jacket extra tight and strutted in the three inch silver stilettos I was wearing. Underneath my knee length jacket was a lace bra and panty set in the sexiest red you could ever imagine.

"Click click, click click", I could hear the steady rhythm of my walk as I eased up the stairs. I wanted him so bad I could feel him inside of me. I mean Cory was a nice diversion but I could never have him, nor did I want him. I had my sights on one man alone and his name was Jason. I stood and thought about his creamy skin as I knocked on the door.

After what seemed like an eternity I finally heard someone coming to the door. They didn't even ask who it was.

"Who is that at the door?" I could hear Jason call.

"What the hell is going on here?" I thought to myself. There were two twin girls standing at the door wearing nothing but the suit that God gave them, there chocolate coated skin seeming to gleam in the moonlight.

"Can we help you?" They said in unison. I know they didn't think that was cute.

"Where is Jason?" I could hear myself about to hit some major octaves. I was about to have an all out bitch fit.

"Who wants to know?" I could hear him call from within.

"I want to know. That's who wants to know, I see why you can't answer my calls." By the time I said all of that Jason was standing before me.

"I don't know why you think I owe you an explanation. I sent two naked girls to answer my door cause I saw your ass walking up the steps. Most people would leave but not you, you still want to push your way into my apartment. You ain't have no invite to my house, which means you shouldn't be standing at my door, and if I didn't answer your call then I ain't wanna talk. So I suggest you turn your half naked ass around and drive it back home. I got what I need for the night." Then he did the one thing that crushed me. He slammed the door in my face. With some people he was such the gentleman just as nice and sweet, but instead of sweet I get two ho's and and slammed do'!

Carmell

Butt-Naked

Well I be got damned. That's all I could think. I sat on my bed in awe because I couldn't believe the past events of my life. This would be my first day back at work in two weeks since what went down with Tina and Louis. Even though I knew I had to go, I couldn't convince myself to move.

I thought I was in love. I thought this man was the one for me but I was sadly mistaken. I remember the events of that night like it was yesterday. I didn't fully understand why Louis seemed to be giving Tina so much special attention. He literally screwed my as I watched him make love to her. It was down right unbelievable. I reached to put my shoes on and immediately became sick to my stomach at the sight of Louis's picture next to my bed.

I hated to admit it but Tina had kicked my ass. Not only had she whooped my ass, she kicked me out the house butt naked. I was pissed as hell. There I was standing outside naked and I had no idea where my clothes were. I remember hearing the calls of some men that were standing outside. Their raspy voices ringing in my ears, "Hey Ma, why don't you come over here, I'll keep your sexy body warm!" That too was disgusting. Not only did I have to deal with the shame of being tricked into their sexual tryst, I had to suffer the further humiliation of being tossed out on my naked ass.

I looked around for my things because shortly before she had slammed the door in my face she had thrown my purse and clothes out of the window. The contents of my purse were scattered underneath the bushes and my dress was caught in the lower limbs of a tree. I quickly gathered my belongings and hit my dress with a stick until it fell to the ground. Once I had my body covered I picked up my keys. I could feel my pisstivity level rising. As soon as I had my keys in hand I headed towards my car. I noticed the happy couples cars parked next to one another. I used my key to write the word BITCH all over her car. After my decorative art I then kicked in the windows of both their cars. I scribbled little lines all over Louis car as I wrote "I hate you" across the hood. Who did they think they were playing with? I couldn't do anything about my decision to have a threesome with them, but I could abuse their property like they abused my body. I took out all of my anger and frustration out on their cars. I don't know what made me want to trust him. I thought he would be the one man that I can count on. I didn't know who I was kidding. If I couldn't trust my own daddy to stand by his word, how could I ever depend on Louis too. I was an emotional wreck, my heart was breaking and I felt powerless to do anything about it. I continued with my ghetto decorating until I had completely defaced their property. I knew I would have to find a way to make her pay for what she has done to me; she had totally humiliated me and then threw me out of her house butt naked.

Natina

Done with Her

The incident with Carmell was completely over rated. I wanted this girl and when I finally got her it was disappointing. The highlight of the night was throwing her light bright looking ass out. She had completely pissed me off. I hadn't seen her at work since that happened and I wondered briefly what happened to her, but that quickly passed when I thought about what she did to my car.

I mean, I can definitely understand why she would have done it but how did she think acting out like a two year old was gonna hurt me. When I went outside that Monday morning I saw that she had done a few hood enhancements to our cars. I just shook my head as I called Louis down to survey the damage.

While waiting on Louis I noticed there was a red Honda Accord parked two spaces behind my car. In the car was a woman I was sure I recognized. I slowly walked towards the car.

"Patricia, what the hell are you doing here. I thought I made it clear to you yesterday I had nothing to say to you and I damn sure didn't wanna see you!" I was trying hard to control myself. What made her want to intrude into my life. What reason did she have for trying to contact me.

"Look, TeeTee I've been doing a lot of thinking and I really think we should talk. There are a lot of things I need to say to you and I can obviously see that you are angry with me still. I want us to talk, I want us to reconcile." Patricia's eyes were pleading with me. I looked at this woman. This was a woman I once thought the world of and now she was nothing more than a memory to me. I wasn't ready to forgive her and I didn't know if I would ever be.

"Leave me alone. I don't know how you found out where I live but don't come here ever again." I didn't give her time to respond because as soon as I was done speaking I walked off. Louis walked outside just in time to see me walking away from the car.

"What's wrong baby, you look bothered. Who was that?" He asked. His eyebrows were raised as if they were asking the questions. I didn't care to get into my family history, or lack there of, with Louis. As a matter of fact, I never discussed my life with anyone. I saw no reason to, people just always looked at you like you were some type of charity case and felt sorry for you because you were so mistreated. I didn't need anybody's pity and I didn't need her.

"Nobody, just somebody wanting directions. Look at our cars and what that damn girl did to them." I motioned towards the cars as I pushed thoughts of that woman out of my head.

He looked at his car and became upset, but that can be expected, he's a man. Men are overly sensitive about stuff like this.

"Calm down baby." I said as I moved towards the car to make sure the valuables were still inside. "That's what we pay insurance for."

"You're right Tina, you're right. I guess she was pretty mad huh? I still can't believe that you threw that girl out with no clothes on." He laughed. I had told him the story of us fighting while he was in the shower.

"Yeah she was pissed, but I don't care. She can be pissed all she wants, she was a got damned waste of my time. You can stick a fork in me cause I'm done with her."

Kendra

Cheaters

Cory and I were still dancing to the same tune. I was begging and he was ignoring. You would think after he had screwed Nicole he would have at least somewhat felt vindicated. I would have thought that after he was finally with a woman that knew the importance of a man, or whatever bs he had said to get her to drop her panties, he would at least be cordial and talk to me, but I got nothing. He slammed doors when he came home, he ignored my calls and he still wouldn't sleep in the same room as me.

I don't know how I was going to fix this but I had to find a way to fix it. I had stopped talking to Gia. It would only pose a bigger problem if I attempted to maintain a friendship with her. It just wasn't gonna work. Some days it was hard. I had found in her a friend, she was someone that was always there to listen or just talk when I needed a friend. We could joke and laugh and be happy and lost in our silliness.

I blinked my eyes to awake myself from the self-induced trance. It was useless to even think of her. That part of my life was over and I was moving forward. I needed to repair my marriage. I looked at the clock and saw it was time for me to go. I was taking a half day in an attempt to go home and prepare a night of romance for my husband. I didn't actually think it was going to work but a girl could have dreams right.

I walked to my car and then my cell phone rang. I frowned to myself. All the technology that Synergy Wireless possessed and I couldn't block private numbers. I answered the phone annoyed.

"Hello." If I didn't answer the phone it would bother me. That was the power of a private number. The average person always wanted to know who was calling them private.

"Hey there, I'm sorry for calling you. I'm in town and I would really love to see you. I blocked my number in hopes that you would answer and I could at least hear your voice. So please say yes." The voice on the other end hit melodies that only she can. A million years could past and I would always know that voice.

"Gia, we talked about this. This is not good and you know I'm trying to make things right with Cory." My heart had already skipped a few beats just from the rhythm of her breathing.

"I know what we talked about babygirl, but I also know what my heart feels. I just want to see you and nothing more. I ain't asking you to drop drawers, just come see an old friend while she's in town."

"Well I have to plan for this evening, but I suppose I could spare a few minutes." I was doing everything I told myself I wouldn't do. I was strong though. I had no intentions of becoming involved sexually with Gia.

She told me where she was staying and then we said our goodbyes. She wasn't far from me at all, actually she was right down the street. I headed towards the Hilton Hotel she was staying in.

I jumped on the elevator and found room 1112. I knocked on the door only once. She opened the door mid knock and hugged me. It was nice to feel arms around me. Cory was showing me no attention so a little affection was welcomed.

She closed the door and motioned me towards the bed. I was somewhat uncomfortable and I knew I was putting myself into a dangerous situation. This was playing with fire and I was praying I didn't get burned. We sat on the bed and talked and it was just like old times. I was so swept up in the moment that I let my guard down and allowed the softness of her lips to brush against mine. The sweetness of her lip gloss drizzled onto my tongue as the fullness of her lips merged with mine. Her kisses were so sensual and I wanted her. My mind told me no but with the way she was touching me it was about to be a yes. Make that a hell yeah.

She began to unbutton my shirt to expose the lavender lace bra I wore underneath. Our bodies began to intertwine as we kissed, rubbed and touched. Her hands found their way to my breast, then her lips. She softly took my nipples into her mouth, teasing and sucking, turning me on as she took more and more of my breast into her mouth. Her biting began to make regions below tingle. What felt so good I knew was so wrong.

"Gia, baby we have to stop." She looked at me and before she could finish her sentence there was a knock on the door. I hurried to find my shirt that had somehow been completely removed as she got up to open the door. Just as I found my shirt I noticed something wasn't right. I struggled to put my shirt on as a flood of TV cameras and microphones rushed into the room. Gia looked at me frantically. I stared blankly back still struggling with the buttons on my shirt and then I noticed why Gia had such a panicked look on her face. It was Cory standing in the doorway next to Joey Greco from Cheaters. My hands began to shake, my mouth went completely dry, for a moment, I thought that I was going to faint.

"You just couldn't leave her alone huh. You couldn't leave your dike whore alone." There was that same fire in his eyes from that night in Atlanta. Is this déjà vu or what? I can't believe that this is happening again, the only difference is it was happening for the whole world to see. I had been caught on camera by Cheaters.

Nicole

Won't Take No for an Answer

●————————————————————————————●

I can't believe that man had the nerves to slam that door in my face. I just couldn't understand, I mean they were cute but they weren't me. There was no way I am taking no for an answer.

I'm so pissed now I can't even bring myself to leave his apartment complex. I need to think so I decide to drive around in a circle. I hate being ignored and I can't believe he is ignoring me. Me of all people, I'm Nicole Neatherly and no one ignores me.

My drive did nothing for me but further infuriate me. I decided to turn around and go back to Jason's apartment. I thought about what my mother would do in this situation. Knowing my mother, she would tell me not to let anything stop me from getting what I wanted, and I wasn't about to let the twin tramps push me away from what was mine. I pulled up just in time to see the double mint twins on their way out the door. At least they weren't spending the night.

I checked myself in the mirror before I walked back to his door. I sprayed myself with my favorite perfume. No man in his right mind could ever resist this scent. He slowly opened the door. As he groggily watched, I stepped back and pulled my trench open to expose my smooth brown skin.

"What the hell are you doing here? I send two half naked girls to the door and you still come back for more?" I took two more steps back as he stared at me. There was anger in his eyes. "Didn't I tell you to go home?" He looked at me, his face blank and void of any emotion.

I began to cover myself and said "I thought I would give you another chance to redeem yourself. You've had a chance to play, now let me show you what a real woman can do for you. One real woman is all you really need." I know that I was challenging him. I wanted him to accept me. I wanted to be the girl in the house and for him to send all the other girls away. I needed to be the one that he craved and the only one that could truly satisfy him. I wanted to be his special girl, his Darling Nikki.

Jason just stared at me. It seemed like the longest minute in history. I looked at him, he still held that fire in his eye but there was also something else there. There was desire and I had to act on this moment. I slowly moved towards Jason. He stood still and watched me. I placed my hand against his bare chest, which bulged with just the right amount of muscle. I used my finger to etch my name around his heart. For me, this held some type symbolic meaning. I was going to work my way into his heart and write my name all over what was going to be mine. I pressed my lips against his and I could smell the faint scent of alcohol along with the fresh scent of soap from his newly showered body.

He stepped onto the porch and pulled my jacket open. He took my left breast into his mouth caressing it softly as he used his teeth to gently nibble on my nipple. I began to moan. This is exactly what I wanted. I needed this man.

His movements began to become more aggressive. He hungrily searched for my mouth as he pushed me closer to the guard rail. Jason pulled my coat until it fell to my feet. I stood there in nothing but my stilettos. He spread my legs as he descended to the ground. He placed his head between my legs and began to taste me. My body began to shiver with the intensity of the wind flowing across my bare body and the subtle movement of his tongue bringing me so much pleasure. Just when I felt myself nearing a climax he pulled away.

My body was so filled with yearning. As if he was reading my mind, he pulled me close to him and entered my body. Jason lifted me on top of the rails as his thrust became harder and harder. He wrapped his hands around my neck. As he held me close, slightly choking me, I began to release a river of wetness. I moaned softly and called his name. I could hear people walking below and I felt their eyes silently judging our public sexual display, but I didn't care. Jason felt so good inside of me I could only concentrate on his hard, deep thrust penetrating through my middle into the very depths of my soul. This was amazing. Sensing that Jason was nearing his climax, I began to move my hips to match his rhythm.

Right before his orgasm he pulled himself out of me, releasing his seed all over my belly.

He whispered in my ear as we held each other in the nude at his front door. "You just won't take no for an answer will you?"

Carmell

Locked Up

•————————————————————————————————•

I'm sitting here in my apartment mad as hell. I can't believe that I fell for her plot against me. I mean this is some soap opera, young and the restless type crap. I never in a million years thought that anything like this would happen to me. That's cool though, I took all my anger out on their cars. Maybe next time they will think about it before they tamper with someone's heart.

Tears slowly streamed down my cheeks. I loved Louis and I thought that he loved me. Every time I think I found the one, it turns out to be the one that breaks my heart. I slowly sipped on my blackberry merlot in complete darkness. This matched my mood. I wanted to be numb. I didn't want to feel the pain of this betrayal. I went against my wishes to please this man, and all the while he was trying to please another woman. Why is it so hard to find a guy that knows how to make a girl feel? Why do I always choose the liars? Questions flowed through my head like the Mississippi River, constantly moving, threatening to penetrate the dams I had built to block out the thoughts of Natina and Louis.

There was a knock at the door. I didn't know how long they had been knocking at the door and I really didn't care. I sat here, hell, I wasn't expecting anyone so forget it, let them knock until their hands bleed. I could care less.

"Carmell Devereaux, ma'am open the door if you're inside, it's HPD!" I could hear a very authoritative voice outside my door. Maybe I do care. I crept to the door and peeped out the peep hole. Sure enough, just as he had said, it was those alphabet boys sporting their blues. I knew better than trying to avoid them and act like I wasn't home, that would only piss them off. I slowly pulled the door open.

"Yes sir, how can I help you officer?" I had all of a sudden become very sober. I didn't want to give him any reasons to become upset or suspect anything.

"I'm Officer Sloane. I'm just following up on a call we received, apparently Natina Mayes believes that you had something to do with the vandalism of her cars.

I stared at the officer. Yes I had everything to do with the vandalism of her cars but I wasn't going to tell him that. I had to think of someway to flip the script. Think Carmell, think girl. I stared at him and then it was on, I was in actress mode.

"Officer, I don't know anything about her cars being vandalized and I don't know why she would say it was me. This is the second time she has done something like this to me. She has tried to have me fired and now I think she is trying to have me arrested." I swallowed, now playing the role of the victim, well hell I was the victim. My mind moved fast. I knew his next question was going to be my where abouts, but where could I say I was. I saw him writing in his little pad. If I volunteered the information before he asked it, it would show I had nothing to hide. Especially if I admitted to being at her apartment. I continued before he could ask the question. "I was at her home early today. We shared one of the same love interests and all of this had come out. We were discussing this and I left. I have been in my home since then." I looked at him. I was near tears but not for the reasons he suspected. I was as wrong as two left shoes, lying to this officer like this, but there was no way I would let Natina win this easy. As long as I said the right things and raised no suspicion this would sit on his desk and then be closed. It was just a vandalism case.

"Well thank you for your time Ms. Devereaux, and I appreciate your honesty. I'm just trying to get all the facts. You have a good night." The officer smiled as he put his pen and pad away.

"No problem sir. You have a good night as well." I closed the door and walked back inside of my home. Guilty or not, there ain't no way I'm going to let her get me locked up.

Natina

Small Claims Court

I had found out that Carmell lied her way out of being arrested. She denied having anything to do with vandalizing my car, but that was cool we can keep doing this if she wanted. It should have been over that night but it wasn't. I kicked her ass and she kicked my car. She really needs to kill all the drama she comes with. No wonder she can't find a man that will commit to her. She becomes upset by the smallest things and she's full of theatrics.

I sat down in front of the tube with my breakfast taco. It was time for my favorite Court TV judge. I tuned in to the People's Court. I loved this show, the red headed judge with her hip Latin flare kept me laughing. Judge Marilyn Milian was hilarious to me. I watched as the defendant attempted to lie herself out of a loan by saying it was a gift. That's typical, just like Carmell, she was lying to keep herself out of trouble.

Then just like a ton of bricks the idea hit me. If I couldn't get her arrested I could definitely get my money back for my deductible. I don't understand why this didn't come to my mind at first. I jumped up from seat to get some information. I wanted to take my case to court TV. I'm going to further embarrass her. I don't care if people know what happen but I know she does. I know she doesn't want people to think she is like that; she doesn't want people to know that she let another chic eat her out, and this way I could tell the world. I decided to leave Carmell a little message on her voicemail. I knew she wouldn't answer the phone but that didn't stop me from calling.   I left the message.

"I knew your ass wasn't woman enough to answer this call. Yeah you lied to the cop when you know damn well you did this to my cars. That's cool though, you know it ain't over. You've been fore warned. I'm taking that ass to court." By the time I ended the call I had replayed the message twice. I wanted to make sure she understood I meant business.

I logged on to my computer. I was going to take this to Judge Mathis; he would tear this case apart. I searched to find his website to find out how to be on the show. This website gave an eight-hundred number. I dialed it from my cell and left all the necessary information for the producers to call me back. I was taking this chic to court!

Kendra

It Wasn't Me

I pulled my car into the parking garage at work. I was in no mood for work today but I had no choice, being at work was better than being at home. I pulled my bag around my shoulder and boarded the elevator. Just as the elevator was about to close I saw Beverly, a co-worker, and stopped it so she could get on. When she saw me she stepped back. This was odd because she was usually so polite, but today her hello was strained. She stood far away from me like we were in third grade and I had cooties. I discreetly smelled my underarms to make sure I wasn't funky.

I sniffed but I was Secret fresh, so I knew it wasn't that. After our awkward ride on the elevator we said our goodbyes. Hmmm, I wonder what that was all about.

I walked to my desk and sat my things down. I felt like the whole world was watching me, or at least the world of Synergy Wireless. I pulled up my email. My box was overflowed with mail. I began to read some of my messages. I ran across a message from one of our cell phone numbers. It was an email sent through the cell phone. I could tell by the email address that read 281-777-6777@synergypix.com. I could tell it was a pix message but who would be sending me a message. I didn't know that number. Before I opened it, I tried to pull the number up in the system but it would not allow me to view that account. My security class was invalid and that meant one thing and one thing only, it was an employee account. I couldn't view it because technically I was not yet a sup and only supervisors and employee accounts can view representative's accounts.

I opened the attachment. The subject was "caught ya on camera". I opened it expecting to see a funny email or something someone got caught doing unknowingly, like digging in their nose, but what I saw was something completely different.

I saw my face. What the hell was this? I saw in the background the Hilton Hotel logo. It was the same Hilton I was at when I went to visit Gia. How had this happened? I watched mesmerized by this moment being played out on camera. Those damn video phones. Is nothing sacred? You could clearly see my face and my unbuttoned shirt. Cory was there, the look of anger on his face brought tears to my eyes. Gia was screaming at Cory and I had jumped between them just as I had in Georgia. There were several clips here since those phones could only hold about fifteen to thirty seconds depending on the phone.

After seeing this I could have just screamed. I felt like my privacy had been invaded. I mean it was going to be on TV anyway but at least I had the option of being anonymous when the *Cheaters* show aired, but this was something totally different. Everybody in my place of work had probably seen this and how do you deny what is clearly you.

Tears began to tumble from my eyes. I uncontrollably sobbed. My life was literally falling apart. Every aspect of my reality had begun to crumble. Little pieces of my puzzle had fallen out of my life, leaving little holes in my heart.

I stood up and walked out because I just couldn't do the job today. I couldn't be around these people and their judging eyes, laughing at me as I walked through the halls. I worked so hard to keep my life separate from my work but somehow the two have become mingled together. There is no longer a line where work and home do not intersect. They have crossed on an interlocking road of chaos and misfortune.

I cried as I walked out of the building and back to my car. On the way to my car I saw Beverly again. She was staring blankly at me. I couldn't control myself at that point.

"What the hell are you staring at? You saw something and decided for yourself that it was me and I was some horrible person. You don't know me and you don't know that it was me." She just stared at me. I wanted so bad just to say it wasn't me. In a way it wasn't because I had become someone that I don't know. The decisions that I have made have caused so much turmoil. Even though I knew that this in a sense was not me, it a literal since it definitely was. Hmmm, it worked for Shaggy, and I knew there was no way it would ever really work for me, I just wanted to shout to everyone one

"It wasn't me!"

Nicole

Please Stop Calling

I'm bored out of my mind. I couldn't find Jason anywhere, but that's nothing new cause I could never find him. I was tempted to show up at his house again, but I wasn't going to keep doing that. One day he may snap and my sex won't work. I don't know. I picked up my cell phone to call him again. I left another message for him.

I thought about calling Cory. We seemed to have amazing chemistry that day and I was in the mood for a little sexual healing. I wonder if he would be willing to accommodate me. I knew what I was thinking was wrong, but in many ways I didn't care. Cory had started this and I was going to finish it. Kendra hadn't exactly been nice to me. I reached for my cell phone to call. I blocked my number just for safety measures. It would come up private if Kendra happened to be the one to answer the phone.

The phone rang several times before I heard his deep voice answer the phone. I could feel my heart pounding. I knew if Kendra answered I was going to simply hang up.

"Hello." His voice was sexy, alluring, and almost erotic.

"Hey you." I spoke in a lowered tone to match the sexiness he was exuding through the receiver. "It's me Nicole, you think maybe you can sneak out of the house? I would love to feel you deep inside of me. Let you work that magic stick you got over there, so can you?" Just thinking about it excited me. I need to relieve this sexual hunger that resided between my legs and since Jason wasn't available, I didn't mind having the next best thing. Cory could definitely extinguish this fire of mine. There was a very long pause and it sounded as if he was moving, then I heard running water. I assume he must have gone into the bathroom. Kendra must be home.

"No, Nicole. I don't think that's a good idea. See, what happened between us was a one time thing. I don't want to have an affair with you or anybody for that matter. Don't call anymore, not like this." His breathing had become heavy.

"Well, Cory I know you enjoyed me as much as I enjoyed you. Kendra can't appreciate a man like you. I know about her going to see that girl again and how yall had another confrontation, don't you want me to make you feel like a man should?" I was working a bit of my magic on him, using the words he had whispered in my ear to get me the first time. I know he has gone through a lot, and I knew I had the means to solve his problems.

"No, I don't. I've already told you no. I'm not going to keep saying it. So when I hang up this phone, Don't call back, please stop calling me." Those are the last words Cory said before I heard the phone disconnect. I just stared at the phone as I heard echoes of the words please stop calling.

Carmell

Unbearable

All damn day my phone keeps ringing. I don't know how so many people got my number. I just want this craziness to stop. The first call I received today was from one of the producers from Judge Mathis. I didn't understand what was happening in my life but apparently Natina was trying to sue me for the damage on her car. It would be a cold day in hell before I go on some talk show. I don't need that mess and I don't need that nut trying to collect money from me. I needed to sue her ass for all the foul crap she did to me. I just hung up the phone in the man's face and he has been calling back ever since. He can keep calling and I will keep sending him straight to voice mail.

The next call was from my mother. I don't know how she found out these things, but she was calling me to find out why the police were at my house. I sat there for the longest time wondering how in the world she knows these things. I couldn't even hold a conversation with her. Too many questions and my patience was just too short to deal with it. So I had to peace out on my mom.

Between those calls I received and all of my life's drama, when the phone began to ring again, I just wanted to throw it into the wall and call it a day, but against my better judgment I decided to answer the phone.

"Hello." I answered the way I usually do, annoyed.

"What's up girl? Where yo ass been hiding?" My heart stopped beating for what seemed to be an entire minute. No he didn't have the nerves to call me. What the –.

"Carmell girl can you hear me now?" His deep baritone voice interrupted my thoughts.

"Why are you calling me? You have some nerve even picking up the phone and calling me. I don't need to talk to you. After what you did to me, after the despicable plan you and your girl lead me right into, the last thing you need to be doing is calling me. Louis, you used me. You made me believe that you cared. That's low you bastard!" I was screaming by this time. I was so angry I swear if he stood before me I would hit him right in his mouth.

"Girl calm down, you don't see me tripping and you messed up my car." Louis responded.

"You deserved that and a whole lot more." I was burning.

"I want to see you." Louis demanded.

"No." I wasn't going to see this man.

"I know you are home because I'm standing outside of your door, now undo the lock and let me in, please. I really want to see you." I walked over to my door and looked out of my peephole. He stood at my door. I looked at him and felt a strange inner turmoil. Part of me desperately wanted to allow him into my home. Allow him into my body and my heart, but there was the other part of me, the part that knew that this would only end up hurting me.

I dropped the phone. I didn't know what to do, but after about five minutes the gentle taps on the door brought me out of my dream like state. Against the rational part of my mind I opened the door. Before I could fully open the door, he was pushing it open. He slammed the door behind him and then grabbed me. Again I felt my heart do a summersault in my chest.

He pressed his lips against mine and slowly parted them with his tongue. His hands became greedy as he began to caress my skin. Louis was like a sculptor, and his hands molded and chiseled the very essence of love and

lust combined within me.   The way he touched me could be considered
nothing but art.

Again our souls touched.   How could this man make me feel this
way? He held me and I could hear him whisper in my ear.   He was saying that
he loved me, but how could he when he had cut me so deep.   He didn't love
me.   He loved the control he had of me.   I couldn't do this anymore.   I could
hear myself scream stop far before the words ever escaped my lips.   He kissed
me and touched me.   He savored the taste of my alert nipples and caused chill
bumps to form down my legs.   Why couldn't he touch me like this when
Natina was around?   I thought about how he just screwed me that night and
somehow I found my voice.

"Louis, you have to stop. Stop!" I pushed his body away from mine.
"I'm not going to keep doing this with you. I can't keep doing it. You don't
love me and you never did. You love the fact that I would stupidly and eagerly
do anything for you. Those days are over Louis, you killed whatever chance
you had by your own actions. Why don't you go home to Natina. That's who
you love and you guys are perfect for one another."

Louis never said a word. He just pulled on his jeans and glared at
me, and then he was gone. I sat on my floor sobbing because the pain to me
was simply unbearable. It was just too much to bear.

Natina

Let's Get Married

When I opened my door, I didn't expect to see the things I did. There, in the middle of my floor stood a girl, stripping for Louis. She was exquisite. I found a seat next to him and began to watch her remove her clothes slowly. Looking at her I could only believe that she does this for a living.

I watched her move her body. She was Asian, with long black hair that was bone straight. Her eyes were slanted upward and her lips were full. Her skin was bronzed as if she had been kissed by the sun. I watched Louis. He was quite taken by her. I stood before him, next to the exotic beauty. I began to assist her with removing her clothes. By the look on her face she was very excited by me touching her skin. If Louis wanted a show then a show he would get. I pulled the girl close to me and danced on her. My movements were erotic. She stood there completely naked before me and I kissed her. As our lips found one another as I pulled her towards the bedroom.

I could hear Louis follow. I laid her on the bed and began to touch her. I watched Louis as I did this. I could feel his excitement and that excited me even more. I stroked and touched her, brought her near climax all for him.

"She's ready for you baby." I looked at Louis and left the girl on the bed. I walked over to him and began to undress him. I kissed him deep and he matched my intensity. I stripped him bare and then led him to her. I kissed her as I parted her legs for him. It excited me to see him enter her. I began to peel the remaining clothes I wore away from my body. Her moans, his thrust, it all turned me on beyond belief. I lie on the bed next to them. His fingers found my wetness and he started to use his fingers to seduce me.

He sensed my readiness for him. He withdrew from her and entered me from behind. I pulled her close to me and began to taste her as he stroked me from behind.

We continued this for hours. Now this was a threesome, that crap with Carmell was a waste of time.

I slept in his arms as did she. When I woke up this morning I was holding her and Louis was in the kitchen cooking for us. He could be so sweet. I sat up to rub the sleep from my eyes and I felt something drop into my lap. It was a blue jewelry box. I smiled to myself. It looked like a ring box. I opened it and there it was an engagement ring. It was platinum, with a single princess cut diamond in the center. The rock was huge and beautiful. I could not contain myself. I was so excited I woke the Asian chic.

"Wow, that's a beautiful ring. I'm Jennifer, he showed it to me yesterday and I knew any woman would love that rock." I smiled and introduced myself to her. I laughed. Most people do the introductions first and we had totally skipped that part. We were so caught up in sexing one another knowing her name was never important to me.

I ran into the kitchen and jumped on him wrapping myself around him. I was so happy about him wanting to marry me. He was actually ready to settle down and it was me he chose.

"Yes, yes yes. I will, I do, I would love to marry you." I hugged him as I said these words.

"You make me happy girl and I realized that it's you I want to spend my life with." He kissed me. "So we gonna do it? Let's get married!"

Kendra

Get Our Lives Back

·————————————————————————————·

I desperately needed to find a way to get my life back in order. I had decided Sunday to talk with Reverend Thomas, he was the minister that married us and I knew that he would give me his guidance. I was determined to be truthful with him about everything. If I withheld things from him I felt that I would be cheating myself out of true help.

I confided in him. At first he just looked at me as if this was some type of sick joke. After he got over his shock he prayed for me and my marriage. He told me that both of us needed to be counseled and it needed to be done together. Then he did what I needed most. He hugged me and told me assuredly that it would be okay. He told me to speak those words into existence. My marriage would prevail because it was joined by God. I remembered his words "don't let satan steal it, believe that you are covered by the hands of God, and not even satan can contend with that."

As I drove home I thought about those words. If I wanted my marriage I would have to fight for it and believe in it. I got out of my car just as the mailman was passing by. I retrieved my mail and thanked him.

I flipped through all the mail that was there. Most of it was bills, bills and even more bills. Just as I reached the bottom of the stack I noticed a letter postmarked from Georgia. I couldn't believe this and didn't want to believe this. If Cory had made it home before me he would have checked the mail and found this. I sat on the steps of the front porch debating with myself about whether to read it or not. I wanted to be able to just toss it into the trash and move on, but I couldn't, so I opened it. I read.

Dear Kendra,

I had to write you. I know that we agreed that we wouldn't have any contact but I just couldn't or should I say wouldn't do that. That night in Houston when I left I felt void and empty. I needed to see you that day and it had turned out to be another fiasco, just as it had when you were here.

In so many ways I know that I would be able to love you better than he ever could, but I've also come to realize that you will never whole-heartedly love me the way I need to be loved by you. You belong to someone else and although I knew these things before hand I thought I could change them. I keep trying to change you but in the end, each time you leave me alone and go home to him.

My love is infinite when it comes to you. Yes I love you enough to let you go. I have been fighting a losing battle for you. You and HIM are married and I am an outsider. I look in on you and say to myself I know this girl would be happier with me, but you are not willing to be with me.

So since you won't be strong enough to end it, I will. I will cherish the memories we have created both good and bad. I will continue to wear the heart bangle that you gave me, and I will cherish it and it's meaning always. But for me, Sweetness, I have to do what's right. I have to move on. I wish you all the best and I hope that you and him can work it out.

Forever Your Cherry,
Gia

After reading this I could do nothing but let the tears spill from my eyes. This was such an emotional time for me that I could cry at the drop of a dime. I know that this was a good thing that she should move on and I should move one to fixing my marriage, but the truth of it was it still hurt. I was losing a friend. I know that since that line had been crossed she and I could never maintain a friendship because there would always be something else beneath that friendship.

I picked myself up and went into my home. I couldn't allow this to let me lose focus. I started to prepare dinner. I pulled out all the ingredients to make one of my husband's favorites. I prepared the meatloaf just like he liked it, along with rice and gravy, green beans and butter rolls to compliment it. He could say no to a lot of things but my cooking wasn't one of them. I showered and waited for him to come in from work. He worked as an engineer for Dupont and sometimes he didn't quite get off when he was suppose to, I was hoping this was not one of those days.

I heard the garage door open and immediately I was nervous. I never knew that I could be so nervous when it came to this man. I didn't know how he was going to react to me. He hadn't been talking to me, he had locked me out of the house, called cheaters on me and cursed me out. I knew that I was no longer on his well respected list. I went to door to greet him.

"Hey baby, let me get that." I took his case out of his hand and leaned in to kiss him. Just as I did this he turned his head.

"Don't." was all he said. I knew he didn't want to kiss me but I had to try.

"Cory, I think it's time to talk. I mean really talk about this. I want our marriage and I think you do too." I looked at him. I was pleading with him. I searched his face for some emotion, but found none. He was void of any hint of feeling.

"I'm going to go take a shower." He walked off. I could hear the water come on upstairs. I sat down ready to give up, but then I thought about my life without him. Gia was right, I would never give him up, and I knew that I loved him to much. I walked upstairs and even though I had just had a shower I removed all of my clothes and got in with Cory.

"What are you doing?" He asked. He was stepping back, away from me. He moved as if I had some type of plague. His face showed how annoyed he was at the thought of me invading his shower.

"I'm doing whatever needs to be done to save our marriage. I know I messed up, I'm not perfect and never claimed to be, but I never, ever meant to hurt you the way I did. Please baby." I stared at him. I was willing to pour the entire contents of my heart out if that would mean that he would show me one ounce of forgiveness. I moved towards him. I longed to feel his arms around me. They were strong, powerful even. I leaned in to kiss him and this time I wouldn't take no for an answer. I kissed my husband. I kissed him as if this one kiss could save my life, and in truth it could. He was my life; the things we shared were my life. I kissed him the way I did on our wedding day, I kissed him.

His arms at first were by his side and my kiss went unreturned, but then something happened, I felt his arms move around my waist. He pulled me into him and kissed me back. I could feel the water running over our bodies. He held me as I lifted my head to look him in his eyes. Tears slowly spilled from his eyes. I had never seen this man shed so much as one tear before, but men do cry. I had taken everything that was precious between us and torn it to pieces.

"I love you Kendra. I didn't want to love you after all of this but I can't stop. I love you." Cory was finally talking to me. He held me and I held him. We held one another and allowed our souls to again become one. Our hearts began to beat together again. He needed me as much as I needed him.

As the water hit our skin, he began to kiss me, slow at first, tender and then with intensity. He looked deep into my eyes and I could see the love in his eyes and I wanted him, I wanted him badly. Cory began to touch me. It had been so long since I had been in his arms that I had almost forgotten how safe I felt when he held me. He entered me, and it sent chills up my spine. The water danced erotically on our skin as my husband made love to me. Feeling the warm substance on our bodies turned me on. Tears rolled down my cheeks and he stroked my pain away. At that very moment everything that had gone wrong between us somehow disappeared. None of the foul things I had done meant anything at this time. The only thing that mattered was Cory and the way he was loving me. I realized that I loved this man, more than any urge or addiction. Gia, didn't matter, my job didn't matter, the only thing that held my concern was him. Cory held my hands as he made love to me. He had propped me up against the wall and I felt him so deep inside of me. I could feel myself reaching a climax.

I whispered in his ear, "Mmmm, Baby, this feels so good!"

"Is this mine?" The question took me by surprise.

"It's all yours baby, it's only yours!" I whispered back to him. He stroked harder, deeper. He found his way to the bottom. With each thrust I begged him not to stop. Then we both reached a climax, together. It was one of the most passionate moments we had shared in a very long time. Then he kissed my neck and held me there in the shower. He spoke no more words, but his actions revealed just how much I meant to him and just how deeply I had hurt him.

I held no false hopes. I knew this moment was one of the many it would take to reconstruct what I had so effortlessly torn apart, but this moment gave me hope that it could be done. This gave me hope that I could, we could, get our lives back.

Nicole

Together

After that night with Jason there's no way you could tell me anything. He was almost mine and I could feel it. When I went into work and over heard Tasha running her mouth about my man I almost lost it.

I have been so tired of over hearing about him and some girl, especially her. I stared at her, she wasn't even that cute.

"What the hell are you staring at?" She asked me.

"That's what I'm still trying to figure out. I don't know why Jason would even waste his time with you." I replied.

"Oh so we back on that again? What Jason does with me is our business. It has nothing to do with you. So you shouldn't waste any of your time trying to figure out anything about us." She was all in my face.

"Tasha you need to back up. Your stank breath is burning my eyes, here have a mint." I pushed a container of altoids towards her but she refused them. She needed them, though she probably thought I was trying to be funny but I was oh so serious. That girl's breath smelled like sewer mixed with stank ass. I still could not figure out what he could want with her. She didn't dress better than me, she wasn't as fly as me and I know she didn't have better head than me. With the skills I was working with, I'm sure I had just as much talent or possibly even more than SuperHead.

It was time for Jason and I to stop playing games. When he was with me it seemed liked there was no one else but the moment it was over he was distant again. I just didn't get that. It was as if he was afraid.

I scanned the room in an attempt to find Jason. I found him engaged in meaningless conversation with Tasha. I couldn't stand her, to me she was like a fungus, anytime she came around my ass would itch. I think I was allergic to her or something.

"Tasha, you need to move around." We stood outside in the parking garage. She was going to piss me off.

"I wasn't talking to you. You can't dismiss me." She was really gonna piss me off, for real this time.

"Tasha, I said move around, I need to talk to Jason." We both stared at Jason, waiting for him to interject. He said nothing though. I believe that he was almost amused at our battle for his undivided attention. He stood there smirking.

"Bitch what don't you understand about no?" Tasha was about to see a real bitch. I reached over and grabbed her by her synthetic ponytail and it came right off. If you gonna wear it please wear it right. She snatched it out of my hand then she pushed me. If it weren't for being at work I would have introduced her ass to my foot.

She tucked tail and ran after that. I guess she was too embarrassed about the ponytail coming off in front of Jason.

"Now that's she's gone I can finally talk to you. Look I'm going to come right out and say it, I want to be with you. I have tried to be your chic on the side, tried to deal with all the other females you mess with, but now I'm coming out and saying it, I want us to be together."

"Girl what are you talking about? You know I don't do relationships." Jason's words hurt but I wasn't taking no for an answer. I leaned in and kissed him.

"You're gonna be my man, one way or the other you will be mine." I just stared at him. I wanted him to look at me and really see me. I was putting it all out on the line for him. I was allowing him to see me vulnerable and pleading. It was something about him. Something in him that made me hunger for more. I was addicted to this man and it wasn't just the sex, it was him. He was just within my grasp but I still couldn't reach him and that made me desire him even more.

"Look I told you that you didn't know how to do anything without bringing the drama. Is that a threat?" He said. He said nothing else after this. His only other response was to just laugh at me. I don't think he thought I was serious, but I was more than serious about making him my man. I had done everything I could to show him that I was the one for him, his down chick that was ready to ride. I watched him shake his head no as I shook mine yes. I guess I had lost this battle, but that's okay. I will find away to be with him. We will be together.

Carmell

Hate to Burst your Bubble

———————————————————————•

I hated being at work. I don't know why I hated doing this type of job so much; I mean it was easy money. All I had to do was take a few calls, help a few people understand their bill, it's not rocket science but still I dragged my tail in here everyday praying for some type of system malfunction.

I figured the only way to make my day speed by was to take call after call. That is exactly what I did. I took call after call after call. Finally, it was lunch time. I went to the break room to eat my lunch. Usually it is packed but today only one other person was there with me. I began to frown as I saw the braids and the back of her head. Why can't I get away from Natina! She makes my skin crawl. I swear her and her man are stalking me. I decided just to take a seat and not worry about her. She had a way of being so annoying, but if I ignored her then she wouldn't be able to get to me. I ate and watched television in silence because I didn't have a need to talk to her.

"Hello Carmell." She walked to my table.

"Go away Tina, I ain't in the mood." I continued eating and ignored her. As far as I was concerned I was alone. Then she held her hand out in front of me.

"I'll make sure I send you an invitation to the wedding. I just know we have your blessings." Natina began to laugh. "Don't be mad cause the better woman won. Let's just say you never even had a chance. He only dated you because I asked him to. I told him I wanted you and he hunted you like a prize animal and delivered you to me to be slaughtered. You didn't mean anything." She gloated.

I was fuming. How dare she invade my space and my time and pour her distorted logic all over my lap. I didn't have time for this and if I weren't careful she was gonna push those buttons that caused me to snap. The only thing that probably held it together for me was the fact that I was at work. I had to control myself cause I needed my cash flow and not even Tina could cause me to lose it here and not be able to pay my rent. I just kept ignoring her but then she did it, she said the words that caused my blood to boil.

"You're a fool. A stupid sap for love and here's the thing Carmell Devereaux he never loved you and you know what else, he never will." Natina smiled a triumphant smile because she felt she had won.

"What makes you think you know a damn thing about what went on between Louis and I?" I was ready to fight back. She wasn't going to continue to tongue spank me and expect me to sit here and take it.

"I know everything. I listened to your conversations. I heard the desperation in your voice for him to love you, for him to accept you. He never did any of that, he never even respected you." I wanted to slap that smile right off of her face. I know my face was beat red.

"Don't assume that you know everything, you'll make an even bigger ass out of yourself." I could barely get the sentence out. Natina stood over me. She was a good six inches taller than me and she stood while I sat. I wasn't intimidated by her I just didn't like her standing over me.

"You need to back up and give me a couple of feet. I don't know why you are even talking to me. We really don't have anything to say to one another. It's over. You got what you wanted right, you just had to have me, had to sleep with me and you did so what the hell else do you want from me?" I just wanted her to go away.

"I just want you to know that he didn't love you. He loves only me."
She was gathering her things.

"You know Tina, like I said, don't assume you know everything. I'm sure he didn't tell you about creeping to my house after that now did he? I'm sure he omitted the fact that he was beating down my door and begging for this pussy, but I sent him home to you." I looked at her and by the expression on her face I knew I had struck a nerve. She didn't know and I exploited this moment to make her feel like the idiot that she was. "Don't look so surprised. I just wanted you to know, your man that loves you so much, still wants me. I'm so sorry, I really hate to burst your bubble."

Natina

Off Limits

When I left work I was furious. I couldn't believe what Carmell had told me. Although I told her I knew all about him going there, I knew nothing of it. I hopped in my car and sped home. We had some serious talking to do.

I unlocked my door and walked in my apartment. The only thing that was audible was a headboard banging against the wall. I opened my bedroom door and there was Jennifer spread eagle in the middle of my bed doing my fiancé.

I watched him. I had to admit it did turn me on. I liked to watch him and other girls. I walked into the room and sat down on the ottoman we kept at the foot of the bed. Louis's body was so beautiful and Jennifer's petite frame seemed to curve to fit his body. She matched each stroke with the rhythm of her hips. I watched his face as he reached his goal. He rolled over and lye in the bed still and silent. After a moment he finally sat up.

"Hey baby, I didn't hear you come in. You enjoy the show." I walked over and kissed him. I had gotten so lost in watching them that I had almost forgotten I was pissed with him.

"Yeah it was nice but we need to talk, get rid of her." I said and then left the room.

I sat down on my sofa and began the dvr playback of one of my favorite TV shows. I watched it as I heard the shower run. I was serious when

I told Louis to get rid of her so I hope he understood. I would hate to have to barge in on her shower and throw her out like I did Carmell.

Just when I thought I was going to have to drag her out by her long black hair, she emerged fully clothed. I couldn't recall if I had ever seen this girl with all her clothes on. She waived at me as she walked out of the house. Louis came over and sat down next to me. He smelled nice. He had sprayed my favorite cologne on. I guess he knew I meant business.

"I had a little talk with Carmell today." He looked at me as if I had just asked him to pass me the remote. He wasn't even going to admit to his wrong doing. He acted as if nothing was out of the ordinary for me to talk to Carmell.

"That's nice baby, but why do you wanna talk to me about that? I thought you said you were done with her." He was doing it. He was trying to change the subject on me. He knew if he got me to talking it would make me side tracked and I would forget what I was saying.

"Not this time buddy, you aren't gonna get me side tracked. She told me you went over there. After that night." I looked at him.

"Yeah so what if I did, I didn't go over there to be with her." He said.

"So just what did you go over there for?" I waited for a response.

"I went over there to see if I could get the money for the cars out of her. That's all baby, I don't know what she told you, but that's what I went over there for. When I got there she started touching all on me and saying how much she wanted me and loved me. I told her right then that I didn't want that, just give me the money for my car." He finished.

I know he was pissed about his car and knowing Louis the way I do he had gone over there for that very purpose. It makes sense, I was showing her my rock and she got jealous. I don't know how I let that girl bother me the way she did. I should have known from the start that tramp was lying.

I don't know why I ever considered the possibility of him wanting her. Louis was mine because I knew how to give him everything he could possibly want.

He wrapped his arms around me and we sat there holding each other watching the television. We laughed at the show and kissed between the commercials. Being with this man was splendid and I had almost let some rumor from a jealous girl mess that up for me.

"Baby, I don't think you should go over there anymore. That girl ain't nothing but trouble and I am trying to take her to court for our cars so don't worry about that. Just stay away from that basket case." He kissed me and smiled. We finished watching our show and went to bed. I lay in the bed hoping he had gotten the gist of what I said. Carmell is off limits.

Kendra

A Talk with the Preacher Man

After speaking with the minister alone, he offered to minister us and we needed it. Even after making love to me I could see that Cory was still upset but at least he was willing to work on it. We wouldn't be going to the church together because we were both coming from work. Besides, Cory's was still upset with me. After being with one another I felt a glimpse of hope.

I pulled into the church lot and saw that Cory was already here. As I got out of the car I surveyed the church. Cory and I were married in this church and we still attended church here together along with the rest of my family. I shook my head and walked inside. I couldn't believe I was about to throw my whole life away. The thing about it is I wasn't unhappy in my marriage. That made it even worse; it took me almost losing him to recognize just how good of a man he was.

I walked inside the church and greeted everyone that was there. The pastor's study was nice and cozy. Reverend Thomas sat behind a solid oak desk and his wife sat to the right of him. I didn't know she was going to be here. He must have seen the question mark I wore on my face because he answered the question before I could even ask it.

"When I counsel I like to have my wife here, she is apart of my ministry and I believe that when I counsel couples they should see a successful couple who have had to endure problems." He smiled at me and then he was ready to begin. He looked at Cory. "Kendra told me about all of the things you guys have encountered." He was trying to put in a very nice tone.

"All that we have had to endure, we've had to endure her sleeping around with a woman. How many men can say that there wife is cheating on them with a woman?" The anger was coming back. Cory spoke through clenched teeth. The minister's wife sat there with an unexplainable look on her face. It wasn't disgust or surprise, it was intrigue. All she needed was a bucket of popcorn, cause you would have sworn she was watching a movie.

"Cory I know I messed up. I don't know what else I can do for you. I realize now how much of a mistake it really was. The second time, the time you called cheaters on me I was only talking to her. I was caught in a bad situation. I was only talking to her and I have to admit that was a bad decision but I made it. It wasn't going to go any further than that." Here I was pleading with him again.

I could here the preacher's wife gasping. I wanted her out of here but I knew he wouldn't go for it at all. She was going to have my business all of the church by Wednesday night at choir rehearsal. Even though it wasn't very Christian like to gossip so many of us did it, and I wasn't excluded. The first chance she could get she was going to be on the phone telling another one of the associate minister's wives and it would spread from there. I had to bring my attention back to what was important.

"If nothing was going on why weren't you wearing a shirt?" Cory asked.

"Because she kissed me and something could have happened but I stopped it baby, honestly." I looked at him and I was close to tears. If I were on the receiving end of this story I know what I would have thought. The obvious answer would have been that this was a damn lie, and a bad one at that.

"Okay, whatever, Kendra. What you should have done is not gone there. To catch you not once but twice, do you know you broke my heart. What did I do to you that was so bad that you had to tear me apart the way you did? You bruised me and you disrespected this marriage and everything we have built together." Cory was hurt and it was evident in the way he spoke to me.

"I'm going to stop you both there. It's good to create a dialogue and I'm glad that you two are finally talking. Just by listening I could tell that there are a lot of unaddressed issues. In situations like this forgiveness is key. I want you guys to think about that, especially you Cory and when you come back next week we will start from that point. Forgiveness." Reverend Thomas ended with a prayer.

We walked out of the church together. Before I got out of the door I heard the preacher's wife say how scandalous I was. Cory thought that was extremely funny. I wasn't as quick to find the humor in it.

"I'm glad that we got a chance to talk about some of the things that was bothering you." I faced Cory. It meant a lot to me that he had come.

"Yeah it's a start huh." He got into his car and I into mine. I pondered the thought of bringing up Nicole in the next session. I mean if we were getting things out in the open should I at least tell him that I know what he did.

I quickly dismissed that idea because I knew I would only be doing it so I wouldn't seem like such a bad guy. I wouldn't bring it up. It wasn't worth it at all. I would allow him to believe he had gotten away with it. He could have his little secret. I have plenty of little secrets of my own.

I sat in the car and prayed a silent prayer for my marriage. I prayed for forgiveness and I thanked God for the opportunity to have a talk with my husband and the preacher man.

Nicole

Stuck on Stupid

It's Saturday and all I can think about is calling Jason. This would be my third time calling him with no answer. I was getting pissed. The phone rang about four times and then his voice mail picked up. He sounded so sexy. It's funny how that man could speak and some of my anger would dissipate. I left a message in my most sexy voice.

"Hey there sexy, it's me your lady or I could be if you would get yourself some act right. I need a little special attention so call me back A-S-A-P." I wanted to talk to him and for him to want to talk to me, but for now this was going to have to do.

I'm not sure how long I could sit here and get no response from him. I called two more times before I decided to go to his house. I just couldn't fathom why he would come to his senses and be with me.

On my way over to his house I left another message. I parked next to his car. Obviously he was home; he just wasn't answering my call. I couldn't believe I was in this same predicament again. It seemed like yesterday when I had come over and found him playing with Barbie and Skipper. I walked to his door. I didn't know how he was going to react to me showing up again. At this point I didn't care. I had stopped and picked up some William's Chicken. Maybe if I came with food he wouldn't be so quick to go off on me.

I knocked on the door. My hand even trembled a bit as I stood there and waited for Jason to answer. Finally he came to the door.

"Nicole, what are you doing here?" He looked annoyed.

"If you returned or answered my calls then I wouldn't have to just show up. I brought food and movies, I thought we could make it a movie night." I pushed past Jason into his apartment.

"Well you thought wrong. Jason is busy for the night." I instantly cringed at the sound of her voice. It was Tasha. I turned around to face Jason.

"What the hell is she doing here? I was fuming. I didn't want to go through this crap with him. Why is it that I could not come over to his house and just get a pleasant hello? It never went down like that with him. He was always laid up with some ho. It infuriated me even further that it was her.

"I told you about questioning me about my house. What are you doing here again, uninvited?" Jason just stared at me. I could tell we weren't going to have a happy ending like the last time I just showed up at his house.

I pushed my way inside the house. It wasn't going down like this. It's about to be a girl fight in here. I don't know how much of this I could take. She seemed to know just how to get under my skin.

"You need to leave!" I yelled at her. By this time I was in her face. I wasn't playing about her leaving. There is no way I would give up without a fight. I want Jason, and what I want I get.

"I don't seem to remember you being the one to invite me in. I know you don't think you're the lady of the house." Tasha began to laugh. If it was possible for me to become any more upset than I was it was happening now. I could hear Jason laughing in the background like somehow all of this was funny. As a matter of fact, none of it is funny. I looked at him. If he had any sense he would shut up.

"Don't think you're getting away with anything. I'm tired of coming over here all the time and you got some girl here and I'm suppose to just deal with it. I will deal with that later, for now our shit's on pause." I looked at him. The amused look he had on his face had turned to anger. I ignored it.

"Back to you, a real woman's here now so you need to go." I told her to get out like I was paying bills here and in some instance I was. I had given Jason money and anything else he needed. In my mind I was his woman and he was my man.

"Shut the hell up and stop issuing demands like this is your house. There is no lady of the house cause I have no lady. Neither one of you are my girl, I don't know how you got that confused Nicole but you are not and will not be my girl, wife or anything else. We have sex, nothing more nothing less. That's the same thing for me and Tasha. The only difference is that she understands that and you won't.

Those words hit me like a ton of bricks. The heaviness of his vocabulary smothered me and I couldn't believe that he had just let them escape from his lips. I knew we had to be more than sex. We made love each and every time that we were together. It couldn't be just sex, because it just didn't feel like sex. Sex was what I had with Cory, sex was what I had with Tina and her man, but with Jason, it was deep, earth moving, sensual love making.

"Yall need to leave." When he began to speak it interrupted my thoughts. I looked at Tasha, who stood smirking.

"You heard the man, leave!" I turned to her and pointed to the door.

"I was talking to both of you, not just her, like I said, leave. Now." Now it was him that was pointing to the door. I felt so defeated. I had only come over to spend a little time with him. When I'm not around him I miss him. This is not at all how I pictured our night. We were supposed to cuddle up on the sofa, holding each other and making love while we watched a movie. "Don't make me call them boys in blue Nicole!" He said. I guess I wasn't moving fast enough. He looked at me like I was the scum of the earth, like I was some type of foreign parasite that had just infected his evening.

"Why would you call the police? I haven't done anything yet." Why would he call the police on me? He never responded to me but the look on his face said it all. Jason wasn't playing with me this time. I snatched my purse from the place it had found rest. I walked out the door and Tasha followed slowly behind. She was smiling as if she had won a prize. All of her big front teeth were showing and her tonsils too cause I could see straight through that driveway of a gap in her mouth. I was mad as hell.

"What are you laughing at? Ain't a damn thing funny!" I turned to face her again. We could get it on in this parking lot if she wanted to. I was tired of her crap and the one thing I would love to do at this time is kick her ass. "You are just begging for an ass whippin'. I'm so tired of the sight of your face. I don't even see what he sees in you." It was time to slang insults at her. She was less attractive than me, fatter than me, and she just didn't have what I had, yet he kept right on seeing her and every body else for that matter.

"I'm laughing at you and you won't be kicking anyone's ass. I don't know why you just don't get it!" I looked at her like she was dumb. If she were smart she would step back and give me fifty feet. She was like a viral infection that I could not get rid of. No antibodies would cure this one. I wanted her to be gone. I can be every woman that Jason needed and I know I was more woman than her. She continued talking.

"You won't ever get it will you? He's gonna keep doing me and keep doing you. He ain't never gonna be your man or my man, he's a playa for life, just can't be tamed. Instead of accepting that; you try to change it. Either you're in love or you just stuck on stupid!"

Carmell

Out His Damn Mind

I needed some quality me time so I decided to take another trip to the house in Galveston. There wasn't going to be anybody there and I desperately needed to be somewhere no one but close family could find me. I wasn't looking forward to any more of Louis's drop by visits and I didn't want anymore of Tina's surprise I'm getting married attacks.

I had to admit that news did something to me. It pissed me off is what it did. I was mad. I was a better woman that she could ever be and he chooses to be with her and marry her. After that night there is no way I would ever take him back, but it hurt so much. I was always so willing to accommodate him. I was always the one that was willing to go that extra mile. I was committed, I know more committed than she would ever be. I don't know why I fell for the wrong guy every single time. It didn't matter who it was or when it was, he was always the wrong guy. The ones that I really like were all wrong for me.

My mind was loaded with a million thoughts and scenarios of how to torture the two the way they had tortured me. With thoughts of throwing them off the Ship Channel Bridge I pulled into my driveway. I grabbed my bags and laughed to myself as I thought about the last time I was here and I introduced Craig to Nina. That crap was hilarious. I wonder if he's traumatized.

I walked into the house and instantly noticed something wasn't right. It was a mess. I hadn't messed up the house the last time I was here and to my knowledge no one else had been here. My parents hadn't been here and my brother was still out of town. I surveyed the living room and there were dirty socks on the floor and empty pizza boxes. This had to have been how those three bears felt when they found out that damn Goldilocks had been in their house.

I walked to the front door and picked up one of the umbrellas that we kept there. This one was long and black with a silver tip at the end. It resembled a cane, but today it would be used for a weapon.

I tip-toed through my own house. I checked the all of the rooms except for mine. As I walked towards my room I could hear sounds. It sounded like grunts. Somebody had to be in pain. I slowly pushed my door open and was stunned by the perverted shit I was seeing.

Right there in my bed, on my satin comforter and expensive Egyptian cotton sheets was Craig and some guy that looked like a weight lifter butt pumping one another. This was some sick stuff, I could have thrown up or either fainted. I felt myself doing that thing I do when I become angry. I was about to lose it. I was about to fly so far off the handle it would be impossible to catch me.

"What the hell are you doing?" They were so into one another that they didn't know I was there until I said something. The look on Craig's face was one of complete horror. He was absolutely terrified. I don't know if it is because he was about to meet Nina again or if it was because I had caught him with his ass in the air gettin' done doggy style by some dude. The world was going to shit. He had broken into my house to have sex.

"You need to answer my question and now!" I looked at Craig. He and his lover were still in the same position I found them. They were staring at me. I moved towards my night stand and fumbled for the key. Craig jumped up. I'm sure he knew what was about to happen next. I pulled my best friend Nina out of her cozy bed. Time to get up baby. I pointed it at him.

"This must be the crazy bitch you told me about man." The lover spoke up. I looked at him. He was tall and well defined, with chestnut brown eyes and dark chocolate skin. If I saw him on the street I would assume that he was straight and I would most likely fall for him cause he was just my type. See I always chose the wrong man. I turned my attention to Craig. I was disgusted by him, at least I was right about him and didn't waist my time.

"Who you calling a bitch?" Nina turned towards the lover as I spoke. They finally began to try to move and put there clothes on.

"Put them down. I don't want you to put any clothes on. You gonna leave my house just like this." I was gonna show him crazy. The lover ignored me and still searched for his underwear. I was just gonna have to show him. I hit the safety and shot towards him. I wasn't gonna shoot him but I had to show him that I meant business. I aimed my shot at my closet door. That bullet sliced through the wood door with ease. There was a small hole now in the door and you could see the bullet lodge in the wood half way. I would have to get that fixed. Later. Now it was about showing this fool he wasn't gonna play with me. When that gun shot it became completely silently in the room and lover man dropped his drawers.

"Craig, why are you in my house?" I asked again.

"I didn't think you would be here Carmell, I'm sorry I just needed a place to relax and I knew were you kept the spare key." His tight eyes were now wide.

"You don't just invite yourself in someone's house cause you need a place to screw your down low lover. This is not the Motel Devereaux. I don't offer a room for twenty dollars or any amount for that matter. It's called breaking and entering. Do you recall my father is a police officer? You must be really trying to go to jail, only a fool would break into an officer's home." I stood there still holding that gun. "Now here's what's gonna happen. You're going to walk into the other room and then you're going to clean up the mess you made, and then you're walking out of my house in your birthday suits.

Lover man, try be fly if you wanna, I'll shoot more than a door the next time."
I made myself loud and clear.

I lead them into my living room pointing the gun at them. I had to keep it pointed cause they were men and if they didn't have the fear of the nine in them they would have thrown me down and left this house a long time ago. They cleaned my living room. Their private parts were exposed and limp. Poor Craig's didn't look longer than two inches. It was resting silently on his gigantic balls. That was just nasty. I looked at his lover man. He was working with a little something. I could tell by how it hung there. Even though it wasn't erect I could see that he was packing in the penis department. To me, that was a sad waste of man, but I bet it had gay dudes across America jumping for joy. Not only did I lose men to women I had to worry about men now too. That's a damn shame.

Once I felt the living room was cleaned to my satisfaction I lead them to the door. My first intention was to lead him to his mom's house and blow him all out the closet, but somewhere in the midst of everything I found a heart. I felt sorry for him. Even though he had violated my home it was not my place to out him to his parents. That's something he would have to do within his own time. I would have hated for my parents to find out about what I let happen with Natina. I was only doing that for my man, well at the time I thought he was my man, but that's besides the point. I would have hated for someone to tell them that. So I was letting Craig off the hook. I could tell he was already embarrassed by me catching him.

"Go get your clothes. I was going to make you leave here butt ass naked, but get your clothes and then yall get the hell out of my house. And Craig, I don't ever wanna see your ass so much as ten feet from my property. You know I'll shoot you right." Craig just looked at me as I spoke. I could tell by the look on his face that he was thankful that I had found a heart. He just nodded and apologized one last time. Once they were clothed they were gone. They didn't hesitate at all getting out of my house. They dressed so fast I'm surprised that they didn't put their pants on backwards.

I don't know what the hell he was thinking. I went to go wash my sheets and disinfect my room. To break into my house and screw a man, he must have been out his damn mind.

Natina

Payback's a Bitch

•————————————————————————————————————•

After talking with Louis I realized Carmell was trying to get to me. My guess is that she is still upset and she will find any way to hurt me. Whatever it was I wasn't going to worry much about it.

I had come to the conclusion that nothing was going to be done about my cars. Even though I wanted her to pay for what she had done, she had become elusive and my plan to sue her was beginning to back fire. The producers of the show were having a hard time trying to reach her and I suspected it's the way she wanted it. She had also lied through her teeth to the officer and now we were dealing with a he said, she said situation. I was going to get my money back one way or another. You can't just vandalize someone's property and expect to get away with it. The cars were insured and currently being repaired but that didn't matter, it was the principle.

It was a clear dark night and I, dressed in all black, was up to no good. I realized the only way I would feel justified is if I destructed something of hers. Even though it was childish, I knew I would be satisfied once I had gotten my hands on her precious Camaro. I wanted to destroy the one true thing she cared about. During my drive to her ghetto ass apartments I thought of all the ways I could demolish her property. I pondered everything from spray paint to sugar in her gas tank. That ass was gonna pay.

I had waited for darkness for a reason. I didn't want to get caught. I had been sitting here for over an hour and she still had not come home. I looked around and decided maybe I should just try again another day. I started the car and shifted into reverse. Before I could pull out of the spot a noticed a red Honda Accord pulling up behind my car. This car looked familiar. I know this wasn't Patricia following me. She just wouldn't give up would she?

Motivated by anger I shifted the car into park and turned the ignition to off. I grabbed my keys by the bottle of mace that I kept on the key ring. My finger was positioned just in case she decided she wanted to start something.

Slowly I approached the car. Before I made it to the door I noticed she had someone riding with her. She stepped out of the car and started towards me.

"Hey baby, I just think that we need to talk." She uttered.

"We don't have anything to talk about and why are you following me?" I was furious. I had told her on more than one occasion I didn't want to have anything to do with her but she continued to thrust herself into my life. She continued to stalk me damn it and if I had vandalized Carmell's car she would have seen. I didn't have time for this.

"But I think that we should talk, I believe we have a lot to talk about." She blinked. Her big brown eyes were full of remorse and the corners had become pockets for the tears that were forming. It was almost believable.

"Bullshit!"

"TeeTee I have been trying to apologize to you. I know what I did was wrong. I know you trusted me, and I should have been a mother to you and not your madam. What I did was wrong but I am a completely different person now. Baby I'm saved, I gave my life to Christ and I know that if God can forgive me you can too. I just want us to start over." She paused. I stared. She continued. "Rodney is here, he wants to apologize too."

My head begin to spin as I looked in the passenger seat. Why the hell would she bring him here? Why would she place me in the same vicinity as my attacker? This bitch was a damn space cadet.

"Rodney? It's bad enough that you're stalking me but then you bring this asshole with you? What the hell is wrong with you?" I could feel the blood begin to boil. My temperature was rising at a very unstable rate.

"Natina, I, I, I, ju, ju, just want to say that I am sorry girl. I was young and dumb, but Pat has been ministering to me and she has me in church and I, I, I was hoping that you can f, f, forgive me." The longer it took him to get the sentence out the more upset I became. How dare he?

"What? You were young, no I was young, I was innocent and your dirty ass took advantage of me. You should have known better and if I would have had a half ass decent foster mother then your ass would be behind bars for what you did to me. It is a crime you dirty pervert!" I was yelling. I couldn't believe he was standing here lecturing me about forgiveness. He didn't deserve my forgiveness and neither did she.

"Natina you don't have to call me names, I'm trying to apologize." He looked a bit annoyed. Patricia just stood here crying. I know he didn't have the nerves to be offended by me calling him a pervert. He was a pervert. I couldn't believe she was crying. She didn't care about my tears when I was fourteen and had been raped by this man that stood before me. She didn't care that what she had done to me had caused me not to trust anyone. Now I didn't care about her need for reconciliation or forgiveness. He was staring at me and it seemed to me he was still the same pervert he had always been. He was watching me with a Chester the Molester stare. She had brought him here and now I can't be held accountable for my actions.

His stare had begun to curdle my stomach. It was absolutely revolting. I stood in complete silence, memories tumbling around in my head. I could feel his hot breath on my skin. I remember the stench of his sweaty flesh as she pressed down on me. I could feel his filthy hands exploring my body causing my skin to crawl. I snapped.

"Motherfucker!" Those were the only words I said as I lunged towards him. My finger was still in place on the mace as I released a flood of pepper spray into his eyes. I wouldn't stop until I got tired. He fell to the ground, begging me to stop as he tumbled and rolled from the pain. I didn't give a damn about his pleas. I had begged him all those years ago and he had ignored them. Now I would ignore him.

I heard Patricia yelling hysterically. She jumped in the car and began to move it back. I was still holding the red button even though the spray was long gone. Rodney's face was contorted in agony. Patricia had somehow gotten out of the car and helped him to his feet and then shoved him into the car.

"TeeTee, you could have hurt him. I'm taking him to the hospital." She ran back to the driver's side.

"Well Patricia he did hurt me! I guess payback's a bitch!"

Kendra

Public Apology

As part of our therapy we had to go on an outing once a week. Our pastor wanted us to spend more time with one another. Go on dates. He told us just because you got married doesn't mean that the dates should stop. Cory left the choice of the outing up to me.

I stood in the mall looking for an outfit to wear. I didn't know if I wanted to be dressy or casual. I opted for a pair of seven jeans with a white cami and pink blazer. This was fly. I loved these jeans cause they made my body look irresistible. Cory and I had not made love since that day in the shower and although I didn't want to push him I was yearning to feel his strong arms around me again. I examined the outfit in the mirror in the dressing room. I had a perfect pair of pink boots that would go with this outfit. I walked to the sales counter to pay for my items. I needed to get out of here before I spent the whole check. That's how it was with me and shopping, once I got started it was hard to stop.

I walked to the car to go home and get ready. I had a special night planned for us. We were going to this nice little spot that had an open mic night on Fridays.

I flipped my phone open and almost called Nicole out of habit. I soon remembered that we were not friends any longer and closed my phone. I never realized just how much I talked to her until I didn't talk to her at all. I quickly dismissed the thoughts of her. I didn't have time to worry with that.

My marriage was the most important thing at this time and all of my focus needed to be on Cory.

I walked into my house. Cory sat in his recliner watching our big screen television. As I walked in the door I noticed him watching a copy of the tape of Cheaters. Dang they were fast. How and why did he have a copy of this? He sat there with no expression on his face. Why was he doing this to himself? I walked over to the television and hit the power button. I turned to face him.

"Baby let's not go down this ugly road. Don't watch this, it's only going to bring up bad memories." I looked at him and tried to make eye contact with him but he wouldn't look at me. He paid no attention what so ever to me. Then he finally spoke.

"It's not that easy Kendra. I think it's a lot easier for you to forget than for me." He pulled himself up from the chair and walked in the bedroom. I heard the water come on so I knew he was taking a shower. I thought about going to take another one with him but quickly decided against it. I would give him a little space. The last thing I wanted to do was push him. I couldn't force him to completely forgive me nor would I try. I was just happy that we had a dialogue going.

I went to the other bath room to take a shower myself. I thoroughly washed my body. Somehow watching that video had made me feel dirty. It was a constant reminder of my infidelity and imperfection. I know I wasn't perfect but I did want to be perfect for Cory. I washed and washed until I felt that I slightly cleaned my misdeeds away. When I emerged, Cory sat dressed and he seemed to be in a better mood.

"Woman hurry up!" He joked. We both laughed as I walked towards the bedroom to get dressed. I smiled to myself. Every small step we took gave me more and more hope that we could one day be the way we were.

As we rode in his car, we talked about small things, what we needed from the store, who was going to make groceries. It was idle chit chat and I was happy to receive it. He had been so mad with me before that when he talked to me without yelling I was ecstatic. It didn't matter what he talked about as long as we talked. When I got out I was so happy to be out with my husband and I was surprised when I thought about Gia and how much she would enjoy this club. It was no sense thinking about her. Again I turned my attention back to Cory. I had called ahead to the club and reserved a table for us. I requested a bottle of Hypnotiq be placed on the table and awaiting us. We sat down and I poured Cory a glass and then myself. We watched a multitude of talented poets grace the mic. Everyone in the house was snapping their fingers and feeling these artist. Then I heard them call my name.

"We have a newcomer to the mic tonight. Ladies and gentleman, lets give a welcome to Ms. Kendra Dubois." The mc announced me and I made my way to the stage. My heart was doing summersaults by this time. I had always been a pretty good writer but I never shared any of my poetry with the world. This would be a first and I was doing to for Cory. I looked out to the table where Cory sat. He smiled and watched me as I stood there, the picture of calm and cool to those on-lookers, but inside I was a bundle of nerves.

I was doing this to let Cory know that I was sincere and serious about starting over.

"This is dedicated to a very special person in my life, my handsome husband." I held my hand towards Cory. "I love you baby and I'm sorry." He smiled at me. "This is My Apology." Some of my nervousness was subsiding. The words began to tumble from my lips and landed rightfully in Cory's lap. They were all for him. I recited the poem that I had written for him.

As I recited the words to the poem, I saw the fingers snapping and the hands clapping. I kept going. I took the cordless mic down to the table where Cory sat. I touched him as I finished the poem. At the end of the poem as requested they began to play *The Way* by Jill Scott. I began to sing the first few versus to him. By this time there was a crowd of people surrounding us and cheering us on. The smile on his face had spread from ear to ear. I knew by his expression that I was doing well. Cory stood up from the table and began to look at me. He looked me in my eyes. This is something that Cory rarely did so I knew I had gotten his attention. He picked me up and brought me eye level with him. As he did this I wrapped my legs around his waist. Then he kissed me. He kissed me in front of all those people. Cory was not one for public displays of affection but he kissed me like we were the only two people that stood in this room. It was such a deep and sensual kiss that I felt the moistness between my legs instantly. I was so turned on by this man and his enthusiasm for me. I kissed him back with the same intensity.

"You better let that man know how sorry you are!"

"Show him girl show him, she sorry baby." The onlookers called out various statements of encouragement. It was like a dream, so surreal. Everything that was going on around me was happening in slow motion. Time had somehow slowed and only Cory and I were real.

The on-lookers were still cheering us on. They were clapping and yelling and singing the lyrics of the song that I had abandoned to receive this extraordinary kiss.

Cory lowered me and slowly pecked me as I moved away to take the mc back the mic I had stolen. People were still clapping as I went on stage to give him his mic.

"Damn girl, you sho know how to give a room a show don't you. Give it up for Kendra." He said as soon as he got his mic back. I walked towards Cory and we soon left after that. We were both excited and I knew we would make love again and again and again tonight. I was filled with anticipation. I wanted him to kiss me again like he had earlier and then make love to me with the same exact intensity. He could be so intense and tender when he wanted to be and I loved every bit of it. He was the one that truly knew how to please me physically and mentally. This evening he had given me a mental orgasm by the sweetness of his actions and tonight he would follow up with several physical orgasms. I looked at him and thought to myself how much I really loved this man. He completed me and he made me a better person. We were finally moving forward and Cory had accepted my public apology.

Nicole

Heart to Heart

I almost jumped out of my seat when that phone began to ring. I didn't think he was ever going to call me again but he had. I grabbed my phone and looked at the picture caller id as the phone rang. I hurried to answer the phone before it went to voicemail.

"I Iello sexy." I answered the phone and even though i had talked with him on many occasions it still gave me butterflies every time I heard his voice.

"Hey there Nicole, what's up? Busy?" He asked. His voice sounded a little different. Like there was something that he called to say but was just being polite. He sounded a bit hurried.

"No, I'm never to busy for you, what's going on?" I answered. The urgency in his voice scared me a little. I really didn't know what he was calling for.

"I was calling to see if you wanted to go to dinner. I want to talk with you." Jason got to his point. It was about time that he had asked me out again. It had been so long since we had done anything more than just have sex. Now don't get me wrong I loved to feel this man inside of me, but I did like to share other moments as well. I was in need of one of those intimate moments that every woman required in some form.

"You know I would love to have dinner with you." I was trying not to sound so excited.

"Okay, well I will be there in about an hour. I would appreciate it if you were ready." He laughed at me. I was always ready when it came to him.

"I'm always ready when it comes to you." I joked with him.

I disconnected the phone and went to get ready. I wanted to shower just in case we did end the night rolling around in the bed. I had to stay fresh.

After my shower I looked through my closet for an amazing outfit. I decided that casual sexy would be good. I grabbed a pair of my True Religion jeans cause I just loved the way they made my ass look. I bought these when I had seen Kendra wearing a pair and they were so cute. Then I grabbed a denim blazer and under it I wore a deep v-neck shirt. I finished the outfit off with some very cute heels and matching belt then examined myself in the mirror. If I were Jason I wouldn't be able to resist me in this outfit. I would want to eat me up because I looked scrumptious.

I heard a knock at the door and rushed to it. I had to slow myself down. I didn't want him to get the impression that every time he called I came running. No matter if it was true or not.

I opened the door and raped him with my eyes. This man was so sexy. I mean he had a style all his own and smelled so good all the time. I hugged him. Just to feel his arms around me made me melt. His embrace was always so strong and he knew just how to hold me. I gently kissed his lips then turned to grab my purse.

"So where are we going to eat?" I asked as we walked to his car. I waited by my door to see if he would open it like he had done the first time we went out, but I guess that was asking to much. He walked to his side of the car, got in and then looked at me like I rode the short bus when he saw me still standing outside. I just opened the door and jumped in the car.

Jason didn't have much to say in the car. We seemed to have an uncomfortable silence. I don't know what it was, maybe he was still a little upset about what had happened at his house. I know that he didn't like the fact that I would just show up at his house, but I hated being ignored so I did what I thought would get his attention.

He pulled in to Saltgrass Steak House. Mmmm, he knew I loved to eat here because they could make the steaks just right. When we were seated and had ordered he leaned in and just looked at me. His stared at me with his pretty eyes and held me with his gaze. There was something else there though. This wasn't a sexy gaze he was giving me it was something different. I don't know if I liked how this night was going.

"I asked you to dinner because I wanted to talk to you. I think somehow you were misled with where our relationship was going." He took a sip of his drink I saw this as my opportunity to turn this dinner around.

"Jason, let's just not think about the..." He interrupted my sentence.

"No, Nicole I need you to listen and truly understand what I'm saying." He looked at me and I could see how serious he was. "I think that you need to understand that this is just a sexual thing. I think you are cool you know, a lot of fun to be around but I'm not looking for any attachments. It is what it is and it's just fun." He paused again.

"Even though you never said it was more than sex I know it is; I can tell that you care by the way you treat me." I looked at him pleading with my eyes not to do what I believed he was trying to do. There was nothing more than silence between us. I stared at him trying somehow to channel those words that I felt he was about to speak out of his head.

The waitress interrupted us as she sat down our dinner. I began to slice the steak even though I could feel my appetite slipping away.

Jason again interrupted the silence.

"I know what you think but what I want to do tonight is set the record straight. I don't want a relationship now. The only thing I want to do is have a little fun, make some money and take care of me. I like kickin' it with you but you want more than I'm willing to give you. You want more than I want to give you. And because of that I think that I need to stop seeing you. I don't think you can handle this type of relationship." He stopped only to take a bite of his food.

"I don't want to stop seeing you. I see the potential in you to be an amazing man. Can't you see that I'm the one girl that's willing to ride or die for you? You know Tasha will never be half the woman that I am." I was on the border of begging this man. I didn't know what kind of power he possessed over me or why I wanted him so badly to accept my love, but I did. I wanted him to receive and return my love.

"This ain't about Tasha, Cole. It's about me and you. It's about the fact that I'm not ready to settle down, or have a girl. I'm not trying to be harsh, just trying to be real about things. There is nothing that can settle me down but a child. When I get ready to have children then I will slow it down and the lucky lady that will be the mother of my child will also be with me. I want my child to have both his mother and father in his life. It's not time yet and I take extra caution to make sure that I don't get nobody pregnant, because I ain't ready for all that just yet. Nicole, you understand what I'm saying. I don't want what you want right now. I don't want what you want for a very long time."

"I'll be right back." I moved my chair back so I could get up. I didn't know how much longer I could hear what he was saying. It was going to drive me crazy. I felt the tears begin to swell in my eyes. I moved from the table because I didn't want him to see me cry. I didn't want him to know that he had hurt me by saying that he didn't want to see me anymore.

I ran water in the sink as the words he said played over and over in my head. Basically the only way that he would want to be with me is if I had his baby, and since I wasn't pregnant how could that ever happen? I thought that was a very harsh thing to say but I had to accept that he said it. I guess I just needed to turn him around. Make him get that idea out of his head. I know that I could do it but I had to get him to see that he needed me as much as I needed him.

I washed my face and started to walk back to the table. As I approached the table I didn't see Jason. Maybe he had gone to the restroom too. I walked back to the table and sat down. I noticed a receipt sitting on the table. I picked it up and could see he had already paid the bill. Something was written on the back of it so I flipped it over and read.

Cole, I decided to leave. I hope you enjoy the
dinner and it's on me. You take care of yourself.

I didn't care who saw at this point. The tears spilled like raindrops from my eyes. I wasn't even important enough for him to finish his dinner with me. I was hurting but I still wanted him. I swallowed and looked at the little note again. He would never know how much he broke my heart with his little heart to heart.

Carmell

Crash and Burn

I was still tripping about finding those dudes in my house bumping. I disinfected my home to the best of my abilities. I sat in house and began to get restless so I decided to go get something to eat at this karaoke bar/restaurant.

I liked to come here because the food was good and cheap and the liquor was strong. Plus it was fun to see the strangers make fools of themselves after they had gotten drunk and try to sing.

I walked in the place and saw they had a full house tonight. That was good. I could get lost in the crowd and not feel so bad about eating by myself. I ordered my food and sat at an empty table. As I ate I enjoyed a frozen margarita. I decided I wanted the margarita far more than I wanted the food. I ordered another drink and I could feel myself getting a little tipsy. I sat back still watching my surroundings when I spotted Craig and his "friend" coming out of the bathroom. They were probably in there getting freaky and stuff, the nasty bastards. I saw them take a seat with two women.

Oh, they were on dates were they? I wonder how their dates would feel if they found out that they were gay. I didn't embarrass him in front of his mama because I felt that would have been taking it too far, but these chicks were something entirely different. I decided to clue them in.

I walked towards the table. As I approached I could see that Craig had spotted me. His entire disposition changed as he leaned over to whisper something in his lover's ear. They were probably talking about me. They both stared my direction and I simply smiled. I felt they needed to be punished just a little bit more. I had let them off easy that night. I let them get dressed and didn't embarrass them, the only thing I had made them do was clean up and they did a poor job of that. Plus they were out here with these women who I know thought they were straight and they were probably gonna have sex with them and then go have sex with each other. Dirty bastards. This would make me feel really good. I was tipsy so my already outgoing personality was heightened, hell I felt like superman.

I took a seat next to one of the girls. "Hi, yall!" I said.

"Hey, I know you. You're Craig's sister. I saw a picture of you in Craig's house." One of the women said. I looked at Craig. His face was blank and he looked not at me but through me. I know he had to know where this was going.

"He told you I was his sister did he. I'm definitely not his sister and that is surely not his house. Craig is almost thirty and he still lives at home with his mama girls!" I winked at them as I finished my sentence. This felt good. I laughed inside as I saw Craig trying to get up from his seat. I continued. "And wait that's not the best part ladies. Hold on cause this one's gonna blow your mind. The other day I came home to my family's home, emphasis on my, and I found these two in my bedroom butt ass naked, doggy style, butt pumping!" This time my laugh was out loud. I know this was cruel but I couldn't believe this ass had been breaking into my home as much as he was. I should have called the police on them but this wasn't bad either. It was definitely giving me a sense of satisfaction. The girls were in obvious shock. Nothing had been said, then I heard the other guy speak up.

"I know you can't believe this crap, yall know we ain't gay. She just jealous cause I wouldn't get with her. She lying." I stared him down. I looked him straight in his eye just to remind him how crazy I could get.

"Ain't nobody lying, I'm just trying to let you know so you're not left in the dark. I wouldn't want to get involved with a man and then find out that his so called boy is his lover. That would piss me off. This down-low stuff is out of hand." I started to move away from the table. "Enjoy the rest of your dinner." I said and then began to walk off. I looked over my shoulder and the girls were up and going off on both the guys. By the time I had made it to the door they were trying to hit and punch the hell out the guys. I don't blame them at all. I would have handled it a little different if I had found out my man was gay but it's just the same. I hoped they got kicked in the balls one good time for me.

I got into the car and tried to compose myself. Dang, those margarita were strong. Okay I wasn't drunk only tipsy so I could drive. I maneuvered my car out of the spot and then my phone rang. Who the hell was that?

"Hello" I answered the phone. The caller id read private so I had no idea who it was.

"Hey baby, it's me. I've been thinking about you." It was Louis. I know I told him to stop calling me but he just wouldn't listen.

"I thought I told you to stop calling me." I said to him. Now it was my turn to be upset. No matter what I did to forget about him, he always popped up to remind me.

"I need you. I don't know how else to tell you. Okay I want you. Can't we just talk about it? To me you're amazing." His voice was so low he was almost whispering.

"Oh I know just how special I am to you. I'm so special that you trick me into caring about you, then when I do you pass me to your girlfriend as some type of gift. I'm so special to you that you use me, my body and waste my time. I'm so special that you lied to me, took my money and probably was spending it on her. You have a funny way of showing that you care." I was practically screaming at him.

"Carmell, I love you. I really do. We can all be happy. All three of us." Louis said.

"What the hell are you saying to me? I'm not interested in being in your harem. I don't want to be apart of anymore of your stupidity." Trying to drive and talk to this man was an extremely hard task. Especially under the influence. It was becoming very difficult to control the steering wheel and the movements of the car. It also infuriated me that he had the nerves to call me and try to influence me to be with him and his woman. I was about to lose it.

"Baby, it's not stupidity." He interrupted.

"You can kiss my ass Louis! I don't want you. Go to hell and don't call me no damn more!" As I finished my sentence I lost control of my car. It spun around three times and then hit the guard rail. I could hear the tires screech against the road. My heart was beating fast and I couldn't catch my breath. I was scared. I felt like my life was about flash before my eyes.

I felt the airbag hit my chest and then my seatbelt grabbed me and pulled me back to my seat. I don't know how long I had been out but when I regain consciousness I noticed a crowd of people around me. I heard someone say that they had called an ambulance and to just stay in the car until they had gotten there. Everything was blurry to me. It could have been the impact or the alcohol, I couldn't tell.

I squinted my eyes to try to clear my vision. Then I saw smoke coming from the hood of the car. I smelled something burning. Oh hell no, there was no way I was going to be burned alive in this car. I was getting out of here. I moved my arms and legs to make sure they hadn't been broken. Once I confirmed that everything was working I attempted to open the door. The driver door wouldn't open so then I tried the passenger door. It wouldn't open either. Well I guess the only way out was going to be the window. I refused to be trapped in this car. The window was only halfway down. I couldn't get them down so I did the only thing I thought that I could at the time. I turned my head to the side closed my eyes and kicked the shit out of the window. I kicked until I could feel myself kicking nothing but air. I crawled out of the car. As I fell towards the ground I could feel someone pulling me away from the car. I could see sparks fly from the car. Just as the nice man pulled me far enough away from the car, the hood caught on fire. The heat from that fire was so intense. I stood there watching my baby burn. That car meant a lot to me, but my life meant much more. I can't believe this crap. I felt this was some kind of symbol. I had to make some changes. Unlike my car, there is no way I would let my life crash and burn.

Natina

The Sting

I stood motionless with the phone receiver in my hand. A cloud of disbelief surrounded me, what I had just overheard could not be true. Just as I stepped out of the bathroom I heard Louis and his attempt whisper. I wanted to know who he was talking to that he felt he had to whisper. I walked into the front room and picked up the phone, hit the mute button and listened in on the call. I couldn't believe my ears. He was talking to Carmell. I listened to their conversation.

"Carmell, I love you. I really do. We can all be happy. All three of us." What did he mean all three of us? I never said anything about him, her and me. It just wasn't going to happen. I just wasn't willing to share him with her any longer. That was over and there would be no all three of us at all.

Why in the hell would he be talking to her when I had specifically told him that she was no longer apart of our lives. What the hell did he mean he loved her and what was all this we could have a good life. I know he didn't think he was going to have both of us. I thought I was a very giving woman when it came to Louis. He had what most men wanted. He could do whatever he wanted as long as he came home. As long as he understood that I was number one he had it made. I let him have other sex partners, I included myself or sometimes I just watched. What was it about her that made him want to have her as a main girl too?

I placed the phone back into it's cradle. I had to handle this. I couldn't believe I was going to have this conversation again. I walked into the bedroom. It was filled with smoke. He was sitting here smoking up all my weed. Although he knows I never mind sharing with him he didn't have to go and smoke it all. I looked at the empty sandwich bag on my night stand.

"Louis, I heard your little phone call. I can tell you right now I am not pleased with it at all. As a matter of fact it really pisses me off that you are sneaking and calling her." I walked over to the bed and stood in front of him, placed my hand on my hips and gave him my best angry black woman face.

"Yeah, so what?" This was his only response. What did he mean so what? How could he be so nonchalant about the entire situation? Didn't he understand how upset it made me every time I heard him even mention her name? What was it about her anyway that made him want to continue to mess with her. She was needy and clingy and not at all his type. She wouldn't and couldn't allow him the space he needed. He was the type of man that needed to be able to have his space. She was the type of woman who thought space was letting him go to the bathroom by himself.

"So I thought I asked you not to call her anymore. We are about to get married and that part of our life is over. She's not gonna be apart of us." I was being as direct as I knew how. I was trying to let him know that I'm flexible about a lot of things but this wouldn't be one of them. I wanted her gone. I didn't even want to think about what happened between the three of us because wasn't even worth remembering. It sure as hell wasn't worth doing again. If you ask me she was frigid and cold. Yeah she talked a big game, told him she would be down but just didn't know how to be down. She could never be me. The more I thought about him calling her the more upset I became. Moving closer to Louis and stared down at him. I needed him to feel that I was truly upset and this wasn't one of our role playing games. This was the real deal and I wanted no more Carmell talk. Ever.

"Girl you need to back up out of my face and stop issuing demands like you running shit." He stood up. I looked up to him. He looked just as serious as I did. He looked so serious that I was nervous. His body language told me he was defensive. Some how he thought me saying this was threatening his manhood. I wasn't trying to question his manhood, just letting him know what I wanted from him. I didn't say it but I wanted him to back off me now. I didn't like him standing over me like this but I wasn't going to back down from him either. I found my voice.

"It's not a demand it's a request. One that I would really like you to comply with, you don't love her, it's me you love. You just hate missing out on pussy. That's the only thing you love about her. Her legs were always open for you, but she don't hold you down like I do. I'm your number one and you can't have two number ones. I told you that we're done with her. Find yourself a new toy." I started to walk off but he grabbed me and pulled me back. His grasp was strong as he pulled me back by my arm. He squeezed so hard I could feel my hand tingle and go numb from the lack of blood flow. He was hurting me. I winced and looked at him, silently letting me know that he was hurting me. His expression told me he already knew that.

"You are my number one and you always will be, but remember this. I'm the man and I run this here. I say when we're done with her." He began to rub my face and then placed his hand around my neck. He squeezed so hard I began to feel a little light headed. "You understand?" He asked me and waited until I shook my head yes. I had never seen him so forceful. I couldn't believe his was getting physical with me. He threw me down on the bed. Then he climbed on top of me and began to kiss me like only he could. Where his hands once held my neck his lips now kissed and sucked. I could feel his tongue trace the fine lines of my body. He was whispering in my ear how sweet I was and how he really loved me. He was so passionate and felt amazing once he entered me. I enjoyed every inch of him. He made love to my body but I could help but remember the words he spoke to Carmell. He had told her he loved her.

When we were done he leaned in and kissed me. "Like I said, you are my number one. I don't want her and I told you that. We are done with her, for good. She's not needed in our life and now that I say she is out she is out." Louis kissed me and got up to take a shower. He made it sound like I was the one that called her and was talking that crazy love stuff to her when it was him. I guess he just needed to be the one that said it was over. I don't know what that was about. I was glad that he was finally done with her. She was the only thing now days that he and I argue over and she definitely wasn't worth it.

I was happy that he had finally gotten it, but I could still hear that conversation and I could still feel the sting of those words in my heart.

Kendra

Unpredictable

I lay in my husbands arms. I loved for him to hold me. He held me tightly like something precious he never wanted to lose. It was quiet throughout the house. I thought that Cory had fallen asleep until I heard him speak.

"Kendra, I want to ask you something." His baritone octaves were so soothing to me.

"You can ask me anything you want baby." I answered.

"Why did you do it?" I wanted to say do what but I knew what he meant.

"I don't know baby, I had a temporary lapse of good judgment I guess." I laughed uncomfortably and hoped that this subject was closed.

"No, I'm serious what was it? I think I need to know why." I guess he was asking for honesty, but I didn't want to go down this road. What if he couldn't handle the truth? Maybe I would only give him part of the truth.

"It wasn't anything that you weren't doing. It was me baby. I think I just liked the sensuality of being with another woman. It was something familiar yet unpredictable about it. Baby, I'm sorry. I don't know what else to do. I'm sorry." I turned to face him so I could look at him but his eyes were closed so I rested my head against his chest.

"I know you're sorry. I just wanted to know. I need to be the one that gives you everything you desire. I don't want you to feel that you would ever have to sleep around or go behind my back." He kissed me on my forehead.

"Cory, that is completely over with. I'm done with that. I don't want to hurt you the way that I know I have. It's over." I didn't want him to have to worry about me. I wasn't going to be that selfish anymore.

We fell asleep holding each other. I hoped that last night was the last time I would have to hear about that. I would answer whatever he needed me to but I wanted to move past this. I felt we were doing well but every time he brought it up I felt like we were slowing our progress. I dressed to go to the store and run some errands. I kissed him good bye and let him know that I would be gone for most of the day.

I went to get my oil changed and sat and paid bills via my pda as I waited. They were very quick at this place and I liked the professional service. While I waited I called Cory just to see if he had any special request for dinner. I didn't get an answer and I thought that was very strange, but maybe he was in the bathroom or something. I closed my phone and looked at my wrist. I wore a bangle that matched one I had given Gia. I promised her that I would never take it off. It meant a lot to me but my marriage meant even more to me. I would have to take it off soon. I didn't need any constant reminders of that and I definitely didn't want Cory to know that I wore this reminder of her. I didn't want to take it off yet and I didn't want to think about it now. I would cross that bridge when I got to it.

When I left I went to the grocery store. I would cook steak tonight and hopefully I could get a little special attention from my husband. I pulled into my driveway and I noticed a car in parked on the street in front of the house. I had never seen this car before. I walked through the door.

It was dark in the house and there was a lighted path of candles and rose petals leading towards my bedroom. I walked the path. How sweet. I could hear soft music playing in the back ground. I opened the door and then I heard the music change. I could hear Jamie Foxx's voice singing to me. He was telling me tonight we're getting unpredictable. This was definitely something new for Cory.

As I pushed the door wider I could see that there were rose petals on my bed and in the center of the bed was a woman. I had to squint cause she looked a lot like Gia. Cory stepped out of the bathroom. His broad shoulders were bare. I could see the muscles in his strong arms and his abs were flat with lines etching a perfect six pack. I know the look on my face had to be one of confusion. Cory finally spoke.

"Hey baby. He walked over to kiss me. This is Jessica, a friend of mine. She looked like your type to me so I talked to her and just your luck she loves threesomes." Cory walked over to a seat that was beside the bed. Was I in the twilight zone or what? This was not real.

I looked at the woman and she was truly beautiful. She was darker than Gia but only about a shade or two. Her hair was Beyonce blonde and her eyes were hazel. She was pretty. She looked as if she were about my height maybe an inch or two shorter than me. She wore make up but you couldn't tell unless you examined her closely. It looked very natural. Her lips were pink and glossy and her eyes were slightly slanted, giving her an exotic appearance. I felt myself getting excited and then I looked at my husband. His chocolate coated skin glowing in the candlelight held my attention. His six foot five stature was one of the many qualities that I loved about him. I had to admit seeing him and this beautiful woman waiting on me, excited me. I didn't know how to react to this. I briefly wondered if he were sleeping with this woman. He would have to be extremely comfortable with her to invite her into our bed. Where there some things about my husband that I truly didn't know? He had completed thrown me for a loop. This wasn't the normal. Caught completely off guard, I didn't know how to handle his spontaneity.

The woman, Jessica, moved from the bed and walked towards me. She touched my face and then took my bag from me. She grabbed my hand

and led me to my husband. I didn't even know he knew people like this. Jessica pushed me towards my husband and then she began to unbutton my shirt from behind. While she did this Cory began to kiss me. Again, just like every other time this man touched my body I began to melt. I felt a puddle begin to form in my panties. With this much stimulation I was liable to flood a block.

By this time Jessica had removed my shirt and began to kiss my back. I remembered Gia's touch. This woman's touch was slightly different but still just as gentle. Cory had made his way to my breast. He used his tongue to taste my nipples. He sucked them softly. Then it became a harder. I felt my clit began to tingle. I was on fire.

Cory picked me up and then laid me against the bed. He kissed me and nibbled on my ear. Then I heard him whisper the words that brought me back to reality.

"Is this what you want? Is this unpredictable enough for you?" He looked at me. He was only doing this because he thought I was some horny freak. He thought he wasn't enough to please me, but the truth was he was all I needed. He turned me on and there could be one other person here or a million I would always devote all of my attention to him.

"No, baby you're enough for me." I said to him and kissed him as I sat up and found my shirt. "I'm sorry Jessica but my husband and I need to talk. I didn't mean to waste your time." She looked a little pissed. I could tell she was really getting into it but this little bit of pleasure just wasn't worth it to me. She grabbed her clothes, dressed herself and then left our house.

I looked at Cory. He was such a handsome man. He was even more attractive to me than he was the first night I met him and his soul desire was to please me.

"Baby, you're all I need. You have everything I need." I touched his face.

"You mean that Kendra. I just want to make sure I give you everything you want. I rather you not go behind my back and do that." He looked at me. I somehow felt he was happy that I didn't allow it to continue. He was doing it for me but somehow I sensed that's not what he really wanted. He wanted to know that he was enough for me.

"You are all I need." I said as I pulled my husband close to me. He finished undressing me then touched my wet place. He just looked at me and smiled. I was extremely wet. He glided himself inside of me. We made love and as usual, it was more than amazing. He laid me on my stomach and held me down against the bed. Then he turned my body to the side and wrapped my leg around his head. I could feel every inch of him. He was deep inside of me giving me all of him. He stroked me and took my breast in his mouth at the same time. Then he flipped me unto my stomach again to take me from behind. I could feel myself about to reach a climax.

He knew just how to work my body and make love to me until I was left trembling in a puddle. Cory did crazy things to me and my body and I didn't need anybody else in the room but him. My husband's love was unpredictable enough.

Nicole

Never the Bride

It has been a full month from the day that Jason said that it was over and I was officially depressed. How could it be over and when it hasn't even began? I wanted him, and part of me felt like I needed him. I craved his scent, I yearned for his kiss and I longed just to be near him. I was getting no attention from Jason. I was alone, my texts went unanswered and my emails were deleted upon receipt. It hurt to be treated that way by him. Shortly after we had our little heart to heart Natina approached me about being her maid of honor. It was only one other girl in the wedding and her name was Jennifer. I didn't know much about the girl but that she was Asian and she seemed to have it bad for my friend's man. She was always talking about Louis this and Louis that. I wonder why Tina never questioned it.

I quickly dismissed the thoughts of Natina and her wedding party. I had to figure out a way to make Jason desire me the way he did before. The day I found out that Tina was moving the date of her wedding up I immediately went to him and asked him to be my date. I walked up to him and he all but laughed in my face. It was humiliating and degrading and I couldn't understand why things could just go back to the way they were.

Today was the day of the wedding and I know many invitations had gone out to the people that we work with. I stood there in my bridesmaid dress. I had to admit I looked good. On the outside, I appeared to have it all together but on the inside, I was falling apart. I don't know how I was going to get past this hump. I wanted someone who didn't seem to want me and that was one of the worst feelings in the world.

I heard the music come on. It was time for the wedding to start but Louis was nowhere to be found. I didn't have the strength or the patience to try to think of reasons why he would be late so I stepped outside the room where Natina and Jennifer were.

As I stood there in the hallway, I noticed Jason entering the church. He should be struck down right were he stood. I was so mad that he had cut me off I wanted to hurt him, but encompassed in that hate was my desire to love him.

After he walked in, I could have screamed because holding his hand was Tasha's skanky ass. I couldn't stand her and at this point, I couldn't control my actions.

I walked towards the happy little couple and blocked their entrance into the church.

"So yall together now or what? Is she the reason that you wasn't gonna come with me?" I looked at him and my face was on fire. I was so angry I could have fought both of them right here in the church.

"You need to back up. It ain't none of your business where Jason chooses to go and who he chooses to go with!" Tasha is the one who had responded to me.

"Hoe I wasn't talking to you so shut the hell up!" I looked back at Jason awaiting my answer. I don't know why he forced us to go through this when he knew we should have been together.

"Nicole, you need to calm down. Don't make a scene you're at your friends wedding. You're in Natina's wedding so stop making a fool out of yourself." He said. The look on his face was not anger but pity. Why in the hell did he pity me? I only wanted him to see that there was nothing better than us. We were good together and when I see him with her and talking to her it infuriates me. I couldn't stand her and he was choosing her.

"Jason..." I called his name but by that time he was walking off. Tasha still stood next to me. Smirking as if she had the final laugh and the game was over.

"You look nice as a bridesmaid, and it's a good thing too, cause you will never be a bride." She left me standing there laughing as she caught up with the date that should have been mine.

Carmell

The Final Laugh

•———————————————————————————————————•

After demolishing my car I was completely out done. That car was my baby and now it was gone. To make matters worse Natina decides that she was going to try and be funny and invite me to their wedding. I know she did it to be funny. She just wanted me to know that she was getting him and I wasn't. That was fine because I didn't want him but what I did want was the last laugh.

She didn't believe that he still wanted me. I know he had lied to her about showing up to my house cause she came up to me throwing accusations that I was just trying to break her and Louis up. She went on to say that she also knew that he didn't want me.

I sat in front of my vanity table applying my finishing touches to my makeup. I could be gorgeous when I wanted and today was one of those days I wanted to be a showstopper. I stepped out the house and got into my new Toyota Solara. It was a champagne color and though it was no Camaro it had grown on me.

I drove to the church she was having her wedding at. I know she would be so shocked when she found out I was coming. I wore the shortest skirt I could find along with the highest heels. I walked into the church and I saw that the wedding had not started. Perfect. I looked for the groom. He was the one I was here to see. It shouldn't take long to find because there weren't that many places he could be. I saw Nicole hanging around one of the rooms and I assumed Natina was waiting to walk out. I surveyed her decorations. She had thrown this wedding together. I guess she had to prove a point when she found out how he was trying to get at me. I continued walking then I finally found the groom. I walked in like I owned it. I was running things and I knew with the way I looked they would get out and I know Louis would want to touch my body. Hell, I look good.

"I need everybody but the groom to leave. Now." I looked around the room. There were two men who stood in the room with Louis. He was dressed in a tuxedo and he wore it well. I was dressed in a skirt and under it I wore a corset. I knew I wore that well. The two other men left the room as instructed but not before I could notice them looking at my ass. I looked at Louis and he smiled.

"What are you doing here? Realize you couldn't live without me finally?" That was the funniest thing that he could have said. That was the farthest from the truth. This wasn't about him. This was about me knowing that I could shatter Natina's world with a moments notice. I chose not to respond to him.

I slowly walked over to him and pulled my skirt down. My bare legs exposed. "Kiss them!" I said. I was calling all the shots and even though I knew that this was wrong, and even more so because I was doing it in a church; I was doing it nonetheless. He began to kiss my legs while mumbling something about knowing that I hadn't stopped loving him. I didn't love him I despised what he had done to me. There was a very thin line between love and hate and his actions had shoved me across it. I could have loved this man forever but instead of receiving my love he was now someone that I hated. I couldn't believe that I had allowed him to do what he had done to me. I had allowed my love for him once to blind me, but things had finally changed. He was a pawn in my feud with Natina.

I made him eat me until I came. I wanted my scent all over his face. I rode his face until I came and I let all of my juices run down his face. I had to admit that it felt good. He was very talented at giving me an orgasm with the movements of his tongue.

There was nowhere for him to shower or wash off and if I played my cards right I had delayed the wedding. I felt like I could stop this wedding if I wanted to. I tried to rid myself of her but she just kept coming at me. She had used her connection to him to get to me now I was using my connection to him to get to her. I had finally turned the tables. I wanted her to smell my scent on him when she kissed her husband to be.

I walked out of the room hurriedly. Just as I was coming out I saw his friends rushing back to get him. Yeah they were waiting on him. I also noticed that Nicole was standing outside the door the very moment I was coming out. She had seen me and I'm sure that she was going to tell Natina. I didn't care, I wanted her to know that I had what she thought was only hers. I wanted her to know that I had used and discarded her man and that he had done it willingly. I wanted her to know that I had the final laugh.

Natina

What's that I Smell?

I had rushed this wedding. My first intentions were to plan the wedding and take my time, but I had quickly changed my mind. I guess I wanted to make a statement directed at Carmell. He's my man and now it would be for life. I stood in the small room preparing to walk down the aisle. I was marrying the man that I loved. We were finally going to walk down the aisle claim and each other for life.

Even though I loved him it wasn't stopping me from being upset with him. The wedding was supposed to start thirty minutes ago but no one could seem to find him. I can't imagine what can possibly make him late for his own wedding. He had asked me to marry him; he should have been here bright and early waiting for me with bells on. I asked Nicole to go out to see what was going on but all she could concentrate on was Jason. Damn, couldn't she put that out of her mind for one day, for my day? Instead of coming back with Louis's where abouts she came back with some useless banter about seeing Tasha and Jason together. So the hell what, I didn't want to hear that on my wedding day so I sent her back out to complete the first task I had given her. Once she came back she told me it was time for the wedding to start and everything was okay. I could tell by looking at her it was something that she wasn't telling me. It could have possibly been me so I dismissed that too. Nicole had been such a space cadet lately I didn't know what her moods or facial expressions meant. She had let that man get to her.

He had her mind so gone that I didn't think she could go one hour without letting him invade his thoughts. I can't believe that she had the nerves to argue with Jason on my wedding day. I had to stop thinking about that. This was my day and I wasn't going to let her get to me.

The wedding had started. I made such a nice bride and was so happy about being the bride that even when I saw Carmell strolling into the wedding it couldn't upset me. Even though she looked like a two-dollar whore and walked in while my wedding party was going in I didn't lose it. I was marrying the man and she was here to watch. Case closed.

I strolled down the aisle and saw everyone looking at me. It was just like I liked it. I thought I would be nervous but I wasn't. This was the way things should be. We should be together and it was always meant to be this way. Carmell was just a distraction between the two of us. I know that he couldn't want her and I was all the woman that he would ever need. I had invited Carmell to the wedding just so she could know that this was for life and that was nothing that she could do to break that up. I wanted to bare witness to us becoming life partners.

I took my place next to Louis as we said our vows. I looked at him and he looked so happy. Can you blame him though? He was about to marry me. I was the woman who was always there for him, always willing to do for him and what more can make him happier. I wouldn't even give him a hard time about being late. I would just let him make it when it came to that. We had our whole lives ahead of us.

As the minister pronounced us man and wife I looked at Louis. He was just as handsome as he had always been. He lifted my veil and leaned in to kiss me. I jerked back some. He smelled funny. I tried to hide the frown on my face but I know people noticed. He attempted to kiss me again and I did just because all of these people were watching. I pulled him in to hug me. It wasn't because I wanted him but because I needed to say something. I smiled and spoke through clenched teeth.

"Louis not on our wedding day, you couldn't even keep it in your pants on our wedding day? I smell it on you. I smell pussy on your breath." I knew I hadn't been with him because we had agreed to not see each other before the wedding. I also knew that it wasn't Jennifer because she was with me the whole time. Forget upset I was livid. I had never stopped him from being with different women but on our wedding day you would think that he had more respect for me. He didn't have the common decency to attempt to wash his face. He just kissed me with another woman's cum on his lips. If we hadn't been in front of all these people I would have knocked the hell out of him.

Every one was clapping for us and I was fuming inside. As we turned to walk out I saw Carmell standing at the end of the aisle, smiling, and I knew then, that it was her that I smelled.

Kendra

Can't Go On

I was dressed and ready for Natina's wedding. I was only going because she had invited me and I didn't want to be impolite. Besides, I would have been devastated if people hadn't come to my wedding. While waiting for Cory to come out of the shower my doorbell rang. Normally I would send Cory to the door but he was preoccupied, so I answered it.

I opened the door to a huge bouquet of long stem roses. They were simply beautiful.

"Aww, those are beautiful. I know they can't be from anybody else but my husband." I smiled. Just as I said that I heard Cory coming down the stairs. The flowers were so large I couldn't see the person that was delivering them. I smiled at Cory but he just looked at me confused.

"I didn't do that babe." He said as he continued down the stairs.

The delivery person began to lower them and there before me in living color was Gia. I could have fainted. My heart began to race and my palms became sweaty. I had rid myself of this part of my life. I looked up at Cory as if to say, I had nothing to do with this.

"Gia, what are you doing here?" That was all I could say once I found my voice.

"I came to see you." She sat the flowers down and on the table in my front hallway and stood there looking at me. Her eyes penetrated me. They were probing and attempting to read me. I couldn't take such an intense stare. Her eyes said to me she knew how I felt. She knew that I still cared for her and I still wanted her to be apart of my life but I couldn't have her. I didn't need this distraction. Cory and I were doing so well and now we had another obstacle to get over. I didn't even know how she knew where I lived.

"You need to leave." Cory spoke up. I was so happy that he hadn't dived across the doorway and started to fight her again. I had no idea what she was doing here. I hadn't talked to her and by the letter that she sent me it was suppose to be over. Why was she breaking the rules? Why was she showing up at my house, at our home? I know that I was wrong for wanting the both of them, but I had made my decision and she was okay with it. At least she said she was okay with it.

"I'm not leaving. I needed to come here. I needed to see you. I come in and out of Houston for work and you don't know how hard it is for me to be in the same city as you and not be able to see you, not be able to touch you. I need you in my life." She stood there and spilled the contents of her heart in front of my husband. I know that took guts. It took courage, the kind of courage that can only be attained by fighting for the one you love.

Cory looked at me. His facial expression was one of annoyance. I felt bad because if it weren't for my bad judgment we wouldn't be standing here having to have this three-way conversation with my ex lover.

"You need to handle this." Those where the only words that Cory spoke. Then he walked away from us and the entire situation.

"Gia, how can you just show up at my home like this? I'm married. I never hid that from you and I thought that you understood that. We had this talk and I know you know how committed I am to making my marriage work." She stopped me from speaking and then pulled me close to her and kissed me. For a brief moment I lowered my guard and allowed her to kiss me. I allowed myself to enjoy the soft sweetness of her lips and then I came to. I couldn't do this. I wouldn't go down this road anymore.

"We can't do this. This can't continue. Cory and I have just come to the point where we can hold a conversation without him cursing me out and this is only going to set us back." I pleaded with her.

"We always talked about what you want but what about what I want. I want to love you. I want to know that I can call you like I used to. I want to know that I can be apart of your life." Gia responded to me. She pleaded with me. She grabbed my hands and pulled me closer to her. She pulled our wrist together and I remembered the promise I had made to her to never take it off. She was trying to remind me that I had cared about her. I didn't need reminding though. I still felt the same way about Gia, but when it came down to it, it would be Cory. She had said it herself. I looked at her face. She was still beautiful but today her amber green eyes were filled with sadness and tears. Feeling as if I wouldn't be able to say no to her, I looked away as I began to speak.

"How can you be apart of my life? When we are together touch each other uncontrollably. I want to touch you and kiss you and I can't hurt Cory anymore. When I'm with you I feel a level of comfort I've never felt before, but I know as well as you do that we can't be friends. The kind of friends that we are will always be more than friends. I can't go down this road anymore. Gia I will always have you in my heart but I have to, I must save my marriage. You know of all people what those vows mean to me. You know how much Cory means to me. You remember the tears I shed when he caught us and how bad I felt when I knew that I had hurt him. I thought it was beyond repair but it wasn't and I can't go back." I turned to face her. I begged her with my eyes. I wanted her to understand that she was special and that I really did care. I also needed her to understand that this was unacceptable for her to show up at my home. It was disrespectful to my husband and it could be detrimental to my marriage.

"You of all people know that I love you. I need you to be apart of my life and I'm not leaving this doorstep until I know that you will be a continuous part of my life. I know what I said in that letter and I also know I didn't mean it when I said it. Those words were for your benefit not mine. I try so hard to give you what you want, but I need you." The tears trickled down her cheeks leaving tiny puddles at the corners of her mouth. I wanted so badly to comfort her and take her in my arms. If I could only kiss her and tell her it would be okay, but I know that's not something that I could do. So I didn't reach out to her. I didn't want to send out mixed signals.

I looked behind me and saw Cory standing in the doorway. The hurt was there in his eyes again. In his eyes I could see the pain just as I did the day he came to Georgia. I then looked at Gia and saw the painful expression. I didn't know what to do. I had hurt both of them by my selfish actions. I really didn't want to have to choose between the two. I thought that I had made my choice already and I thought that she understood but she didn't. I wanted her in my life but I couldn't have the best of both worlds.

"Gia, that's not something that I can do. It has to be over. I miss our conversation, I miss the way you get me, and the way you understand me. I miss being able to talk to you about everything, but I would miss my marriage even more if I lost it. You said it better than me. It has end and we have to do it so we can both move on with our life." I moved towards her and hugged her. I held her tightly because this was truly going to be the final good bye. I wanted to savor her scent as much as I could. I sniffed, taking in her sweet scented perfume and then I let go. Cory had heard the entire conversation. My feelings for her were apparent. She could still make my heart beat fast. She could still make my head spin with a kiss but the fact remained that I loved my husband. "This just can't go on."

She hugged me back and began to cry. I knew I had hurt her and I didn't mean to hurt her at all but I had. I turned and watched her walk back to her rental car and I realized that I was crying as well.

I slowly closed my door and faced Cory. Instantly changing my mind about the wedding I walked up the stairs to remove my clothes. I wanted to say something to Cory to reassure and console him but I had no words. There was nothing that I could say. He had heard the conversation and he had also heard that it can't go on.

Love Lust and A Whole Lotta Distrust

The Aftermath

Nicole

Caught Up

It had been three months since I slept with Cory. I couldn't believe that it happened and I couldn't believe that it had been that good. I had tried to make it happen again, but he wasn't hearing it. I had to admit I felt used. After he was done with me he discarded me. I even felt stupid as I sat on the bathtub waiting for my pregnancy test to finish. I knew I was pregnant; I was only going through the motions. I also knew that it was a strong possibility that it was Cory's. The only other person that I had been with was Jason. I slept with Jason a month after Cory. I am almost certain that is would be Cory's.

I leaned over the *EPT*. There were two pink lines.

"Dammit" I said aloud. I was pregnant. I needed to go to the doctor right away. I felt a sense of urgency not because I wanted to find out if I was pregnant. I knew that much but I needed to know just how far I was. I prayed more in this very second than I had in the last year. I didn't want this to be Cory's baby. I couldn't stress that enough to God. I threw on a t-shirt and sweat pants and headed towards the door. I knew that the Planned Parenthood could give me an ultrasound and tell by the baby's growth how far along I was and they took walk-ins.

I walked into the office and signed my name on the sign in sheet. The room was almost empty. That was good. I had called in to work today because I felt so sick. I had spent half of the morning with my face in the toilet. When I couldn't keep down anything I ate I knew it was time to take a pregnancy test. I sat there and let the twenty-inch tube entertain me as I waited.

"Nicole Neatherly" I heard my name being called. I gathered my things and strolled passed the nurse and into my designated room. There she left me with instructions to strip myself of clothes and put on this drab hospital robe. I lye silently on the table, praying that it was Jason's baby. That would be easier to deal with than it being Cory's. Kendra hadn't found out about that day and though we are not the same she does hold a bit of conversation with me. She doesn't totally ignore me.

The nurse walked in and introduced herself. I didn't care I just wanted to get this over with. She applied a cold jelly substance to my belly and then she began to do what she does best. Within a matter of minutes the examination was over. I sat up.

"So what's the verdict?" I asked.

"Well sweetie congratulations! It looks that you are about twelve weeks." She smiled and handed me pictures that she had printed from her contraption. "I will leave you to get dressed. Your paperwork and prescriptions will be waiting up front for you.

I slowly started to dress. I didn't know what I was going to do. I left trying to figure out what it was I could do. I know there was no way that Cory was gonna leave Kendra even if I was pregnant. I was only a one-time thing. Something he did to make himself feel better. I couldn't help but to cry and to beat myself up for all of my bad decisions. I had to fix this for real. It would have been so much easier if it had been Jason. He wasn't married and I really liked him. I am sure that if he had a kid with me everything would work out between us. I don't know how I had got caught up in this soap opera bs. As I started my car an idea came to me. I picked up the phone and dialed Jason's cell.

"Hello, Jason hey this is Nicole. Can I come up there to talk to you? We need to talk it's really important." I was gonna get myself out of this mess. I headed towards my job, on my way to fix a problem that I had ultimately created by being to careless and free. I didn't think about my actions or the consequences of them and now I was going to pay for my illicit behavior. If everything went well with Jason, I could finally have the opportunity to have him as a constant part of my life.

I saw Jason walking towards the car. He really was sexy. Just watching him walk I know why all the girls wanted him. His movements were so graceful as if he floated when he walked. I knew I wanted him and I started thinking about my plot. Most likely he was not the father of this child but he was going to be. I looked at him, for my sake I do hope this baby comes out looking like me. That would make it easier, instead of the baby not looking like either one of us.

"Hey there, Stranger." I looked at Jason.

"What's up girl, do you know how to do anything without bringing the drama?" He laughed.

"I'm pregnant." I didn't know how to say it, it's not like I had passed another man's child for someone else's before.

"You're what? So how am I supposed to know that it's mine?" Although he had every right to ask, it still pissed me off.

"Because I'm telling you, I'm pregnant with your child." I looked at him.

"Damn, I thought you were on the pill or something." He just looked at me.

"So you gonna make this my fault now? You gonna act like I was the only one there and I forced you not to always wear a condom?" I just stared at him. I needed him to go along with this. I didn't want my child to not have a father. Silence surrounded us. Jason's face was twisted as if in deep thought, then finally he spoke.

"Hey, well I am not the kind of man that's not going to be there for his child. I want to do what I can for you and the baby. Just let me know whatever okay." He leaned in and kissed me on the forehead before he got out of the car.

"So much for being caught up." I thought to myself as I drove away.

Carmell

A Trip to The Clinic

I hadn't talked to Louis since that day that Natina threw me out of her house. Actually that was fine by me. He was an asshole with a capital A. I don't know how I allowed myself to fall in love with someone like him. They both played me for a fool and I had fallen for all of that game. Even though I was smarter than that, he was smooth and everything out of his mouth was a lie.

As if the lies weren't enough I had contracted something from my little interlude with those two nuts. I was sitting in this office waiting to find out the results of last weeks test. I received a call telling me to come into the office and that could only mean one thing. Something was wrong. I waited patiently in the room for my doctor. She didn't come; instead a nice looking Hispanic man in his late twenties opened the door. Oh my goodness he was too cute to be meeting in clinic under these circumstances. I glanced at his left hand. Humph, no wedding band. I smiled to myself. I didn't think there was any chance that he would be interested; I was here for a STD. He would think I was nasty.

"Hi there," His sexy Latin accent was attractive. "I am Dr. Alejandro Escalante, you can call me Alex if you like." He smiled revealing dazzling white teeth neatly arrange in his mouth as if he were the spokes person for Crest.

"Well pleased to meet you, my name is Carmell, you can just call me." I laughed at that corny line. I sounded so stupid. What the hell is wrong with me? I looked at the floor and I could feel the blood rushing to my cheeks.

"Why are you blushing?" He smiled at me again. "What's to be embarrassed about? I just might call you." He winked at me. He sat down on the little rolling stool that so many doctors owned. His tone was gentle and caring, yet utterly professional when he began to speak.

"Carmell, I know a woman as beautiful as yourself should value your life. Do you often have unprotected sex?"

"No, Alex. I made a very stupid mistake this time but that is not something that I would normally do. I was taught better than that and I have been beating myself up since I had my check up."

"Well sweetie, we are gonna thank God for small favors okay. Gracias a Dios. What we found was Chlamydia. It is a STD but it's one that can be cured. I have prescription that will clear that up for you in no time. All of the other test that we ran came back negative. So don't let there be a next time. Comprendes?" he smiled again at me. He was really sweet. His skin was the color of toasted almonds. It was beautiful and so was he. I wondered if he was seeing anybody.

"Sí." I said showing him that I had pearly whites of my own. I didn't speak a lick of Spanish but I thought it was cute that he was throwing it into our conversation. I just smiled and stared into his hazel eyes.

He made small talk as we walked back to the front of the office. I was ready to get my medication. Even though it could be cured I felt dirty to know that something bad was inside of me. I felt as if my body were tainted. I gathered my prescription and said my goodbyes to Alex. I was a little saddened. I knew that I would never see him again. He had given me his card. As I placed the papers into my purse I noticed something scribbled on the back of it.

"Tu eres bella, mas bella que las estrellas y la luna ajuntos. Llama me :)... 281-777-1946." I smiled to myself. I don't know what the hell he just said but there was a phone number here. I smiled at the thought of the doctor and I. He was handsome and successful. I couldn't believe he was even hitting on me. Being my doctor I thought that he would have been hesitant, but it made me feel good. I felt like the doctor obviously found me irresistible and with the things that have been happening lately my self-esteem was a bit shattered. He probably didn't even realize how he had made my day.

I walked out of the clinic desperately wanting to know what was written on this card. This was one of those moments I really wish I had paid attention in Spanish class. I stood here for what seemed like ages. I saw a young man pass by.

"Excuse me, can you read Spanish?"

"Sure." The boy replied. As he stood there I pulled the card out of my purse and handed it to him.

"It says, "you are beautiful, as beautiful as the stars and moon. Call me" Who wrote this corny stuff?" The boy laughed as he handed me the card back.

"Thanks." I handed him five dollars and left. It wasn't corny to me. I could feel all of the color rush to my cheeks. He had gotten my attention and I wanted to call him. It was amazing to me that my doctor wanted to know me and even with everything that was going on inside of my body he saw passed that. Most men would think I was some dirty disgusting tramp, but he didn't. He wanted me. I had to work up the nerve to call but I was definitely going to do it. I wanted to tell Louis or maybe Natina about the STD, they needed to know. I would want to know.

Louis had been a waste of time and was not worth all that I invested in him. He was nothing compared to the man I had just met. This morning as I got ready for my day, I was nervous, but the Latin doctor with the sexy smile had given a new meaning to the words a trip to the clinic.

Natina

Bad Karma

It was always my belief that Louis and I were soul mates. I thought that we would be the perfect couple once we were married. Louis and I had decided to get married three months ago. It was nothing fancy, just a small, simple wedding to seal our love. At first things were the same. We had more good times than bad, but lately everything seems all wrong. Many times since we have been married I have come home to find women in my bed. Normally I wouldn't trip about it because I would be involved in it. That was the agreement. No hoes in this house unless I do em too. I thought to myself about the constant disrespect he showed. I guess somehow I had started this with my acceptance of this wayward lifestyle. It was fun for me too but I would never go as far as to bring a man or woman into our home without his permission, but he didn't care about permission, everything was fair game for him. His lazy ass didn't want to get a job either. He had used the school excuse for long enough and now that he had finally finished he couldn't use that anymore. Now it was he couldn't find a job that was willing to pay him what he was worth. Every day I left this house to go to work and everyday he pretended he searched for a job. Then I would come home and find a girl in the bed, a few times I just jumped right in bed with them and we did our thing, but it was more to life and marriage than just sex. I started to think if that is all we were built on we couldn't be made of much. I knew that it had to be much more to Louis and I than good sex.

I turned to face Louis. "Baby, all this little extra curricular activity that you have going on has got to stop. I'm out there working my ass off with school and work and you are just sitting on your ass. Use that damn degree that you got and things would be a lot better for us." I had a lot on my chest that I needed to say.

"What? Don't start with me Tina. I don't want to hear that bullshit tonight." Louis just glared at me. I sensed he didn't like that I was telling him what to do, but who cared. I didn't have time for this. I remembered this was the very reason that we weren't together in the beginning. I thought since he had gone back to school that maybe he had also grown up. What I saw before me was not a grown man. He was a big baby. A child in my eyes and I didn't have any children. He actually thought if he kept giving me good dick then I would keep taking care of him. This is getting old. Either he had to get his stuff together of he could leave.

"Look if you can't get your shit together then you can take your shit and get out." I yelled at him. Louis stood up over me and slapped me. I felt the sting of his hand against my face and my heart. He kept hitting me until he drew blood and then he grabbed me by my braids and dragged me into the bedroom.

I yelled and kicked my hardest. He was beating the crap out of me because I had attacked his manhood so he was going to show me that he was indeed the man. I didn't want to believe this was my life. I couldn't understand how we went from loving one another to this. I couldn't understand why he would want to beat me, bruise me and harm me. He at one time told me he would do anything for me, he vowed to love me forever.

He threw me on the bed. We had rough sex before but this was violent. His left hand was wrapped around my neck and used as an anchor to hold me down as his right hand ripped my clothes off. I could feel the sting of his nails scratching me as he tore at my underwear.

After he had successfully removed my panties he pushed himself in me. Each thrust was a stab at my heart. I would have given anything to this man and this is what he gives me. I lay stoic. I was completely void of emotion as he used my body. His breath was hot on my skin. I could smell the awful stench of beer and weed mingled on his breath. Once he was done with me he stood above me and readjusted his clothes.

"You're not leaving and neither am I, it's 'til death do us part or did you forget about that." He laughed and closed the door and locked it. I couldn't get out. Our door had a keyhole on both sides and without a key no one could get in or out for that matter. I sat there crying. I began to beat against the door. I was about to have a damn fit. I analyzed my situation. How could this be me here a prisoner in my very own home? All of these things I had worked hard for and purchased yet he seemed to make all the rules. What the hell was going on? What happened to my old Louis?

"Am I being punished for my sins?" I thought to myself and crawled into bed. It had to be bad karma..

Kendra

Blackmail

———————————————————————————————————

I sat across from Jason having lunch. I told him about my latest meeting with the marriage counselor. One of my professors who has an outside practice agreed to see us. I had to admit it was truly helping. Being in her presence again made me remember why I wanted to be a Psychologist, maybe I could one day help someone's life. I started to think long and hard about my career path. Maybe it was time to use that degree in psychology. Cory and I were actually on speaking terms and loving terms for that matter, being counseled by the minister that married us was turning our marriage around. I was proud of the progress that we had made in the three-month period.

"Kendra, I need to talk to you about something. Nicole told me earlier this week that she is pregnant and that she knows for a fact that it's mine because she hasn't been with anybody else. I'm gonna be a daddy." Jason smiled that foolish smile that so many of our men smiled everyday. One of the preachers in my church always said that the bad influence of a woman was witchcraft and this was a woman's influence at it's worst. Now I knew for a fact Nicole was with someone else because I had caught her with my husband and I had the pictures to prove it.

"So how far is she?" I asked. Before I blew up anyone's spot I wanted to make sure that my assumption was correct.

"I think she said twelve weeks." He boasted proudly. "I hope that it's a boy, I want a lil shorty to carry on my name." Jason had that glazed over look in his eyes and it hurt a bit to ask my next question.

"So do the times add up? When were you last with her?"

"I guess about two or three months ago. I am sure that it's mine, she says she hasn't been with anyone else and you know how she was jonesin' for me. She been hooked on this daddy dick for a while." Jason laughed as ego and testosterone took hold of him. I was lost in thought. I had a unwavering feeling that this was Cory's baby. I know just how bad he wanted kids and my fertility drugs weren't working. Maybe we can love this baby as our own. I felt that it was fifty percent ours anyway. I told Jason that I would be right back and ran to my car to retrieve those pictures. I had to keep them in my car so that inspector gadget didn't get a hold of them. I had to admit my husband was nosey and I didn't want him to know that I knew. I would leave that were it was. I came back into the building and searched for Nicole. I laughed to myself. I didn't know what I was doing when I took this that day, but now I am glad that I did. I thought at the time that I would maybe have to use them if he threatened divorce or something, but they were about to come in handy. I knew in my heart what I was about to do was wrong but I couldn't help it. She was going to deprive Cory of knowing his child just so she could save face and trick a man into being with her. I wouldn't blow her entire spot up but I was gonna get what I wanted too.

"Hello Nicole. Why don't you come with me for a minute? We need to talk." She gave me a look of total confusion. I motioned her to follow me into the private session room. I needed a secure place.

"Is this Cory's baby?" Nicole looked at me with a look of disbelief.

"I don't know what you are talking about Kendra. Why would this be Cory's baby?" She looked away as she said it. Her shifty eyes were tattle tell signs of her lies.

"Well maybe these will refresh your memory. Could these be the reason why this could be Cory's baby? Have you finally recovered from your lapse of memory? Nicole you are the only one I know that can have ten second amnesia." I said as I laid all the pictures out on the table.

"Honestly Kendra, I went over there with hopes that we could reconcile our friendship. I didn't mean to sleep with him. It just happened." She began to cry.

"Please Cole don't give me that. It is not like he tripped and fell in your pussy. Those kinds of accidents don't happen. You can save your theatrics and fake tears. You slept with my husband and now you trying to lie your way out of it. That's okay. I am okay with it. I have come to terms with a lot of my anger and I have realized a very important fact. My husband used you for exactly what you are. A whore" I stated.

"Wait a minute Kendra. How you gonna call me a whore when you were the one screwing some woman. You were the one that got caught not once but twice with this woman. All that bumpin' you were doing, somebody had to take care of your husband. I mean every chance you got you were out there doing this woman. You were out there living the lesbian life I guess, carpet munching ever time you thought you could get away with it. I bet you thought I didn't know."

"Frankly, I don't give a damn. Like I said you are a whore, you slept with any and everybody and now you gonna try to past this kid off as Jason's. So maybe you are not a whore, just very whorish!" I stared her down. The anger was still fresh in my heart. How dare she sit there and judge me when more guys have run through her than can be counted. I mean this bitch was just like motel 6; she left the light on for everybody.

"You don't know that it's Cory's." She glared at me. I was pushing all of her buttons.

"You're right, I don't know that it's Cory's and I don't know that it's not either. I do know that I can count and it's a strong possibility that this is my husband's child. Do me a favor Nicole and stop acting as if I am stupid. Do you see the dates at the bottom of this picture? This date is almost exactly three months from today. You slept with Jason at least a month after you did Cory. I know cause he came back bragging like all men do. I over heard him talking to Curtis one day and I remember thinking how much of a whore you were then. You are like the call center whore. Every time you spread your legs for someone here every one knows. You didn't think Jason talked to his boys, hell he just got through telling me how hooked on his dick you were. I know about those calls to Cory. Bitch I know everything. I know he turned you down and no he didn't tell me. He thought I was sleep. I over heard you that night you called. I picked up the phone the same time he did and I heard your voice. You have no shame do you? Any man will do when you're horny huh, no matter if he was your best friend's husband. You were telling him how much he needs a real woman. You even told him about how someone recorded that mess with Gia and cheaters on the video phone. I over heard the entire conversation. Do you wanna know what the best part of that conversation was to me, the part where I heard my husband say, "I don't want to have an affair with you stop calling me please". Funny ain't it. You thought you were more than just something to screw. You came into my house and had sex with my husband and now you gonna have to deal with the consequences of that. You're going to have to deal with me." I laughed out loud. I could be cordial with her if she agreed to what I was about to proposition, but things could never be the way they were.

"What do you want from me Kendra? Are you planning to tell Jason? Why would you do that? I don't have a husband, I don't even have a boyfriend and now that I have a chance to have either one of them you are willing to destroy that for me." She looked terrified.

"No you two can live in your little make believe world if you want to, but Cory and I will be apart of that child's life because you are gonna make us the God parents and we are going to see him. My husband is his father and although he won't know it. He will be apart of his first child's life."

"You can't make me do this." Nicole said.

"Oh I can, and you will or I will make copies of these for Jason's viewing pleasure. I suggest you play along unless you want your child to be a bastard." I started to get up from the table.

"Kendra, I never thought you were capable of this. This is not you. You are blackmailing me. I will just tell Cory." I guess she thought she was getting to me.

"Well get over it, Nicole. When it comes to you this is me. What's the matter, mad that I beat you at your own game of deceit? As far as telling Cory, that's fine too. After paternity is established I will see you in court for custody. Given our income and success and your background as a unstable whore, I would say we would have a pretty good chance. What court in their right mind will allow a whore to raise a child." I gathered my evidence and left the room. She was gonna play ball. Blackmail. This shit really did work.

Nicole

The Arrangement

I had agreed to Kendra's plan. It was a small price to pay. Jason wanted to try a relationship and everything. The financial help that Kendra and Cory could bring was more than helpful. I guess I should have been more careful when I asked for Kendra back in my life. She was going to be a non-stop part of my life now. I wanted Jason in my life. I wanted him to be the father of my child and if this will make that happen so be it.

Kendra and I smile at one another but I know that she hates me. I can feel it. Chills went down my spine when I thought about the last talk we had when she blackmailed me. She didn't hold anything back. She kept calling me a whore and even threatened to take me to court for custody of my child. She was vicious. I know I was wrong for the things I did. The choices that I made were far from the best but I will live with them day by day. Kendra had begun to soften just a bit after I told her okay. I just didn't know she could be so cut throat. Once I told her okay and she told Cory they started to help me with everything. Cory and Kendra have actually been good to me; buying me things and helping out with expenses. Cory is almost as proud to be a godfather than an actual father. One day while shopping Kendra had ventured off to look at strollers. I was left there with Cory and I felt so awkward. Then he said the words I had been dreading.

"Nicole, is this my baby?" He looked at me. "Is that why you made me and Kendra godparents?" I was terrified by this question, but I somehow found my voice and let the stream of lies fall from my mouth.

"No, Cory it's not your baby. I'm sure of that. We were extra careful so I know it's not. I was already pregnant when we slept together. I don't think this is anything that we should be talking about while your wife is here, she could over hear us." He just nodded his head and walked off to find his wife. I could see it in his eyes. He didn't believe a word I had just said.

After that day I had been extremely careful not to be alone at anytime with Cory. I just knew if it bothered him enough he would bring up the "is this my baby" subject again and I didn't want to have to tell my lies again.   My child was going to have a father and I was finally going to have Jason and I didn't want Cory's curiosity to mess that up for me.

Jason and I have agreed to move in together. We wanna make this family thing work. When I told him I wanted to make Kendra and Cory the God parents he thought it was a great idea. I believe he's in love with the idea of having a child. He should know that the dates don't add up, I slept with him again about a month after Cory, but I honestly don't think that he cares and that's fine by me. Like Kendra said we can live our make believe world and that is exactly what I want to do.

I have made a promise to myself. I thought about all the things that I used to do. All the parties, drugs, and sex had to cease. I was about to be a mother. Unlike my mother I wanted to be a good example for my child. When Kendra called me a whore it did have some truth to it. Although she didn't believe me I was sorry for all the pain that I caused. I still needed her as my friend and only a true friend can boldly stand up and tell me my flaws. I knew that in time I could win her friendship back, and we had at least eighteen years to do it. I looked over at her staring out of the window. Yes, things would only get better with time. The arrangement that she thought would only work for her would bring our friendship back together. If she could forgive Cory I knew mine would come with patience. I rubbed my tummy thinking how much we were going to love this child, both sets of his parents. It was win-win for both of us when it came to the arrangement.

Carmell

Let Go

I held so much anger in my heart sometimes. It was truly pathetic. I hadn't noticed it until Alex pointed it out. He was an exceptional person. He had a wonderful outlook on life. I didn't know how he did it. Alex was always upbeat and happy, and he had a positive outlook on life. My mother would always say that people came into your life for a reason. I had to have Natina and Louis in my life to teach me things, if it weren't for fooling around with them I would have never had to go to the doctor and I wouldn't have met Alex. Everything he brought to our relationship was constructive. He is the reason that I could finally be somewhat nice to Natina. Granted we would never be best friends but I could look at her without calling her a bitch.

I had talked to Alex everyday since that day. He was so intelligent. When comparing him to Louis, I sometimes wonder how I ever made it without him in my life. He is passionate and caring and he actually listens to what I have to say. We have agreed to take things slow and even though we haven't slept together I know that it will be perfect. I'm just grateful to meet a man worth something. Alex was teaching so much. We studied the Bible together and other things also. When he discovered that I had what he called a vengeful spirit he made me get down and pray for guidance and strength to cast out the evil that was within me. At first I was offended by this, but then I realized that the only way to make a change was to acknowledge that I had a problem and that I did. I had a horrible anger problem that can get me into a lot of trouble. So after I got pass being offended I joined him on his knees and prayed. We prayed for my growth mentally and spiritually. We prayed for our relationship, and asked to be guided in the right directions. I asked forgiveness for placing men above my love for God, and then I asked the Lord to help me forgive my father. I wanted to understand that my father did not create this anger within me but I did by allowing his actions and the actions of the men I dated to dictate my happiness.

I looked over at Natina. She had come to work with a black eye for two weeks. I felt sorry for her. I knew that Louis was whipping her ass. Part of me felt that is what she deserved, but in my heart I knew that know one deserved that. There were parts of me that wanted to hurt her and see her hurt because what she had done had shattered me. I guessed that I could tell her that she should be checked. Alex had lectured me on the importance of notifying all of your partners if possible. I told him I wasn't going to tell her but he quickly told me how something like this untreated could cause all kinds of problems in the future. This would be a big step for me cause the old Carmell wouldn't give a sh–, crap. I was also working on not using so much profanity.

I was going to tell Natina about the std. I guess we weren't the only two that Louis was sleeping with. I had so many times thought of the million ways to try and get back at Natina. It's not worth it though. She looks as if she is already getting more than she has dished out. She did some pretty nasty things to me and although I knew I couldn't return to the friendship that we had I could learn to let go of the hatred that I felt towards her. I wasn't gonna tell her about the std. I was going to let them find out on their own, but something in me told me I had to move.

"Hey there, can I talk to you real quick?" I asked. She motioned towards the empty seat next to her.

"I took a little trip to the clinic and found out some very important news that I think you should know." I was talking to her but it was like she had checked out. She just stared at me or through me rather. I continued anyway. "I just wanted you to know that you should be checked. I went and I had an STD, thankfully not one I can't get rid of but still one. I think you should be checked too cause the only person who could have given it to me was Louis."

I told her all about my trip to the clinic. I also told her she didn't have to put up with someone kicking her ass. She looked horrible. Her eyes were swollen from crying and there were bruises along her arm. If she didn't get out now he would probably kill her. I sat and stared at her. I thought about thanking her for it being her and not me but that would be in poor taste. I couldn't help think how that could have been me. He could have been kicking my ass, I mean butt like that.

"Natina, why do you have all those black-eyes?" I was going to ask her whether she liked it or not. There is no way I could sit here and pretend like I didn't see it. I saw it and everyone else around us did too.

"What black eyes?" She stared at me blankly. I could see the pain in her eyes. She was on the verge of tears but I guess she didn't want to break down in front of me of all people. She swallowed so hard that I heard her. Natina looked at me but it was like she didn't even see me.

"We can pretend if you want. I'm only going to say this once. I'm willing to put my true feeling of dislike for you on the back burner because I feel that you honestly need to hear this. You need a wake up call! You can become a victim of your own actions. If you keep allowing this type of behavior from him you will find yourself not questioning it and blaming yourself. If he abuses you what makes you think next time will be different. What if the next time he doesn't know how to stop himself? What if he hurts you and it can't be repaired? Have you ever thought about any of those things? No matter what you did to me and how much you hurt me, no one deserves what you are going through. I don't wish that on anyone. I've been through it myself and it's part of the reason I held so much anger. Don't be that person Natina. You can turn yourself around. You just have to know how to walk away from a bad situation. Your man is a user and an abuser. He gave me an std and you probably have the same one. Walk away while you can." Natina never said anything. I don't know if it was that she couldn't say anything or didn't want to say anything. I hope I had reached her. Domestic abuse was nothing to play with and many women had died because of it. I started to stand and she gave me a half smile and went back to working on the account she had been working on.

I left her with a few more kind words and then walked away. I still had some anger left but in time I would learn to let go.

Natina

Nobody's Punching Bag

I guess the last straw would be what Carmell told me about this std. She sat there and counseled me even though I was responsible for so much pain in her life. She opened up to me without all the anger that I was used to receiving from her. I know if she could make changes within herself, I could too.

My mind wondered to Patricia, I hadn't heard from her since the last time that I cursed her out, after all of the craziness in my life settled down, maybe I would give her a chance or at least allow her to apologize.

Strength encompassed me, I finally felt like I may be able to leave. Maybe what I am going through is bad karma. I dished out a lot of nasty stuff. I didn't care who I hurt and now the man that I loved has done nothing but hurt me. My mind is made up. I'm leaving this hellhole.

When I left work I found a letter on my windshield. It wasn't signed by anyone but the words hit home. I sat in my driveway reading the words of that poem to myself.

Now listen close to what I say
Let your heart show you the way
Walk out that door cause he's no good
It's to late for whata, shoulda, could
The love he gave was soiled and dirty
Keep on moving, cause he's not worthy

You gave your love, no questions asked

You put him first and yourself last
You were there, always on time
You were his Bonnie, his partner in crime
He's the one who chose the end of this story
Don't look back, cause he's not worthy

Now listen close, a broken heart can mend
Time heals wounds with the help of friends
Women are beautiful; know your worth
For it is you who delivers life to earth
I know it's hard because you're hurting
But let him go, cause he's not worthy

Those words rattled around in my head. After the talk I had with Carmell I knew it couldn't have been anyone but her to leave that on my car. I know she used to write poetry all the time and it amazed me that she actually took the time to give me a word of advice, even after all the things I had done to her. I was amazed that she had changed so much. She seemed to be miles away from the person that I once knew, the person I once tortured. Maybe it was happiness that I now saw in her. I don't know, and at this time figuring out what about her had changed was not at the top of my list. I needed to figure out what I was going to do about my marriage. I had made up my mind. She was right, I should not allow him to abuse me in any kind of way. Knowing the things I now know, I would have never rekindled what we had. I thought of all the reasons we weren't together before. I thought that Louis had changed and I thought that finishing school had some how made a man of him and he was ready for the responsibility of life. He was careless with my heart. I realized that our relationship was one based on sex. Once you scratched pass the surface there was nothing there. He loved me because I allowed him to do whatever and whomever he wanted, but I had finally made a decision. It was ending today.

Again I have come home to find a woman in my bed. I guess I'm supposed to disregard this as if it is a normal part of life. I think that for the most part I was pretty giving. He is the one that exposed me to the bisexual lifestyle. Granted he couldn't make me like it but he definitely held the door open for me. I was leaving and it was going to be today. I knew that I couldn't say anything because if I tried to leave he would lock me in the room. He had done that on more than one occasion to keep me from leaving the house. I never in a million years thought that our marriage would be like this, but it is and I accept that.

I walked to the bathroom. I could hear the headboard bang against the wall as he started round two with the Asian chic that lay in my bed. I took a long shower and drowned out those moans. The water splashed against my battered body. It was scolding hot as if I could somehow disinfect my life by rinsing every trace of him from my body. Stepping out of the shower, I grabbed a towel to dry myself. I looked at my thighs, blackened and bruised. I eyed myself in the mirror. He had taken my face and bruised it. My body is battered and tired. I can't lift my left arm and my legs are sore from being repeatedly held open while my husband violently took what I would have so willingly gave.

Those words from our wedding day rang in my head. Until death do us part. Well at the rate we are going it's gonna be my death and not his. I grabbed a pair of wind pants and a t-shirt to put on. The lovers were sound asleep in my bed. I remembered that this was once my apartment. I smiled remembering that we had put everything in his name when we did the Carmell thing. So this really wasn't my house. We had re-signed the lease in his name. He could have it all. I could easily get another apartment. I know he didn't have the money to pay the rent, so either he would have to get a job or some other fool to pay his bills. I didn't care which route he went but I knew I would no longer be the fool footing the bill for him. I laughed to myself as I gathered my things to leave this hell we once called a home.

I moved cat-like through the house careful not to wake him. I put on a pot of boiling water and added some grits to the pot. I would need just before I left. After I loaded everything I went back upstairs for one last finishing touch.

I grabbed his car keys and tossed them over the railing. Along with his clothes and some of his most expensive shoes, then I tossed his precious magnum condoms. He hadn't been using them anyway, because he had given me and Carmell a std. I emptied an entire bottle of Clorox over his belongings. Through all this he never so much as rolled over. He was knocked out cold. Damn, guess the sex was good.

I picked up that pot of boiling hot water and carefully walked into the bedroom. I placed the key into the lock of the door before I entered. I stood over them. I had found this chic in my bed on more than one occasion. Her name was Jennifer. I had even been apart of a threesome on more than once. What was even more twisted is that she was in my wedding. She must be his main girl on the side. Well if he wanted her he could have her. I became upset. He violated my life, my body, and my heart. She was sleeping in my bed as if she belonged here. Well like I said, she can have him and everything that goes along with him, including this. I tossed the pot of water into the bed and on them.

"I ain't nobody's punching bag!" I screamed as I threw the pot in his face. Before he could realize what happened I ran towards the bedroom door grabbed it and locked it. Let's see how he liked being locked in the room. When I got downstairs I looked at his pile of belongings on the ground. I didn't want him to be able to salvage anything, so I went to my car and got a lighter and torched the clothes right there on the ground. I didn't give a damn who saw. I didn't care that this was arson. The only thing that matters is I was getting out. I wanted to inflict some pain on him, he's lucky I didn't set him on fire.

I got into my car and turned the radio up as I drove off. I would have the divorce papers mailed. Hmmm, I wonder if it was too late to have it annulled. I smiled. I was about to start my life anew and the next time I won't be nobody's punching bag.

Kendra

Love, Lust, and A Whole Lotta Distrust

As I stood at the window near my cubicle I thought about the job I was recently offered. My supervisor wasn't coming back and they wanted me to take her job. I wasn't really sure about that. I mean, the money was good but this place was filled with mess.

When I came into this job I thought it would be nothing like this. I have seen some of everything in this place. There were orgies in the stairways, stealing, you name we've got it. I guess this is just what comes with working in this sort of environment. There are far too many people and so many different types of personalities that you were bound to have conflicts and controversy. I just didn't' know how much more I could stomach.

Cory and I are doing well. I know he felt guilty about sleeping with Nicole. That was enough for me. Cheating on him was selfish of me and I thought that he would never know. I learned it by watching and listening to so many stories here at this place. I guess eventually it will get the best of you. It had gotten the best of me and almost cost me one of the most important things in my life, my marriage. I accept responsibility for my actions. Even though it has surrounded me at work doesn't mean I had to let it change me and that's exactly what I had done. Somehow, through all the madness and drama I had found myself again, the real me. The me that remains faithful and loving to my husband instead of deceptive.

Life for me has completely done a 180. Nicole tells me everyday how she is sorry about what she did. I really believe that she is. Nicole and

254 LOVE LUST AND A WHOLE LOTTA DISTRUST

Jason are working together on being together. I guess she finally made that man hers. It is funny how things work out. A baby that was made out of lust has brought all of us together. I can see the change in all of us. We are growing while we await the arrival of our baby. In time I am sure that the child will come to know the truth, but no time soon. I just wanted to give my husband what he wanted most. A child. One day God will bless us with our own and then we will have two, but until then we would love this child as our own and keep it safe from harm. I think Cory has been wondering is this baby really his. He is not a stupid man and I know he can do the math. I know that he too will come to know in time, but for now the secret is safe with me.

It is almost time for my vacation. I don't know if I am gonna make it a permanent one. I didn't know what I would do when I left here, would I go back to school or get another job or just stay at home. I didn't know but I did know that I couldn't do this much longer. Maybe I would write a book about all the horrible things that went on here and outside of here. I'm sure people would love to read about this mess. I would decide eventually. I have to talk to my husband. The church counseling has been most beneficial to us. This is something that God joined together and no one can keep it together better than him. I have become active in the church again, working like I use to. Cory has even become a Deacon. God does answer prayers.

I smiled out of the window. I would have to seriously think about returning to this place after my vacation. This call center had become a strain on my life. I got tired of overhearing all of the rumors and lies. There was once a time that I would have been listening to the hype. I guess all that changed when I became the hype.

I walked pass Nicole on my way out and stopped to rub her bulging belly. It was small and she had just begun to show. She glowed like all pregnant women. I know a lot of it stemmed from having this baby and Jason in her life. She smiled and we shared a few words.

"Kendra, I just want to apologize for everything that I have done to you. Every thing." Nicole stared at me. I could see so much remorse in her eyes. I knew by the emphasis on everything that meant sleeping with Cory mostly. That was the big everything. I needed a little time to heal those wounds but we had begun the road to recovery. I believed this was sincere but I didn't have any words at this time. So I just hugged her. I hugged her tight. She was once like a sister to me and that apology meant everything because it was from the heart.

I think that gradually I can befriend her again. I forgave Cory why shouldn't she deserve the same. Hating her used too much energy. It was now useless to me to exert so much energy on hating people. It would kill me inside to carry on hatred and distrust rather than just forgive. I would gain nothing from holding hate in my heart and when it was all said and done, I would be the one left holding all the baggage. I wasn't prepared to live my life that way. Rediscovering myself has left me with a feeling tranquility. I feel so much peace within. That's why I had such a struggle with the decision to come back to this job. It was a job that is filled with stress and I don't want to disturb the calm I now possess. It was so hard to continue to be upset day end and day out. Besides that just wasn't me. I didn't have it in me to be completely spiteful and mean. I knew that meaning of forgiveness I just had to take that first step with Nicole. Since she had apologized and taken the first step it would only be right for me to meet her halfway. I wanted to be able to open my arms whole-heartedly but I just wasn't there yet, but I knew that it was coming.

I walked out the door, waiving bye to co-workers for what might be my last time. I was ready to move on to something bigger, something better and I knew that life had something more in store for me than this place. I knew there was something else out there for me. There had to be something else out there for me. I walked in these doors expecting to do just a job; I walk out knowing about love, lust, and a whole lotta distrust.

Epilogue

J**ason Edwards**

Five years of my life, it had been five long years of my life. I didn't know that I loved her. I cared but I didn't trust her, not as far as I could throw her ass. I sat at that bar even though I knew she would be mad that I hadn't come home. Every day I walked into that house it was harder and harder for me. Everyday I looked at my son I realized he didn't look anything like me.

When I met Nicole she was so much fun, so full of life but she never got that I didn't want a relationship. When she found out she was pregnant I think she saw that as the perfect opportunity to have me. I have to admit back in those days I was dumb as hell, I would have asked for a paternity test but instead I took her word for it. Now it was too late. I would be that little boy's father forever now. He was apart of me just as much as I was apart of him.

I had to admit that I was angry with her. I didn't know if it were true or not but I had a suspicion that he wasn't biologically mine, but I knew I wasn't going anywhere. I had made a vow to be there for my child blood or no blood I wasn't walking out on the boy. I just needed a moment to calm down. I needed a minute to get my mind right and convince myself again that this was my son.

I remember when I told my friend Kendra about her being pregnant. She just kinda looked at me in the oddest way and said, "Are you sure?" I was so sure then, but I wasn't nearly as sure now.

I looked over at Tasha. She wasn't as pretty as Nicole was to me but Tasha knew how not to cross that line. She knew how to just take it at face value. She never questioned a good thing. She never demanded anything from me and she never tried to make this more than it was. I wish that I could give Nicole what she wanted but I can never be who she completely wants me to be. Hell I'm me.

Tasha never gave me any mess about being married to Nicole. She never said anything about Nicole and that's what I loved about her. Nicole was so full of drama until it just about drove me crazy. I think that's why I kept Tasha around. I knew what to expect from her. I knew what she expected of me.

Maybe I would make an attempt at our marriage. I had made this promise of marriage I wanted to honor it and I was trying my hardest. Perhaps I would just try a bit harder. I would try harder to ignore the fact that this may not be my son and that my wife tricked me into marrying her. I search for that same strength every time I go home so I don't strangle the bitch. I had invested all of this time in her might as well make it last, right?

Louis Broussard

I watched the look on Tina's face as she wobbled to the bathroom. She was carrying my child and to me it was a beautiful thing. I turned to watch her walk to the restroom and that's when I saw her. Carmell, standing there waiting on her food. She was just as beautiful as the day I met her. She was a sight to see. Watching her stand there made me remember why I was so drawn to her. She was so sweet and caring and willing to do anything for me. I had abused that. I had taken her kindness for weakness, taken advantage of her.

I did the things I did to her out of devotion to Natina, but Carmell was truly the one that got away. There was something special about her and Tina knew it. That's why she had gone through such great lengths to be with her.

I tried to waive at her. I raised my hand but quickly put it down when I saw the look on her face. She looked hurt. I had nothing to say for my actions and for a long time I blamed Natina for what had happened.

When Carmell showed up at our wedding I thought she was there to stop it, I thought she realized she wanted to be with me, but she was only there to get back at Natina. She was only there to use me as I had used her. I smiled at her but it went unreturned so I turned back to the table and looked straight ahead.

When Carmell refused to talk to me I took my anger out on Natina. I hit her, no I beat the hell out of her. I never meant to hurt her like that and I will never do it again. I believe that if I did she might try to kill me. I rubbed the burn mark on my neck. Five years had changed me a lot. I wasn't the man I used to be. Even though Natina allowed me to have other sex partners I limited my extra curricular activity and I didn't disrespect our home as I did when we first got married.

Tina was coming back to the table. Even though I harbored feelings for Carmell, I knew Natina was the one for me. She was my lady and we were meant to be together.

ia Llorens

G I stood next to the woman I loved. I stood next to the woman I compromised my beliefs to be with. I knew this was wrong, but I wanted her; I desired her. After five years, I was still here to pick up the pieces when she fell apart. She needed me as much as I needed her.

Her husband was clueless to what she wanted. I could give her the world and more if she would only let me. I wanted her to know that I could love her better than him.

I smiled at her. If only she could realize I was here for her. Cory didn't know what to do with a woman like Kendra. She was special; no, more than special she was exceptional. I longed to touch her but she wouldn't allow it. She hadn't allowed it for years.

I stared at her. I know she cared about me. I know that she needed me and walking away from me was not an option.

Still, it wasn't enough. I only had her for stolen moments. I only got to see her when he wasn't around. He was in the way and I didn't know how to get her away from him. I had in fact stepped into the fire and even though I was burned, I couldn't move my hand away. Being around her was something that my soul yearned for. I craved to hear the singsong cadence of her voice or her mindless chatter. I loved to hear about her and her day.

The one time I had her to myself in Atlanta was like heaven to me. Then he showed up and ruined it for me. He had hit me and even though I was scared, I wasn't going to back down from him. He was a huge man but I wasn't going to show him that he scared me. I took those licks so the woman I loved wouldn't have to.

We walked outside and that's when I saw him approaching. I wasn't surprised, he's had us followed before but this time he was the one that was doing the dirty work. I steadied myself as he moved closer. I didn't know what to expect from him. I hope we didn't' have to fight. I hoped we could talk like adults but when it came to her, I knew he was just as crazy about her as I was. He wanted me out of her life. I wanted to be a constant part of her life and I wasn't going out without a fight. I never had and I never would when it came to Kendra.

Cory Dubois

I followed her in my car. I didn't know who she thought she was fooling. I saw the way she tensed every time her phone rang and she wasn't near it. I wanted to know where she was going and who she was seeing. I had a suspicion it was her. This woman was like the black plague and she wouldn't go away.

I watched my wife and the woman go into Chuck E. Cheese's with my godson. The godson I thought to be my actual son but his mother had denied it. I looked at Jaden and he looked like me when I was his age. I dismissed those thoughts. I had to deal with the matter at hand.

I waited in the car for hours. My wife was my wife and I didn't plan on sharing her with anyone. I thought we had gotten rid of her, but she kept coming back. Kendra had made a mistake and now she was about to make another. I didn't know how many times I could continue to catch her running around town with another woman. I think in some ways it was worse than finding out she had been with another man. I can at least compete with a man. There is nothing that a man can do that I can't, but her being with this woman was something totally different to me. It was the unknown. I didn't know what bound my wife to this woman and why in the hell she couldn't walk away from her. We had undergone counseling and I wasn't prepared to see that go down the drain because my wife has a temporary lapse of judgment.

This wasn't my first time following them. I had seen them before. I don't think that had been having sex but she was giving her my time, which was even worse. I saw them coming out and I moved to open the door. I walked over to Kendra's car where she stood with her.

"Kendra." I said her name calmly. She turned around and her light brown skin turned beet red. "You're going to stop." I pulled her close to me and looked at her.

"Gia, why don't you go away? She's mine; she's my wife and I don't want to ever see you with her again. I don't ever want to see you again." I said to her. I knew she was in love with my wife, but that was just it. She is my wife and nothing is going to change that, not even some little carpet munching lesbian. It didn't matter to me that she thought she could treat my wife better than me. Kendra had made her decision and I was it. I just wanted this woman not to exist. It was a constant battle between us, but I was fairly certain that I would be victorious.

I stared at Kendra, this time to let her know that I meant business. I was angry with her for getting us involved in such nonsense and carrying it on for so long. I was ready to wash my hands of it and she was going to wash her hands of it as well. The look on her face told me that she understood. Her eyes said I understand and for a brief moment, I thought I saw a hint of gratitude.

I watched her get into the car and drive away from that woman for what I hoped to be the last time.

About the Author

Born and raised in Houston, Texas, Deilra Smith-Collard's passion is writing. Her writing style embraces life's beauty and imperfections and compels her to write from the heart. Deilra Smith-Collard writes novels, poetry, short stories, and children's fiction. She resides in Houston, Texas with her husband and two children.

VISIT DEIIRA ONLINE
www.writerwithinonline.com